Praise for Skye Taylor

"A compelling tale of love, compassion and being true to your heart."
NY Times and USA Today bestseller, Caridad Pineiro

"Taylor has done it again - grabbed us by the throat with a complex story of love, loss, and second chances - don't miss this powerful new Camerons of Tides Way story. Your collection won't be complete without *Keeping His Promise*."
N.L. Quatrano, OnTargetWords.com

"From the haunting prologue to the tender finish, *Keeping His Promise* delivers. Skye shows us that love, and honor, are treasures that last."
Betty Carpenter, author of *Christmas is a Timeshare*

"Falling for Zoe is a deftly plotted and delightful story of family, of real life, and love, and trying to do the right thing. *Falling for Zoe* is a romantic gem."
Cheryl Reavis, Best selling, award-winning author

"Bravo Zulu for *Healing a Hero*, filled with turmoil, tenderness, and painful secrets from the past. Will Gunnery Sergeant Philip Cameron have to choose between the Corps and the woman he loves?"
Heather Ashby, author of Love in the Fleet series

Is this a second chance for Jon and Kate, ... or a second chance for heartbreak?

After losing her husband, Kate Cameron Shaw has rebuilt her life with a lot of help from her childhood friend, Jon Canfield. But falling for the handsome small-town police officer isn't part of her plan to grab this second chance at making a name for herself as an investigative journalist.

Twenty years ago, Jon Canfield watched helplessly as the only woman he's ever loved fell head over heals for his best friend. Two years ago that friend died in his arms, but not before begging Jon to take care of "his girls." Is keeping his promise a second chance to lose her all over again?

The Camerons of Tide's Way Novels

Falling for Zoe

Loving Meg

Trusting Will

Healing a Hero

Keeping His Promise

Loving Ben (Short Story)

Mike's Wager (Short Story)

Also by Skye Taylor

Iain's Plaid
(a time travel romance)

The Candidate

Dedication

In Memory of:

John Scott Parker

My brother, my friend and often, in my youth, my partner in crime. You believed in me, encouraged me to follow my dream, and you were always there to help when things didn't go the way I planned. We both had our share of second chances. I miss you, Scotty – this one's for you.

Keeping His Promise

Book Five, The Camerons of Tide's Way

Skye Taylor

SandCastleBooks.net

This is a work of fiction. Names, characters, places and incidents are either the products of the author's imagination or are used fictitiously. Any resemblance to actual persons (living or dead), events or locations is entirely coincidental.

SandCastleBooks
Print ISBN: 978-1-7322287-0-2

Skye Taylor enjoys hearing from her readers.
Visit her at: www.Skye-writer.com

Cover design by Carrie Richter
Interior design by Skye Taylor
Anchor © Natis76/Dreamstime.com

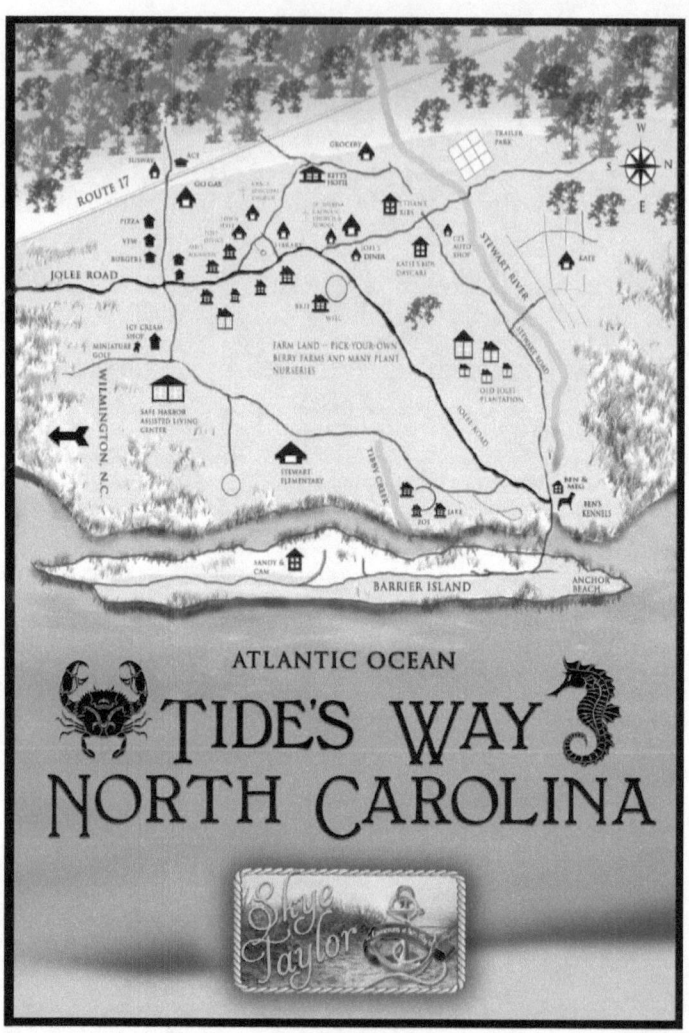

Prologue

JON CANFIELD SAT in his cruiser listening to a ballgame while keeping an eye on Calico Jack's. Tide's Way, North Carolina was a quiet, law-abiding town, but it was also a beach town and it was Saturday night, a night when young people with nothing better to do after a day at the shore hung out in bars and drank too much.

Three guys staggered out of the bar with arms laced across each other's shoulders singing off key. They reeled toward a black SUV with out-of-state plates. Jon reached for the door latch, but then a fourth man appeared and strode purposefully toward the driver's door. *Good for you!* He silently cheered the designated driver.

Only one truck left. Jon was ready to call it a night when Bart Onslow stepped out of the bar and crossed the lot to his truck on steady feet. According to the bartender, Bart usually nursed the same bottle of Budweiser for the whole evening. Jon fired up the cruiser and waited to pull out onto Stewart Road behind Bart's truck.

Bart took his time pulling onto the road, then drove slowly toward town, maybe even a little too cautiously. Best to check him out. Jon flipped the switch for his lights.

As if Bart had fallen asleep and the lights woke him up, he immediately sped up, veered left then right and lurched off the pavement toward the darkened parking lot of the local rib joint.

Bart's truck struck a dark figure crossing the lot and sent him flying through the air like an oversized rag doll. Jon slammed on the brakes and leapt from his cruiser, speaking urgently into the mike on his shoulder.

When he realized the victim was his friend Ethan Shaw, owner of the rib joint, anguish slammed into Jon's gut. Ethan lay on his back staring up at the sky gasping for breath. Even in the dark, the blood soaking through Ethan's gray sweatshirt was obvious.

Jon put a second urgent call over the radio as he dashed back to the cruiser for his first aid kit.

"Ethan?" Jon yanked up the blood-soaked sweatshirt to reveal the injury. He pressed his hand over the wound trying to staunch the bleeding. "Can you hear me?"

Ethan turned his head. "It hurts . . . like hell." He closed his eyes. His face twisted in agony.

"Ethan! Look at me."

"I'm . . . done . . . for," Ethan said without opening his eyes.

"Hang on, buddy. It's not over until the fat lady sings. And she isn't singing," Jon urged desperately.

When Ethan opened his eyes, the pain was starkly clear in his eyes. "Take care . . . of my . . . girls."

Jon's heart raced. It hadn't been more than two minutes but it felt like twenty. Where was the ambulance?

"Promise me." Ethan clutched Jon's uniform with desperate hands.

"You're gonna be okay," Jon said with a rehearsed assurance he didn't feel.

"Promise . . . me," Ethan begged, his voice breaking as he gulped for air.

Jon worked around the clinging hands, still trying to stanch the flow. *Where the hell are they?*

"Prom—" Ethan coughed, and a trickle of blood ran from the corner of his mouth. His eyes pleaded with Jon.

"Okay. I promise." *Please, God, don't let him die.*

+Ethan's hand's weakened and fell from Jon's shirt. A tear rolled down the side of his face. "Tell her—" He coughed again. More blood. "Tell Kate—I'm s-sorry."

Sirens blared. Headlights rounded the corner and swept across the unlit parking lot.

Sorry for what? "Tell her yourself," Jon insisted as a paramedic jogged toward them with bags of life-saving equipment in both hands.

As the EMT took over, a desperate prayer ran through Jon's head. Ethan's eyelids fluttered, and a spasm of pain flashed across his face.

The EMT slit Ethan's sweatshirt up the middle and slapped a quick clotting sponge on the wound.

Ethan made a desperate grab for Jon. "Promise."

Jon captured the hand and squeezed. "I promise." He mouthed the words as Ethan's broken body was eased onto the stretcher.

"Sir?" The EMT glanced at the clasped hands.

Jon squeezed one last bit of encouragement and released Ethan's hand so the stretcher could be rushed toward the waiting ambulance.

"Anyone else hurt, sir?"

Jon glanced at the county sheriff's deputy who had just arrived. "Yeah. The drunk who hit Shaw. I didn't have a chance to check on him yet." He nodded in the direction of a pickup truck with its hood buckled under the lip of the dumpster at the far end of the parking lot.

He jerked himself back to business and jogged toward the dumpster with the deputy on his heels. This was his fault. He should have checked Onslow out before he let him drive away from Calico's. He'd failed to protect and defend either man. Then, seeing his friend down, he'd ignored Bart entirely. What kind of cop was he?

Steam boiled out of the fractured radiator, but the truck was remarkably intact considering the size and heft of the dumpster.

Jon pulled the driver-side door open. Onslow stared straight ahead.

"Bart?" Jon touched the man's shoulder. "You hurt?"

Bart turned his head slowly in Jon's direction. His eyes were wide. It took a minute for his eyes to focus on the cop standing beside his truck.

"Don't let him move until I assess his status." The deputy, who had been a Navy medic, climbed in on the passenger side.

While the deputy asked Bart a series of questions, Jon turned back toward the front of the lot.

The rear doors of the ambulance bearing Ethan's battered body slammed shut, and the siren screeched to life. As the flashing lights disappeared, racing toward the hospital in Wilmington, Jon gazed up at the inky, starless sky and began to pray as the first drops of rain fell in his face.

Chapter 1

Two years later

KATE SHAW IGNORED the ache across her shoulders and feet that were sore in spite of the comfortable running shoes she wore as she bussed tables on one of the busiest nights at Ethan's Ribs. *Oh Ethan, I know you loved this place, but it's killing me now.* She scooted a full bin of dirty dishes across the counter toward the dishwasher, grabbed an empty bin and returned to the dining room.

Ethan's dream had become *the* place to go for ribs for miles around. Especially on a Saturday night. But Kate wasn't supposed to be here tonight. She was supposed to be at her father's birthday party out on the island. And she would have been if two members of the wait staff hadn't broken down on their way back from Raleigh and the frantic young hostess had called Kate asking what to do until the men arrived.

Once upon a time, Kate had enjoyed working at the restaurant, just being anywhere Ethan was and helping him make his rib joint a success. But that was before she became a widow raising two girls on her own, earning a living in her own career as a journalist for the *Port City News* and managing the restaurant because Ethan's brother and majority owner didn't want to sell it.

Had Garrett chosen to sell the business, there would have been regret over saying goodbye to a place where she and

Ethan had spent so much time together. But it was just too much, and Garrett was career Navy so he wasn't around to do any of the work until he retired in another four years.

She set her bin on the corner of a newly vacated table and began piling dishes and glasses into it. The air held the enticing scent of Ethan's signature barbeque sauce and the happy chatter of the suppertime crowd. All was well in Ethan's world. It was just hers that seemed stalled out.

"Come sit with me a minute."

Kate turned to find one of Ethan's longest regular customers pulling out a chair at his own table.

"You look totally done in," the man said, his faded blue eyes full of concern.

Kate shrugged, finished clearing the table, set her full bin on a tray stand next to the table and wiped it down.

"Please." The older man urged again. "Take a load off. I don't get many chances to sit with a pretty woman and chat."

Mostly because he had grabbed the apron tied around her waist and didn't appear ready to let go unless she did as he'd asked, Kate glanced around the dining room and didn't see any tables needing her immediate attention. She gave in and sat.

"How are you doing, Mr. Delong?" She pulled a towel free of her waistband and mopped her brow.

"I'm doing just fine. It's you I'm worried about. Bustling around when you should be home with your girls."

"I should be at my dad's birthday party," she admitted. "But Cory and Al broke down and they'll be late. The hostess is new, and she was in a state when she called me. So here I am."

The old man reached across the table to pat the back of her hand. "You work too hard. I saw that article you wrote in the paper the other day. Two important jobs. Not counting raising two fine young gals. Ethan would be proud of you, but I doubt he expected you to carry such a heavy load."

"He didn't expect to be gone," Kate replied. A pang of loss sliced through her. Not as sharp or unbearable as it had been a year ago, her loss was more tinged with melancholy now. Missing Ethan was more about missing a companion and life partner. When he'd first died she felt like she'd died too. Well-meaning friends and relatives had told her time would heal, but she hadn't believed them. Not back then.

Healing had come slowly. Little by little in unexpected ways. She would always miss Ethan and the love they had shared, but time had done what she'd thought impossible. Life had gone on. She'd learned how to cope. Most of the time. She'd learned how to be happy again.

"I miss him, too," the man murmured gently. "I miss the moments he stopped to keep a lonely old man company while he ate ribs at a table for one. He was a good man."

"Yeah, he was," Kate agreed. "And he'd be hollering for me to get my butt in gear and get these dishes to the kitchen if he was here."

As she got to her feet, the missing Cory burst in from the kitchen and scanned the room. He caught Kate's eye and headed in her direction.

Kate kissed the old man on his cheek and thanked him for his concern and for making her take a break, then turned to greet Cory.

"I'm so sorry, Miss Kate. I shoulda—"

"But you're here now," Kate cut him off. "And I'm outta here. I've got a birthday party to get to." She reached into her apron pocket and handed the young man a handful of bills. Then she took the apron off and plopped it on top of the bussed dishes. "Good luck tonight. Share my tips with the rest of the staff. Okay?"

Cory nodded, shoved the money into his own apron, snagged the bin and headed for the kitchen. Al had appeared and was already delivering water and cutlery to a newly seated table. Ethan's Ribs was back on track for the night.

KATE HURRIED UP the stairs to her parents' house and burst into a living room filled with laughter and people. Nathan "Cam" Cameron was leaning forward at the edge of his recliner with a game controller in his hands and his grandchildren gathered around him.

"Mom! You're here." Kate's younger daughter, Becca, leapt to her feet and rushed to give her mother a hug. "Look what Uncle Jon gave Gramps." She pointed toward the coffee table.

Kate didn't see anything but a coffee table and a floor littered with cast-off gift wrapping. Then the paper moved and a tank appeared. Emblazoned with the Marine logo, the little tank plowed its way through the paper and over Kate's brother, Jake's toes as it headed in her direction. It stopped at her feet, the turret turned and lifted, aiming at Kate's midsection. Then a little puff of smoke appeared.

Kate laughed. Jon knew her father as well as he'd known his own, and he'd picked a gift that was so something her father would love playing with. She glanced across the room at the man who'd grown up next door and been her best friend since forever. A man with a big smile and a mischievous sense of humor. Jon winked at her.

"I suppose once supper's over, there will be a trip to the beach to see how it goes in the sand."

"We're going to build a fort for it," one of Kate's nephews piped up.

"And walls for it to mash down," his brother added.

"Men just never grow up, do they?" Kate's mother shook her head.

Another of Kate's brothers set a small pile of magazines behind the little vehicle and her dad put the thing in gear. The little treads made short work of this new obstacle and it was cheered on as it crunched back across the litter to its new owner. Cam picked it up and set it and the controller on the table at his side.

Kate followed the tank and bent to give her father a hug. Her father's blond hair was liberally laced with silver and crows' feet crinkled the corners of his blue eyes, but he was still fit and looked at least ten years younger than his age.

"Happy birthday Dad. Sorry I'm late."

"Not a problem," Cam answered returning her hug. "As you can see, I've been amply entertained, but I saved yours until you got here." He reached for the package she'd hastily wrapped and sent with her girls as she'd dashed out the door to the restaurant.

"It's not nearly as exciting as a remote-controlled tank, but I hope you enjoy it anyway." She knelt at his knees to watch him pull the wrapping off. Her father loved to read and he had a library full of books, but Kate thought it was time he moved into the digital age so she'd purchased an e-book reader for him.

Cam sighed as he revealed his gift. "First it was a smart phone. Now I need a smart book?" He grinned at her.

"There are already four books on it I thought you'd like, and I opened a new book account for you so you can download more. I hope you like it."

"I know I will." He hugged her again and began turning the gadget around looking for the on button.

The sound of a baby crying interrupted the group inspection of Cam's latest gift.

"That would be for me," Philip said as he got to his feet. "Alex wants his dinner."

As Kate's oldest brother hurried up the stairs to get his son, the rest of the crowd began to move toward the kitchen. It was time for everyone to eat.

"At least you didn't miss dinner." Jon Canfield wrapped an arm about Kate's shoulders and gave her half a hug. "But you look beat."

She rested her head briefly against her best friend's shoulder. "I am kind of tired. Thanks for bringing the girls out early."

"I was coming anyway. Not a problem."

Jon had always been there for Kate to lean on. All the way back to when they were kids. She'd been the only girl in a gang of boys that included her brothers and Jon. Her brothers had always treated her like one of the guys, assuming she could fend for herself, but Jon had always watched out for her. He was a very caring friend and always had been.

These past two years, he'd become even more watchful. With his last words Ethan had wrangled a promise out of Jon, and Jon had been diligent in keeping it. Watching out for Ethan's girls.

"You're a better friend than I deserve," Kate murmured as she pulled free of his arm and looked up into his familiar green eyes.

"We're going to have to agree to disagree on that." His gaze intensified with something Kate didn't understand. They'd always been good friends. Even before Ethan Jon had been her friend. But that fiery green gaze was something new. It made something inside her stir, and her breath caught in her throat.

"You guys coming to eat or not?" Jake's wife Zoe interrupted the oddly tense moment.

Jon grinned and turned toward the table overflowing with Kate's family.

The scarred old table that had once been more than adequate for Kate, her four brothers, her parents and most of the time Jon, had been replaced with one twice as long and half again as wide with extra leaves for gatherings like today with spouses and grandchildren added to all the family events. Thankfully the kitchen/dining area was big enough to hold them all.

Kate squeezed in between her daughters on one side of the table while Jon found an empty chair opposite. As they held hands while Cam said grace and thanked God for his loving wife, his kids and all his grandchildren, Kate glanced across the expanse of food-laden table and caught Jon looking at her. The intense green gaze was back.

Chapter 2

"JUST WHEN I thought I had my life under control again." Kate wrung her hands and gazed at Becca's pleading face.

"Please, Mommy. Please can we stay at Uncle Jon's? I don't wanna sleep at Gramma's again."

"It's not a problem," the handsome cop standing just inside the kitchen door said. "I'm off duty tonight, and I've got plenty of time to get the girls on the bus for school in the morning."

"But—" Kate stopped, considered her options. She glanced at her watch, then sighed in resignation. Her mother lived out on the beach. Most kids would be all over spending time at the beach, but Becca wasn't most kids. "Okay. This time."

Becca flung her arms around Kate's waist and hugged her hard.

"If you've got a plane to catch, you better get moving," Jon reminded her. "I'll get the girls and their gear collected and lock up."

"Thanks, Jon. *Again.*" Kate reached for the handle of her carry-on, but Jon beat her to it. A spark of electric excitement raced up her arm from the connection of her hand and his on the suitcase's handle. Startled at her reaction to the small moment of contact, Kate let go immediately and turned to give her daughters a goodbye hug.

"You be good and don't make Uncle Jon wish he hadn't invited you for a sleepover."

"We won't," the girls chorused in unison. Their eyes were alight with a spirit of adventure. They loved their grandparents and enjoyed spending time at the beach house, but of late, they'd grown more attached to Jon. Perhaps they were trying to fill the gaping wound Ethan's death had left in their young lives.

Guilt nagged at Kate as she followed Jon out to her ancient, high-mileage minivan. She shouldn't let him take on so much. He should be spending his free time dating and finding a wife. He was a kind, generous man who deserved his own family, not a borrowed, broken one that had been wished onto him by a dying man.

"I still feel like I'm imposing," Kate muttered as Jon deposited her suitcase in the rear and slid the door shut.

"You're not." He opened the driver's door for her. "It was my idea."

She peaked her brows. "I thought Becca came up with the plan." She hiked herself onto the seat and slid her keys into the ignition.

His hand gripped the top of her door as he bent his head to peer in. "Drive safely, and don't worry. The girls will be fine. Call when you get to your hotel if you want to say goodnight." He hesitated a moment, then shut the door and stepped away from the car.

Kate started the engine and buzzed the window down. "Thanks, Jon. You're too good to me." A strange haunted look flitted across Jon's face. But then it was gone and Kate wondered if she'd imagined it.

She and Jon had been friends forever. They'd grown up next door to each other, raced on the beach, played pirates aboard the abandoned hull of a boat in the dunes between their homes, made up fantastic stories about the things they'd do when they grew up, and sat at the kitchen table doing homework and sharing slabs of her mother's fresh baked bread slathered with butter. Jon had been her best friend when they were kids. He'd introduced her to Ethan and held her sobbing in his arms the night he'd come to tell her Ethan was gone.

Jon was still her best friend. His perpetually tousled brown curls and green eyes were as familiar to her as the face she greeted in the mirror every morning. They thought alike . . . most of the time. They cheered for the same ball teams and still talked about what they were going to be when they grew up. She had close girlfriends too, but no one knew her better than Jon did. And no one had been kinder or more supportive of her while she worked her way through the minefield of an unmoored life.

She backed out of the driveway thinking about that odd look in his eyes. Maybe she was leaning on him too much. Best friend or not, maybe it was time to pull up her big-girl panties and manage for herself instead of letting him drop everything to help her out all the time. She'd stopped crying on his shoulder, literally, months ago, but he was still around bailing her out of the nagging little problems of being a single parent.

Traffic was light on the way to the airport, which was good considering her time crunch. Her boss had planned to cover the hearing in Washington, but then his wife had been rushed to the hospital and he'd asked her to take his place at the last minute. She'd been corralling her girls and their things, hoping her mom would be able to come after them and take them out to the barrier island house Kate had grown up in while she was in DC when Jon popped in on his way home from work.

Not that his popping in was anything new, either. Jon had been Ethan's friend as much as hers, and he'd stopped by a lot before Ethan's death. But over the last year, he'd come by more often and she'd begun to feel incomplete when he didn't. Not being much of a mechanic, he hadn't been able to do anything about her minivan, but he had rolled up his sleeves and helped out at Ethan's Ribs. He'd advised her on the repairs to the restaurant's security system and helped her untangle some of the bookkeeping.

But Ethan's Ribs wasn't Jon's problem, either. Ethan's brother Garrett was the majority owner because he'd sunk a huge chunk of his savings into it to get Ethan started. Until Garrett decided to leave the Navy and manage the place himself, Kate felt she owed it to Ethan to keep the place running. But she didn't want the responsibility. She wanted more time for her own career. That had been the argument Ethan had walked out on the night he was killed. The argument had been her fault.

The sudden flare of taillights ahead brought her attention back to the road. Traffic came to a standstill. She drummed her fingers on the steering wheel and tried not to keep looking at the clock. She had time. Deliberately loosening her grip on the wheel, she sat back and tried to relax.

Allison, who along with Jon and Chief Atkins made up the minuscule Tide's Way police force, stepped into view, blew her whistle and waved the stopped cars forward. Her ash-blonde hair glistened in the sunlight as she tweeted and urged the backed up cars past two other cars that had obviously had a minor collision. Kate glanced once more at the clock on the dash and stepped on the gas. She'd make her flight after all.

"HURRY UP, MAX." Jenny urged the two-year-old golden retriever to stop sniffing around in the grass and catch up to Becca who was already skipping up the stairs to Jon's back door.

Jon looked forward to spending the next two nights with Ethan's girls. The girls Ethan had made him promise to watch out for. But they were Kate's girls, too, and he'd do anything for Kate. Even if all she ever wanted from him was friendship.

Guilt over coveting his best friend's wife nagged at him regularly, but he'd loved Kate first. Long before he'd introduced her to Ethan. He'd been watching out for her since they were little kids. And he loved her more than he'd ever loved anyone else, then or since. Was it wrong to want her for himself now that Ethan was gone? Was it wrong to let Becca and Jenny look up to him as a stand-in for their father?

The more time he spent with them, the more his presence began to eclipse their memories of their father. That couldn't be denied. But keeping his promise to Ethan without becoming a significant part of their lives didn't seem possible.

Jon bent and scratched the fur between the dog's ears, distracting the animal from whatever had caught his attention. Max turned his head, licked Jon's hand, and then obediently followed Jenny up the stairs.

"Can we have grilled cheese sandwiches for supper?" Becca dropped her backpack on the bench beside the door and came to wrap her arms around John's hips. "And chocolate ice cream?"

Jon ruffled her short curls as he gazed down into her eager face.

"No dessert until you do your homework," Jenny said as she toed her sneakers off, plopped onto a kitchen chair and began rooting through her own backpack. At twelve going on sixteen, Jenny was a bossy big sister. Kate had started leaving the girls home on their own now and then with Jenny in charge, and Jenny took her new responsibilities seriously.

Too seriously, maybe. She was still just a kid. When Jon had been twelve, no one in their right mind would have left him in charge of a nine-year-old. He'd barely been responsible for himself at that age. But he wasn't their father, so it wasn't his place to judge.

"Jenny's right. Homework first, then I'll fix us some supper. And ice cream."

Through the routine of homework and supper, Jon stopped fretting about his increasing attachment to Kate's daughters and theirs to him. It wasn't until the girls were in bed, and he'd retrieved a beer from the fridge while tuning into Thursday Night Football, that it came back to him.

He sipped his beer while the Patriots whipped a lot of Texan butt, but after the rookie quarterback's surprising run for the end zone, his mind wandered away from the game and back to the guilt that sat uneasily on his conscience. He loved Kate, but he'd let her husband die. He'd let a drunk driver rip Jenny and Becca's daddy out of their lives. All of which made it impossible to just enjoy the here and now without a lot of self-recrimination. And without wondering if he had any right to enjoy it at all.

He drained the bottle and set it on the table next to the remote and glanced up. Becca stood on the threshold of the TV room, a tattered stuffed Dalmatian in her arms and Max at her side. There were tears on her face.

"Becca?" He sat forward and opened his arms. "What's wrong?"

The little girl dashed toward him, flinging herself into his arms. "I had a bad dream."

Jon lifted her into his lap and wrapped his arms about her trembling body. He snatched an afghan off the back of the couch and snuggled it around her.

"You want to talk about it?"

Becca shook her head vigorously and burrowed closer.

Kate had mentioned that Becca had begun having nightmares recently. Just when it seemed that that girls had started to heal, the nightmares had started. They were always about Ethan's death. Becca hadn't been there the night a drunk driver mowed her daddy down, but in her dreams she always was. In her dreams she was always shouting to warn her father to jump out of the way. But her father couldn't hear her.

Kids had amazing imaginations as it was, but in nightmares, Jon could only guess at how horrifying the scene would be to a nine-year-old. Kate had taken Becca back to the therapist both girls had seen for a while right after Ethan's death, but whether the woman was making any headway in sorting out Becca's nightmares, Jon didn't know.

He'd been only seven when his mother had succumbed to breast cancer and he'd been devastated, but never had he experienced the nightmares Becca did. Maybe he'd been more fortunate. His mother's dying had come after a long illness and not as a shocking surprise. Kate's family had lived next door back then, too, and Sandy Cameron had accepted Jon into the Cameron family circle, loving and caring for him just as she did her own boys. He recalled spending many nights at the Cameron house that first year when his own father was on the night shift, falling asleep with Kate's mom sitting on the side of his bed singing to him.

He hugged the little girl closer and began to hum.

Chapter 3

"IT WASN'T YOUR fault, Jon." Kate slid a steaming cup of coffee across the table and took a seat on the bench opposite. "If anyone is at fault other than Bart Onslow, it's me. If we hadn't been arguing, Ethan would never have been at the restaurant at that hour of the night in the first place."

Apparently, Becca had not shared the part of her dream that included her mother and father shouting at each other before Ethan stormed out the door and headed down to close up his popular ribs establishment. He'd sent the staff home and buttoned the place down for the night in their stead, probably trying to cool off before coming home to face Kate. Or giving her time to calm down and consider his side of the discussion rationally.

She'd been waiting for him armed with a whole new list of reasons to support her view. But he'd never come home to hear them. And here she was. Unable to ask for his forgiveness. Unable to let the guilt go and move on with her life. But Jon thought the blame was his.

"If I'd pulled Onslow over sooner—" Jon pushed his fingers through his hair, leaving it even more disheveled than usual.

"It's what? Not even a mile between Calico Jack's and Ethan's Ribs?" Kate interrupted. "Not much time to make much of an assessment about how incapacitated Onslow was."

They'd had this conversation before. Jon seemed to believe that turning on his light bar when he had was the sole cause of Onslow's veering recklessly off the road and into the parking lot at Ethan's Ribs instead of placing the blame, as the courts had, on Bart Onslow, who'd consumed far more than his usual one beer and then chosen to drive himself home.

Had Jon been so attentive to her needs and those of her girls for the past year because he blamed himself for Ethan's death, or because Ethan had wrung a promise from Jon to watch out for his girls? *His girls*, apparently, included her. At least in Jon's mind.

Jon shook his head. "I shouldn't have let him get into his truck in the first place."

Kate reached across the table to cover Jon's free hand with hers. He jerked his hand away, startling her. Surprised at both her own desire to touch him and by his reaction, Kate sat back. Time to change the subject.

"Thanks again for taking the girls. I appreciate it."

"Did you enjoy the chance to get out of Tide's Way and report from the capital for a change?"

Kate glanced out the window to avoid meeting Jon's gaze. "It wasn't New York, but I did enjoy covering our representative's speech on the house floor. DC is . . . different. It's such a crazy mixture of power and money and memorials. It has a different vibe." How to explain the feelings she'd had walking into the house chamber and knowing this was where things got decided that affected everyone's lives? Or the sense of urgency and importance everyone seemed to carry with them as they moved through the city? Or the frightening sense of vulnerability she'd felt personally?

Jon's brows lifted. "Sounds as though there's a but to go with that."

"Something weird happened—"

Alarm filled Jon's eyes.

Maybe she shouldn't have admitted that. But now that she'd started, it was too late not to finish. "When I left an after-hours meeting, I got an eerie sensation like someone was following me. It was creepy."

Her sudden awareness of Jon's amazing green gaze caught her by surprise. The warmth curling in her gut was unexpected, too.

"Why were you walking? DC is full of cabs." His question was laced with concern rather than condemnation. Ethan would have called her stupid.

"It was only a couple blocks. And I didn't think—I should have, I guess." She shouldn't have told Jon about the unsettling episode, either.

This time, it was Jon leaning across the table to enfold her hands in his. The comforting strength of them warmed more than just her icy fingers.

"That's all? No one actually accosted you or anything? You're all right?"

She shook her head. "I probably just imagined it. Maybe I just got spooked over nothing."

"Promise me you'll take a cab next time." He didn't take his hands away.

"If there is a next time." With the election heating up, she'd be stuck right here in Tide's Way for the next couple months. "I'll call a cab."

She turned her hands over, squeezed his briefly, then reluctantly withdrew them from his grip. It was amazing how bereft she felt now that she'd broken their physical connection.

"You're good at what you do. There'll be a next time," he said reassuringly.

"Yeah, well, for the next few months I'm stuck right here covering JJ's campaign to unseat Gordon Quinn."

"What's wrong with covering the campaign? Someone's gotta do it."

"I want to feel like I'm doing something important. Like my life makes a difference."

"You make a difference to Jenny and Becca. And me," he added softly.

"Oh, Jon. I know that." She sat back in her chair and lifted her empty palms. "But I meant . . . I want to make my mark on the world."

"Like winning a Pulitzer?"

She shook her head. "That would be sweet, sure, but I meant just every day. I want my life to count every day."

"Don't underestimate how much you mean to the people who love you."

His gaze was intense and his words sweet, but she ignored both in an effort to explain her frustration.

"My brothers make a difference. Will talks psychos into releasing hostages when he isn't training new troopers. Jake rescues people from burning buildings and puts out fires, and Ben trains dogs that save lives. Philip and Meg help soldiers put their lives back together when they come home from war. And you. Every day you make a difference, but I feel like I'm just treading water, keeping things afloat. Especially since . . . since Ethan has been gone.

"The rib joint is doing okay, but it feels like I'm always playing catch-up instead of looking ahead. The girls were coping, and then Becca starts with the nightmares again. And my chance to make something of my career as a journalist never seems to get out of Tide's Way where nothing, but nothing, ever happens." In frustration she slapped her palms down on the table, and Jon blinked.

"And nothing's going to change because I can't keep expecting you to watch the girls, and it's not fair to keep dumping them on my parents. Or one of my brothers."

"I loved having them," Jon reassured her again. "One nice thing about being a small-town cop is I get to make my own schedule. More or less."

"But you need to spend more time doing what you do, not less if you want to take over as chief when Don retires."

Jon made a face, drained his coffee and set the mug back on the table. "Allison's latest broadside is that when her Aunt Jennifer gets elected, she'll be the new chief and she'll give me the boot."

"She can't do that, can she?" Kate's frustration and self-absorption evaporated.

"Do what? Get herself appointed as the new chief or get me kicked off the squad?"

"Either!" Allison thought bearing the last name of Jolee was like an entitlement, but firing Jon? "What grounds would she have? Say JJ wins and Allison did con her aunt into giving her the chief's job, what reason would she have to fire a man who's given years of faithful, unblemished service to Tide's Way?"

"It's a small department in an even smaller office space. With my luck, she'd accuse me of sexual harassment if she decided that was the only way to be rid of me."

"That's ridiculous. Anyone who knows you would laugh."

Jon pushed away from the table and stood. "It might seem laughable to you, but it's a strange world we live in. Straight, white, Christian guys don't have much going for them anymore. We're considered the enemy. The privileged class who've kept women and minorities down for far too long."

"Well, I might be covering JJ's campaign, but I don't have to make it easy for her. I already don't like some of her ideas, and I'm going to be asking a lot of hard questions. And praying Quinn keeps his job."

"You do that." Jon retrieved his cap from the hook by the door and settled it on his head.

"Did you know she wants to turn the Jolee Plantation House into a home for criminals?" Kate followed Jon to the door. "In Tide's Way!"

"I'm not sure I agree with using the Jolee place, but her idea isn't a bad one." Jon stopped with his hand on the doorknob. "And it's not hardened criminals. Just young men who got afoul of the law as teenagers and never had much of a chance to get straight."

Kate planted her hands on her hips. "They're still criminals. God only knows what kind of chaos they'd bring to Tide's Way. That's why Ethan didn't want to raise the girls in the city. This isn't the right place for that kind of people."

"And the city is?" Jon raised his brows challengingly.

"Criminals just escalate. First it's a charge for drug possession, next they're selling the stuff. And stealing. And where does it stop? Rape? Killing? We don't want that kind of element in our town." Outrage boiled in Kate's breast. "Some disgruntled psychopath who goes off the deep end because life wasn't fair and he arms himself to the teeth and shoots up a school full of kids?"

"Whoa, Kate." Jon put his hand on her shoulder and squeezed.

Another shot of hot excitement began in her gut and flared outward.

"The kind of place JJ has in mind is for men who've just had a lousy start in life, got in a little trouble with the law, did their time and then got out, determined to go straight. All they need is a chance. A place to live, people who believe in them and support them. And a job. It's a good plan."

The excitement burning in her gut drowned her indignation. She'd been without a man for too long. That's all it was. She hadn't felt the touch of a man since Ethan. Other than her brothers, and her dad. And Jon. But before now, Jon's touch, his hugs, had always felt sympathetic or affectionate. And brotherly. This—this—whatever it was—was different. A flush warmed her cheeks as she moved out of his reach.

"Well, I don't like it. And I'm not going to make it easy for her. I'm going to stick it to her and make sure we get answers."

Jon smiled. "That's your job. You're good at it. And you do make a difference." He tossed her a mock salute and stepped out onto her porch. "By the way, I promised Becca I'd go to her soccer game this week. I hope that's okay."

"Of course," she murmured as he turned and headed for his cruiser.

Her body continued to hum with unexplained excitement as he folded himself into the vehicle, waved, and backed out of her driveway.

Chapter 4

TIDE'S WAY WAS quiet this sunny Tuesday with all the kids back to school and the rush up to the holidays not yet begun. After promising his boss to be present for tonight's town meeting, Jon had taken a walk around the town square, stopping in at Abby's Book Nook, Emmy Lou's Antique shop and the Tide's Way Tea House. Between Abby, Emmy and the ladies at the teahouse, there wasn't much local gossip he didn't know. It was a good way to keep tabs on the goings on around town.

Today he'd learned that Aaron Cavaleri didn't approve of his mother's new boyfriend. The teahouse ladies hadn't had much good to say about Lonny Ward, either. It sounded like a situation Jon needed to take an interest in. Two fall weddings were coming up he hadn't known about, and the fall fair at the Baptist Church was postponed due to the head of the ladies guild's illness.

Completing the circuit, he climbed into his cruiser for a mobile tour of Tide's Way. Not that there were a lot of trouble spots in his quiet little town, but it was always good to be seen and available.

He started with a trip out to the trailer park where Aaron lived. The Cavaleri doublewide was deserted with no cars in the dusty driveway. Aaron would be at school and the last Jon knew, Aaron's mother was employed over in Wilmington, so that wasn't surprising. Jon wasn't sure why he'd come this way at all. He headed back toward town, then turned left on Stewart Road and headed toward the waterway and the barrier island. The now familiar jolt of remorse hit him as he passed Calico Jack's. Even if he had no reason to feel guilty, seeing the place still hit him with a sense of what might have been.

The weather-beaten façade of the old Jolee home surrounded by unkempt lawn and fallow fields sidetracked his melancholy. He really did want the chief's job when Atkins retired. But it was a position appointed by the mayor, and come January, that might be JJ. And Allison wanted the job, too. She might be a Jolee, but this was his town just as much as it was hers. He'd been born and brought up here. Literally, since his mother had never made it to the hospital in time for his delivery. Allison had been born in Charlotte and only moved to Tide's Way for her high school years, then returned to Charlotte until she'd been hired on as a fellow officer. He'd only abandoned Tide's Way for the six years he'd spent in the Marine Corps and his first four years as a cop in Wilmington.

Six years he'd hoped would quench the fire burning in his gut for Kate Cameron. His father had been appalled when his only child had signed on the dotted line to become a Marine, but the day Jon had discovered Kate was following Ethan Shaw off to college, he'd driven aimlessly trying to outrun the crushing news. The Marine recruiting office was the first thing he'd actually taken note of during that drive, and suddenly joining the Corps had seemed like a first-rate idea.

By the time his tour was up, she was married to Ethan, and he'd convinced himself he could come home and not covet his friend's wife.

It had been easier at the beginning, while he was on the Wilmington police force and living in an apartment on the outskirts of the city. But when Tide's Way had decided they could afford more than a one-cop police department, he'd applied, and some demon of self-flagellation had beguiled him into purchasing a beautiful old house on the hill overlooking the little development where Ethan and Kate lived. They were all friends, he'd assured himself. He could handle it.

Jon passed Kate's brother's kennel and considered pulling in to check out Ben's new service dog project, but once again there were no vehicles in the driveway. Meg was probably up at Lejeune where she'd counseled Marines suffering from PTS and other deployment related issues. Ben's truck was gone as well, so Jon drove on, headed for the bridge to the barrier island. The subject of Allison and his history with her returned to his thinking.

Allison had come onto the Tide's Way force a year after he had. Working with her at the beginning had been pleasant enough, but when she began to make unwelcome passes at him, things had gotten less comfortable. She was a beautiful woman, and if he hadn't known her history, he might have been flattered. Perhaps even attracted. In high school she'd had a reputation for sleeping around, and he had no interest in getting involved with her. In spite of his disinterest, she'd found excuses to corner him in ways that were all too suggestive in situations that were totally inappropriate. She hadn't taken the hint even when he got less tactful about dropping them.

Their complete falling out had come at a Christmas party. She had clearly had too much to drink and spent most of the night latching onto him at every opportunity. A kiss with a lot of tongue under a sprig of mistletoe had sent him into retreat in another room where a basketball game was on the television and half a dozen guys were cheering for the Tarheels. Without warning, Allison had plopped herself in his lap, wriggling against his crotch with total disregard for all the watching eyes. When she groped his junk, he'd jumped to his, feet dumping her unceremoniously on the floor. It had been anything but tactful, but he'd been too shocked to react otherwise.

She'd never forgiven him.

Whoever had written that line about hell having no fury like a woman scorned knew what he'd been talking about. Ever since that fateful party, Allison had had it out for him. If her aunt won the mayoral race, she might very well ask her niece to become the new chief. And Jon would quickly be out of the department for good.

He turned the cruiser around in the Anchor Beach parking lot and headed south on the island lined with lovely weathered homes. Most were summer homes, or at least weekend retreats, but there were several year-round residents. The Cameron home was one of them. The house next door that had once belonged to his dad had a new coat of paint. Gone was the faded gray, replaced with a peaceful sea green color. It looked good and well cared for. He pulled his cruiser to a stop and rolled down his window when he saw the new owner headed out to check his mailbox.

"Something wrong, officer?" The man was tall with a full head of white hair and stooped shoulders.

Jon shook his head. "Nope. Just admiring the new paint job."

The man glanced over his shoulder at his home, then back at Jon. Then his eyes focused sharply on Jon. "You're the guy who grew up in this house, right?"

"I am. Jon Canfield." Jon stuck his hand out the window. "And you're Greg Jensen. The place looks good."

Greg Jenson smiled. "Glad you approve. I've heard good things about you from Cam and Sandy. You want to come in and check out what the wife and I have done to the inside?"

"I'd love to, but another time, maybe?" His dad had been gone less than a year. The idea of touring the house and seeing nothing of his father inside was too painful. "I'm on duty and supposedly keeping tabs on the whole town. Gotta keep moving."

"Well, it was good to meet you Officer Canfield. Another time, then."

"Just call me Jon."

The man nodded and reached to retrieve his mail. Jon put the cruiser back in gear and continued past the Cameron home, rounded the circle and headed back the way he'd come. He left the window down. It was a beautiful day out here at the shore. Too bad so few people were here to enjoy it. He could see the ocean from his home, but the scent of salt and sand didn't drift that far except on foggy days. Perhaps he should have sold his home instead of his father's. But that would have meant moving away from Kate and maybe only seeing her when she came out to visit her parents. Just dropping in on her would be less casual and harder to justify in spite of his promise to Ethan. He should get a life . . . of his own.

Few minutes later he crossed the bridge back onto the mainland. He considered taking Shoreline Drive up past the elementary school and the assisted living center but decided a quick tour of the Jolee place might be good considering the item he knew would be on tonight's town meeting agenda.

Something needed to be done about the Jolee Plantation now that the town was responsible for the place. A year and a half ago, Kate's brother Will, who was a State Trooper, had discovered the remnants of a meth lab in one of the out buildings. The county sheriff's department and the Tide's Way force had kept a closer eye on the place ever since, but it required a visit by one or the other just about every day.

Jon pulled his cruiser around the gravel drive overgrown with grass and pulled to a stop. Checking the place out was more than just a drive-by. It required getting out of the cruiser and walking the grounds to check all the buildings.

The rotten well cover where Will's adopted son, Sam Reagan had broken his leg had been replaced and locked to keep other kids from falling in. Deadbolts had been installed on the doors to the main house and the windows boarded up but the barns and old slave quarters remained a hazard. Tide's Way had inherited the property from the previous owner and it had seemed like a gift at the time, but nothing had been done with it, and now the property was a drain on the town budget.

The current mayoral candidate challenging Gordon Quinn's long reign wanted to turn the empty mansion into a facility to give young men who had gotten off to a bad start a second chance in life. JJ was passionate about her project, and Jon was on the fence about the idea. On the one hand, the property would become a tax paying entity and someone would be living there, preventing transients and other trespassers from making free of the place. On the other side of the debate was the historical significance of the property. Then a heated grass-roots opposition to a home for grown-up delinquents had gotten into the fray.

Kate wasn't alone in her objections. None of the property owners close to the plantation acres were happy about the idea of former criminals living there, however minor their offenses had been. Trouble was brewing in Tide's Way. The kind of discord the town hadn't seen since the aftermath of the Civil War.

Jon made the rounds peeking into the disused buildings. He wondered what JJ's plan included regarding all the outbuildings. Nothing seemed out of place today, at least. He climbed back into his cruiser and headed back down the drive.

Chapter 5

WITH HIS BROAD uniformed shoulders propped against the wall, arms folded across his chest and his eyes searching the room, Jon Canfield looked like a man who was expecting trouble.

Kate scanned the town hall meeting room, following his lead. There seemed to be a number of people here she didn't know. Out-of-towners. Were they here in support of JJ's proposal on tonight's agenda? Were they the trouble Jon was watching out for? Why?

Her gaze returned to Jon. He stood a head taller than most of the men in the room, a formidable deterrent just by being there. His curly brown hair was laced with early strands of gray, but his body looked as fit and strong as it had when he was fresh out of the Marines. Lean where a man's body should be lean and broad where it counted.

Amazing that no woman had ever rounded Jon up and gotten him to the altar. The thought flitted unbidden through her mind and left her feeling a little unsettled. He'd had a woman once. Back when he was on the Wilmington Police Force. They'd lived together with her son from a previous relationship and everyone who knew him assumed they'd marry. But then, shortly after they moved to the house just uphill of the row of poplars that divided Kate's new subdivision from the older homes in Tide's Way, Candy had left. No argument or falling out that anyone knew of. Candy and Brian Dillon just up and moved to Georgia. And Jon hadn't appeared to grieve their going.

Kate's friend Jacqui was always trying to hook him up with some hopeful single lady, but none had managed to snag him. That was fortuitous for Kate, considering this past year. Jon had been around a lot, taking over little repairs around the house that had once been Ethan's job, taking the girls when she needed a sitter on short notice, being a good listener when she needed a sounding board. If he'd had a wife, that wouldn't have been the case in spite of any promises Jon had made to Ethan.

Kate tore her thoughts away from Jon and the changes the past year had made in their friendship. She had a job to do, and it wasn't ogling handsome cops. Or wondering about their love lives.

Miss Jennifer Jones, white hair perfectly coifed and dressed in a tailored charcoal suit with an eye-catching magenta scarf, sat in the front row. Kate didn't know the woman on JJ's left, but the stunningly beautiful blonde woman on her right was all too familiar. Allison Jolee. Jon's fellow officer and nemesis.

Jon hadn't told Kate about Allison's unwelcome pursuit, but her brothers had. She didn't blame Jon for not wanting anything to do with a woman who went through lovers like most people go through tissues, using them and tossing them aside once she'd gotten what she wanted. At least that was the reputation Allison had earned in high school. Kate had no idea whom Allison was shacking up with now. Whoever it was, she was showing a lot more discretion about her love life than she had even two years ago. Maybe it had something to do with her desire to become Tide's Way's new chief when Atkins retired.

The crack of a gavel brought Kate's attention back to the meeting. She grabbed her notebook and flipped it open to a new page. She should get herself a tablet and learn to take notes on that. Notes that could be transferred anywhere, to her computer or that of her editor via email or Dropbox. All her associates were tech savvy, but the urge to hold a pen and scribble in a notebook kept her from moving into the digital age.

Mayor Quinn opened the meeting with all the usual formalities. Kate recorded just the pertinent details. They weren't the story tonight.

"Miss Jennifer," Quinn nodded toward the front row. "The floor is yours to outline your proposal."

JJ stood and walked to the podium provided for townspeople from the floor to address the assembly. Her heels clicked decisively on the hardwood floor.

"Good evening." She smiled at the crowd. "Most of you know me and that I'm running for mayor, but for those new to Tide's Way . . ." she glanced toward the back where Kate had previously noticed the row of unfamiliar faces.

"I've been a resident of this town all my life, and I'm proud to say I've had a hand in many of the civic groups and efforts to make Tide's Way a better place to live, but this is my first foray into the political arena. I admire Gordon Quinn who has done much for our town, but he's been our mayor for close to fifteen years and it's time for some new and fresh leadership.

"Mine."

JJ was a confident politician. Kate would give her that. Quinn had been a good mayor and much admired. That JJ could so confidently assert she brought something new to the table was a bold move, even if a little out of place at a regular town meeting.

"But it's not my life or my qualifications for mayor that I wish to speak to tonight. It is, perhaps, even more important to me than stealing Gordon Quinn's seat." She winked at the current mayor in a show of good will, and then her face became serious again.

"Some of you have probably heard bits and pieces of my proposal, or at least heard rumors. I'd like to ask you to leave judgment aside until I've had a chance to share my vision with you and how I feel it will benefit both Tide's Way and the people my plan will serve."

There was a murmuring in the crowd, some sounding vaguely hostile, but JJ didn't falter as she began.

"As you all know, the current state of the physical building, the original Jolee Mansion that was built in 1842, is not good. Termite damage has been found and if not treated in the very near future could destroy the historic old mansion. There are other maintenance issues that need to be addressed as well. But the building, currently belonging to the town, does not pay taxes, and there are no funds allotted to do what needs to be done to keep a piece of our history from crumbling into the ground."

"What does a halfway house have to do with maintaining history?" A rude voice in the crowd interrupted. A number of assenting murmurs greeted the question.

"Please," JJ went on, apparently unfazed. "There will be plenty of time to discuss and ask questions after I've presented the plan."

JJ waited until the murmurs of disapproval died down, her hands folded serenely on top of the podium.

"I'd like to tell you a story," she began. "About a young man named Matthew. In his early teen years, despite coming from a good home with supportive, loving parents, Matthew got caught up in the wrong crowd at school. His first brush with the law was nothing more than a fistfight with another student that neither boy would ever reveal the reason for.

"His next encounter with law enforcement was for drag racing on a public road. Four months later he was caught driving while his license was still under suspension, and this time he had also been drinking. His license was revoked for two years."

Kate scribbled furiously, making sure not to miss any details that might turn out to be important. She had no idea where this story was going, but the more information she had when she began digging deeper the better.

"Matthew eventually went to prison for two years on a breaking and entering charge. An unusually harsh sentence for the crime, but in light of the string of arrests and convictions preceding that offense, the judge apparently felt time in prison would straighten the young man out."

The townsfolk were beginning to squirm with impatience.

"Matthew's mother was diagnosed with cancer when he was barely into his teens. Matthew's father was too wrapped up in caring for his wife and worrying over her future to notice his son's slide from a straight-A student and well-behaved young man to a boy failing both in school and out. Maybe all Matthew wanted and needed was a little attention, but we'll never know.

"The things that happened to Matthew in prison were not nice, but he endured and was released, according to the prison chaplain, determined to make a new beginning for himself.

"Unfortunately, during his time in prison, his mother died and his father lost his life in an automobile accident. Their home had been sold to pay off huge medical debts, leaving Matthew nothing with which to begin his new life. With nowhere to go, he ended up on the streets. With his criminal record, he was unable to find stable employment. With no family to offer support and encouragement, he was drawn, once again, into a life of crime."

JJ paused. It was hard to tell whether her moment of silence was theatric, or whether she was touched in some personal way by this unknown Matthew's story. Kate waited, her pencil poised. Jon still leaned against the wall, but was reading something on his cell phone, perhaps not even listening to the long tale about an unfortunate young man no one knew or probably even cared about. He glanced up as if the sudden silence had caught his attention and met Kate's gaze. He smiled, but it wasn't his usual generous smile that added a sparkle to his sea-green eyes. He nodded his head briefly, and looked back down at his phone.

JJ was talking again. Kate had missed the first part of what she'd said during those moments of wordless communication with Jon.

"That's why I am so committed to creating what I'd like to call Second Chance House for young men like Matthew. The Jolee Mansion has been vacant and unused for far too long. This would be a worthy way to put that grand old home back to use."

She broke off as a low grumble of dissent began to swell. She nodded toward Allison, who jumped to her feet and thrust a manila file folder into JJ's hand. JJ opened the folder, then looked back at the crowd. She began reading statistics for recidivism in several different cities as compared with small towns and rural areas.

The restive clamor grew more specific.

"Not in Tide's Way." A burly man standing against the wall not far from Kate spoke up. "Not in Tide's Way!" Another voice joined the refrain. It became a chant.

Brianna Cameron jumped to her feet. Kate's sister-in-law was an ardent supporter of having the Jolee Plantation restored to its original glory with the idea of making it a showplace recounting an important piece of Tide's Way history. Zoe, Bree's friend and Kate's youngest brother's wife, stood up, joining Bree. Then two men got to their feet, flanking the women.

Tony Jenkins, a member of the Rotary, was active on at least a dozen committees. His sidekick, Bob Cahill, was another active member of the historical society. The two men and Kate's sisters-in-law made up the committee spearheading the restoration drive, and they had a bond issue on the fall ballot to fund it. It stood to reason they would oppose the idea of turning the property into a halfway house for recently released felons.

Kate drew a line down the middle of a blank page and began adding names to the pro and con columns. JJ and presumably Allison were on the pro side. Kate flicked a glance in Jon's direction, and then wrote his name under Allison's and put a question mark next to it.

As different residents popped up to add their opposition, the list grew under the first four names Kate had started the con list with.

"Our kids wait for the school bus less than a hundred yards from the end of the drive leading up to the Jolee place," a woman in a sweat suit with a messy bun spoke up. "I don't want to worry about what could happen to them when they get off the bus and I'm still at work."

JJ waited patiently while everyone who felt inclined to add an opinion had their chance. When the last of the objections petered out, she straightened her shoulders.

"How would you feel if Matthew was your son?" JJ pointed directly as several of the townsfolk who'd made the loudest objections. "Or your nephew? Or grandson? Or brother? Wouldn't you want the community they grew up in to support them?"

Argument erupted again. This time more strident. One man in the row next to where Kate stood gave his neighbor a shove and the other man staggered into the aisle bumping into Kate. She sat down hard. The man muttered an apology but didn't bother to help her to her feet before he turned to address his assailant.

"Are you okay?" Jon had a hand under her elbow, helping her to stand. He peered into her eyes, a frown of concern furrowing his brow. A moment ago, he'd been on the far side of the room. How had he gotten across the room so quickly?

"I'm fine." She bent to retrieve her notebook from the floor. "Really," she insisted when he seemed uncertain.

Jon nodded and turned away. A moment later, he had the original pusher by the upper arm and was escorting him from the room with the second guy trailing them.

38

"Perhaps we should hear from law enforcement." JJ brought Kate's attention back to the discussion. "Chief Atkins? Would you care to add anything to the conversation?"

Don Atkins strode toward the podium, and the crowd settled back in their seats. Surely their chief of police would be on their side.

Skye Taylor

Chapter 6

KATE TYPED FURIOUSLY. Who knew tonight's town
meeting was going to turn into such ruckus? Suddenly, the
assignment to cover JJ's campaign had gotten a whole lot
more interesting than it had sounded when her boss tasked
her with it.

Miss Jennifer, as some people knew her, JJ to most of
Tide's Way, had never married. Wealthy and without a
husband or children to fill her days she'd dedicated herself to
a variety of civic causes. Only recently had she decided to get
into politics. She was an elegant woman who had been a
pampered southern belle in her youth and was still beautiful
at fifty. She was well liked and highly respected.

Gordon Quinn had been in office for several terms, but
since his first campaign, this was the first time anyone had
seriously challenged him. He had come into the job when the
mayor before him had dropped dead of a heart attack. Quinn
had taken over without missing a beat. An energetic man
with an eye to bringing a small tidewater town to the notice
of more than just tourism, he'd easily been elected in his own
right, and he'd done much of what he'd promised. They had
lovely beaches but not much else, and he'd had plans to
change that.

Tide's Way's lovely setting and proximity to the city of
Wilmington and its airport as well as miles of beautiful
beaches had brought business as well as tourists. Just a year
previously, a handsome conference center had been built as

40

an annex to Kett's Hotel, and Kate's sister-in-law, who had worked for Kett's for just over two years, had been tagged to manage the new center. Quinn's plans for Tide's Way had kept the new facility busy, almost as soon as construction was completed. The place nearly always had some function going on, and Bree worked long hours. It was probably a good thing Will had transitioned out of the highway patrol and into a position with more reliable hours.

Now JJ was challenging both Quinn and the town with an even more radical plan. No one seemed to know what had put this particular bee into JJ's bonnet, but that was half the fun in being a good journalist. At least for Kate. Digging where others hadn't thought to dig and looking at all angles of a story, finding the story beneath the story, were the aspects of her job that drove Kate and had from her first days as an intern for a well-known New York paper while she was still in college.

Miss Jones was a generous donor to several charities and her hand was often a guiding light on projects for the welfare of the community, but Kate had never known her to seem this emotionally invested.

At least that's how it had struck her when JJ blinked a little too rapidly at one point in her recital about the life of this unknown young man who'd gotten himself into trouble over and over again. She hadn't backed down in the face of considerable opposition, in spite of how that might impact her run for mayor.

To Kate, at least, the overwhelming opinion of the townspeople who attended the meeting appeared to be decidedly in the Not-In-Tide's-Way camp. Tide's Way was a peaceful little seaside town where everyone knew everyone else, even the people who flocked to beaches for the summer season and swelled the town's population to nearly double. Petty thievery, an occasional domestic dispute, traffic accidents, drunk driving, and the rare beach party turned raucous were the extent of the troubles the small Tide's Way police force were ever called on to deal with.

Although when a drunk driver had ended Ethan's life, it had not seemed very minor to Kate. Her chest tightened as it always did when she thought about Ethan and how angry she'd been the last time she'd seen him alive. She closed her eyes and tried to force the memory away.

They'd rarely argued, and Ethan had never walked out on an unresolved difference. Until that night. The blame was not all hers, but still . . .

An image of Jon standing on her porch just before midnight with tears in his eyes filled her head, and a wave of regret washed over her. Ethan had been where he was because of her refusal to see his point of view as equally import as hers. Because she'd wanted to move back to the city so she could pursue her dream of becoming a journalist for a major newspaper and he didn't want to leave the restaurant he'd spent years building into a going concern. There had seemed to be no compromise to be made.

It had been a row like nothing they'd ever had in their ten years of married life. His parting shot as he'd stormed out of the house was that he didn't want his little girls growing up in a city where they would never be safe. She'd slammed the door behind him, more out of frustration than disagreement. Tide's Way was a great place for kids to grow up. But working for a small-town newspaper just wasn't what she'd envisioned for herself after the bustle of her internship with the *New York Times*.

She shot from her chair, headed to the kitchen, and began the ritual of making herself a mug of tea, trying to forget the last thing she'd said to Ethan. The words had been cutting and unfair. And she'd never gotten a chance to take them back.

I'm sorry, Ethan. I'm sorry you didn't come home so we could make up again.

She hugged the hot mug to her chest and let the litany of apology play itself out. In her soul, she knew he was in a good place and he understood. She hadn't uprooted the girls the moment he was gone, but that was more from shocked inertia and guilt than acquiescence to his point of view.

She moved toward the hall, setting the mug on the corner of her desk on her way by. She went into Becca's room first. Becca, who looked so much like Ethan, or at least as Ethan had looked in photos taken of him when he was this age, lay sprawled on her back with the covers sliding off the bed onto the floor. Kate pulled them back into place and tucked Becca in. She kissed her on the forehead, tucked her tattered stuffed Dalmatian next to her, and moved on to Jenny's room.

Jenny, twelve and eager to be all grown up, curled on her side, nearly invisible under her down puff. Kate pushed a fold of the coverlet away from her daughter's face and kissed her cheek. She straightened and gazed down at her older daughter for a long moment. Ethan had been certain Tide's Way was the best place to bring up their girls, away from the dangers a city held.

But what if this halfway house for delinquent young men became a reality? Would he still think so then?

She returned to her desk.

She studied the list of pros and cons again. After a moment, she added kids. All kids, not just hers, to reasons against.

Another as-yet-unheard-from group should be added to the con list, too. It was surely a given that the non-voting, wealthy property owners with fancy homes on the barrier island, who were here only part time, wouldn't like the idea of having ex-cons camped on the other side of the waterway, separated only by a few miles and an easily accessible bridge.

Another negative was JJ's dream, a pipe-dream in Kate's opinion, that these young men she wanted to help would be able to find meaningful employment in Tide's Way. Most of those who actually worked *in* Tide's Way were skilled tradesmen or college educated. The entry-level service type jobs were scarce and hard to get except in the summer, and even then they'd be in competition with local high school and college kids. Unless these men had their own transportation, they wouldn't be able to get to places like Wilmington or Jacksonville where jobs were more plentiful. Wouldn't it make more sense to create this halfway house in either of those two cities?

She brought up the help-wanted section of the last issue of the town's weekly, *Tide's Way Anchor News*. Unless these young men wanted to paint, considering the number of listings for painters wanted. It seemed like half the town must be in the process of getting their houses spiffed up. But that was temporary. Not like having a position at the diner or the hotel. What would these men do to earn their keep and stay out of trouble?

With no new ideas for her list of whys and why nots, Kate typed in Jennifer Jones, Tide's Way NC. A long list of links popped up on her browser. All of them things about JJ Kate already knew. She typed in Jennifer Jones and Matthew.

She sat back and chuckled. There seemed to be quite a few Jennifer Joneses and Matthews by a number of last names on a site called The Knot. All about weddings. She hunched forward and scrolled through the list, but none were her Jennifer Jones. These all appeared to be young people recently married, but really! Did everyone create a website about their weddings now?

Several links were articles about the life and death of an actress born in the last century with and without any Matthew connection.

This was getting her nowhere. If, in fact, Matthew was a real person and not some composite poster child JJ had made up, what Kate needed was Matthew's last name.

IGNORING THE TELEVISION currently tuned to a news broadcast, Jon crossed the living room to stand by the sliding glass doors opening out onto a patio that overlooked the development that had grown up in what used to be an orchard surrounding his house. From his upstairs windows he could see the Intracoastal Waterway and the ocean beyond, but not from down here.

The house had been purchased on a whim with perhaps more than just a little masochistic desire to live near Kate, even though she did belong to another man and that man was his best friend. But the condition the house had been in when he bought it turned out to be a good distraction. Both from Kate's proximity and Candy's sudden departure from his life. It had needed a lot of fixing up, and he'd enjoyed the work.

He was in the midst of the last of the big projects now, replacing the cracked old patio bricks with pavers. The patio and the stacks of waiting pavers were in darkness just outside the door, but there was a light on in Kate's house. The one in the little den she'd turned into her office. The space where she did most of her writing. He couldn't see her or the desk she was probably sitting at, staring into her computer screen with tired eyes, but he could picture her there typing up tonight's story for tomorrow's evening paper.

There was probably something wrong with his pining after a woman who had never thought of him as anything more than a friend. If only he'd been able to find more than a passing interest in someone else, he might have had a family of his own by now. Sons to wrestle with on the floor or shoot hoops with in the driveway. Or maybe he would have had daughters who would have him wrapped firmly around their little fingers from day one. Girls like Jenny and Becca.

This past year, standing in for Ethan whenever Kate needed help or one of the girls had a father-daughter event to attend, had filled an aching void in Jon's life. Kate had been a widow for more than a year. So far as he knew, she had not dated anyone in that year. Nor did she appear to be even thinking about returning to the singles scene.

What would she think if he asked her out on a date, just the two of them without Jenny and Becca? Would Kate be shocked by the idea? Perhaps she'd just laugh at his nonsense. For the zillionth time, he wondered how their lives would have turned out if he'd never introduced her to Ethan in the first place.

Neither of them would have become the people they were today. He'd have gone to college instead of becoming a Marine and then a cop. But back then he'd had no idea what he wanted to do when he grew up, so who knew what he would have been doing now. Kate had followed Ethan to school in New York City and caught the journalism bug between her sophomore and junior years.

Wishing for might-have-beens wouldn't change anything. If he wanted any hope of a second chance to win Kate's heart, he'd have to put the fear of rejection aside and pursue her before another Ethan appeared in her life. Except that meant getting past his guilt over the fact that she was free to be pursued in the first place.

Ethan had asked him to take care of Kate, not seduce her.

Jon turned back to the news broadcast, doing his best to shut out his troubled thoughts about Kate.

"Everyone is asking, who is Matthew?" A perky late night news desk personality with an elaborate braid of hair and a cherry-red blazer leaned toward the camera as if she were going to share some titillating gossip. "Miss Jones' touching story about Matthew's journey from a typical teenager who got on the wrong side of the law and ended up in a situation he couldn't find his way out of felt kind of personal. But there don't appear to be any Matthews in her extended family. Nor has this station been able to find . . ."

Jon turned the television off.

He didn't care who Matthew was. He knew plenty of young men who fit the description, with as many different names. He also knew several young men who didn't end up where Matthew had because someone had cared enough to give them a second chance.

His old partner on the Wilmington Police force was one of those who cared. It had started with a kid he'd separated from a number of known gang members who were being arrested for peddling drugs. The cherubic looking kid, ironically named Gabriel, had been on the verge of getting sucked into that gang. An orphan living with an ailing grandmother, he'd been eager to become part of something, and the gang was better than nothing.

Jerry Brady had offered the kid a job, then a place to stay and finally a place at the Brady dinner table. Gabriel Hunter had recently been sworn in as the newest member of the Wilmington PD. Since saving Gabriel, Brady and his wife had opened their home and their hearts to three other troubled young men too old for foster care and too young to make a go of it on their own, and so far their batting average was a thousand.

Sometimes all it took to keep a kid out of trouble was someone interested enough to give them an alternative. JJ's idea for a second-chance house was just that sort of alternative. Except for the involvement of the Jolee property, he was one hundred percent behind JJ's project. Kate was one hundred percent against. And if he knew Kate, she was just as determined to find out who Matthew was as she was to stop the town from turning the Jolee mansion over to JJ.

Chapter 7

KATE WAS LATER getting home than she'd expected. She had stopped in at Ethan's Ribs on her way to check on things and had run into a problem with inventory that had taken longer to straighten out than it should have. Trying to be her brother-in-law's on-site manager was complicating her life despite her nostalgia about the restaurant Ethan had spent so much of his time and effort building up.

But whether she could bring herself to sell out wasn't the issue anyway. Garrett wasn't ready to pull the plug. Maybe he was hanging on to memories of his brother, too. Once Garrett had retired from the military in six or seven years, the brothers had planned to grow old together running the place. It just hadn't worked out that way.

She pulled into her driveway, gathered up her stuff and ran the driver's side window down. Reaching out the now open window, she grasped the door handle and opened the car door. One of these days, maybe when she got her next paycheck, she'd get the darned latch mechanism fixed so she could go back to opening her door from the inside.

She climbed out, her arms full, and kicked the door shut. She'd come out and close the window later. Jenny called the old van a rust bucket. Kate wasn't sure where she'd heard that expression first, but the term fit. The faulty door latch wasn't the only thing wrong with it.

Ethan had been good with cars and had tinkered with her van often, but since his death it had gone downhill fast. She stopped in the middle of the front walk as an image of Ethan, his shaggy brown hair falling in his eyes as he teased her about the van, flashed through her mind. The pang of loss had been so sharp a year ago that it had brought tears to her eyes, but today she smiled at the memory.

How long had it been since she had felt that breathless stab of pain? She deliberately pictured Ethan on his back on the crawler, scooting out from under the car to grin up at her. She still missed him, but the ache had eased. Her life had gone on without him in spite of how impossible it had seemed at first.

It had been thirteen months and three weeks since that dreadful night. She'd lived through all the firsts: first birthday, first anniversary, first Christmas, first vacation. Was getting through all those firsts a rite of passage and once achieved a woman could get on with her life?

She shook her head and resumed her way up the driveway. She wasn't sure how she felt about the change. Ethan had been her first and only lover. He'd swept her off her sixteen-year-old feet and never let her down. Until his heart had stopped beating. *When was the last time I cried for him?*

She rapped on the door with her toe, expecting one of the girls to open the door for her. Neither did. Juggling her things, she managed to turn the knob, step inside and dump her load onto the end of the couch.

"Jenny? Becca?" She kicked off the high heels she'd put on that morning and regretted for the rest of the day.

The kitchen was empty. The girls should have been at the table doing their homework. That was the deal. If she let them come home instead of getting off the bus at their cousin's house, they were to come straight inside, change out of their school uniforms and start their homework.

"Jenny? Becca?" Kate raised her voice and called down the hall.

Still no answer.

Maybe trusting them to come home on their own should wait another year or two. She crossed the kitchen in her stocking feet, heard the giggling coming from the back yard, and stepped out onto the back porch.

Her girls were covered with suds. Becca held the hose while Jenny clutched Max's collar. Max sat in a puddle of lather, his ears laid back and not looking happy. Jon was doing his best to keep the hose aimed at sluicing the suds off the dog.

He was soaked. And still in uniform.

"Surely this isn't in your job description." Kate moved across to the railing.

Jon looked up and grinned. "I took an oath to serve my community to the best of my ability, ma'am." He winked and went back to seeing that Max got properly rinsed off while Kate bit her lip to quell the fluttering in her gut at the sight of his well muscled shoulders flexing beneath the soaked uniform.

A moment later, the dog sprang free and began to shake. Jon jumped to his feet and backed up. Not that it made much of a difference. His knees were soaked and his shirt liberally spattered with suds and dog hair. Becca ran to shut off the water. Jenny just looked up at Kate and shrugged.

"He ran away." Becca dashed back to foot of the stairs. "We called and called and called. But he didn't come home. Not until Uncle Jon got here and called him. I think Max only listens to grownups."

"But why the bath?" Kate stayed on the porch, well out of reach of wet dog and soaked kids. Her favorite suit had just come back from the cleaners and she wasn't eager to get it soiled.

"We didn't think you would like the way he stinked." Jenny shrugged again.

"I think he found a dead animal to roll in," Jon explained, coming to stand beside Becca. It was a toss-up as to which one looked wetter.

Max bounded past Jon and up the stairs, clearly intent on greeting Kate with his usual tail-wagging enthusiasm.

Kate squealed and jumped out of the way as Jon made a grab for the dog's collar.

"Go get a towel," Jon said to Jenny.

Jenny dashed past her mother and into the kitchen, appearing a moment later with the requested towel.

"You both need to get changed again and get back to your homework. We'll discuss how Max came to be running free later."

The girls rushed past her, happy to put off the reckoning.

Kate sighed. "Did you volunteer to get involved with the bath, or was it because the girls couldn't manage without help?"

Jon surveyed the damage to his uniform. "It did get a little out of hand. Had I known, I'd have tied the disgraceful animal up and gone home to change first. I guess I'd better go do that now."

"Are you done for the day?" Kate didn't want him to go. Besides not wanting to wallow in the unhappy mix of irritation over problems at Ethan's Ribs and nostalgia, she had an ulterior motive. She had put Jon's name in the pro column under JJ and Alison's, but she wasn't really sure where he stood. He'd seemed vague about using the Jolee mansion, but okay with the idea of a half-way house. She wanted to find out for sure which camp he was in.

"I am unless something unexpected comes up." He retrieved his cap from the picnic table and set it on his head.

"It's nothing fancy, but you're welcome to join us for supper. If you want to."

"I'd like that. Let me get out of my soggy duds and I'll be back." He saluted, turned and jogged across the lawn to the fringe of young poplars that divided her property from his. A moment later he appeared again walking up the hill to his house with long easy strides.

Kate watched him go, praying he was going to stick with his objections to the Jolee place even if he did support JJ's idea for a second-chance home. She needed her best friend on her side in this fight. And a fight she expected it was going to be.

JON REACHED FOR the last slice of pizza. Even frozen pizza was good if he was sharing it with Kate and her girls, and it appeared no one else was going to eat that last piece. Kate had pushed her plate away after one slice, and Becca and Jenny had abandoned the table once they'd had their fill. There was apparently something on the Disney channel that was way more interesting than the discussion their mother had introduced to the supper table conversation.

Kate pulled one foot up and tucked it under her other knee. She'd changed into sweatpants and an old T-shirt with her honey-colored curls partially caught up in a clip of some sort. She looked adorable in spite of the mutinous expression on her face.

"Ask your brother if you don't believe me," he told her picking up where the conversation had left off when the girls had asked to be excused.

"Which one?" Kate challenged. "Jake thinks the place is a fantastic representative of the era and in remarkable shape considering the lack of care in recent years."

"I was talking about Will, and you know it," Jon replied trying to ignore the curls escaping around her face that made him feel like kissing her instead of continuing the discussion about JJ's second-chance-house plans. "He's seen evidence of trespassers on a regular basis and criminal behavior on several occasions. If the place had permanent occupants, that would go away."

Kate threw up her hands and dropped her foot to the floor, her eyes shooting him an obvious dare. Was she trying to start a fight?

"Are you kidding? If we let ex-cons live there, seems to me that's just an invitation to make criminal behavior an everyday event."

Jon wagged his head in disagreement as he finished chewing the bite of pizza in his mouth. He swallowed, took a drink of beer, and tried to think of a better way to explain his position.

"This place isn't going to be a refuge for hardened criminals. JJ intends for it to be a place for guys that are basically decent people who just got off to a rocky start and ended up on the wrong side of the law. Guys who desperately want to get back on the right side."

"But once one of your *nice* guys moves in, what's to stop worse men from following him?"

"You think JJ's plans don't include a careful vetting program to make sure the men chosen are the kind she wants to help?"

"I think she might think one criminal is an okay guy, but then once he's there, what's to stop him from letting other men he met in prison crash at his place when they get out?"

"You're forgetting that one of the things these young men want as much as a job and a place to live, maybe even more than that, is a way to get away from the bad actors who got them into trouble in the first place. They aren't going to want to let that kind of ex-con ruin their only chance to make good."

"I don't believe it." Kate crossed her arms over her chest and glared at him. She was the most stubborn woman he'd ever known. It made her the tough, resilient woman he couldn't help caring about, and she was a fearless champion for causes she believed in, but she could also be frustrating when she refused to consider the other side of an argument.

"You don't believe me? Or you don't believe a man can have regrets he'd like to fix?"

Kate bit her lips and looked away. What was going on in her head? When she looked back, the mutinous glare was gone, but she didn't relax her arms or her posture.

"How can you know which ex-cons are worthy and which are lying to get a free ride?"

"Like I said, there will be a vetting process. They'll need a sponsor who can be trusted. Besides, it's not a free ride. They'll be required to participate in maintaining the place and paying rent as soon as they have employment."

"What about sex offenders?" Kate's chin jutted in defiance.

"There's a huge difference between a pervert who molests or rapes his victims and an eighteen-year-old who got caught having sex with a fifteen-year-old who lied about her age. JJ has no intention of accepting rapists or anyone else charged with serious felonies."

Jon sighed with frustration.

"You remember Mike Kennedy? He was in Jake's class in school, I think."

Kate nodded. "What's Mike got to do with any of this?"

"You know he runs a program over in Wilmington to give veterans who were down on their luck a second chance, right?"

She nodded again, so Jon went on.

"Dominick Masiac who's the manager over at Vets For Vets, has a son who's currently at Forsyth. Adrian's due to get out in about six months, and he'll have nowhere to go. He can't stay at Vets For Vets because he's not a veteran. His mother kicked him out of the house when he was fifteen. He's nominally a sex offender, but he's as unlikely to commit a crime as I am. He was just out of high school and attending UNC Wilmington where he met a girl at a party. They hit it off and started dating. It wasn't until the girl's father caught them in the act in the back of Adrian's car that Adrian found out the girl was only fourteen. She'd told him she was older than he was. And she looked it.

"The father pressed charges, and Adrian got convicted of statutory rape. He's never done anything criminal in his life, but that conviction is going to be a problem to finishing college, getting a decent job or a place to live. Adrian is one of the young men JJ wants to help. And he's no more dangerous to the kids who live in the area than any of the other neighbors."

"He must have family other than his dad or the woman who gave him life." Kate's tone had softened a bit.

"None. A raft of step-siblings by a variety of fathers, but no one else."

"Well, look," Kate leaned her elbows on the table. "I feel sorry for this Adrian guy, but that still doesn't change how I feel about turning the Jolee place into a rescue project just so he doesn't have to find a run-down apartment somewhere on the wrong side of Wilmington. Why can't JJ find some place other than Jolee for this second-chance-home? Somewhere more suitable? Someplace where there aren't a lot of kids living so close by. Maybe some place like Wilmington.

Jon's phone buzzed in his pocket. He was off duty, but in a town as small as Tide's Way with only three officers on the force, he was always on call. He pulled the phone from his pocket and got up from the table, holding up one finger to ask Kate's permission to take the call. She nodded.

"Jon here," he said as he put the phone to his ear without looking at the caller ID. "What's up?"

"It's Ty. And I'm headed your way."

Chapter 8

JON'S FACE LIT with surprise before he turned away and stepped out onto the porch.

Kate slid from her chair and began clearing the remains of dinner from the table. Jon's deep voice could be heard as the conversation continued, but she couldn't make out any of the words. It couldn't have been an emergency or he'd have been trotting up the hill to his cruiser already.

"Well, that was interesting," he remarked as he stepped back into the kitchen. "Have you heard from your brother-in-law lately?"

"Garrett? Why?" Kate stopped what she was doing and faced Jon. "Is something wrong at Ethan's Ribs? I stopped there on my way home, but the only problem they had then was a shortage of napkins with the logo printed on them. I took care of it."

"Nothing wrong." Jon held his hands up, palms facing her.

"Who was that?" Her curiosity bubbled. "And what did it have to do with Garrett?"

"That was an old friend of mine. Ty Halloway. He's Navy, but we served on the same ship once. He says your brother-in-law offered him the job to manage Ethan's Ribs. And he accepted."

"Garrett what?" Shock replaced curiosity. "He hired someone to take over my restaurant without even consulting me?"

"Your restaurant?" Jon's brows rose.

"Well, partly mine. But still. How can he just up and hire someone to take over without even consulting me?" Shock was turning into resentment.

"Because he's the majority owner." Jon crossed the floor and put his hands on her shoulders. "Kate. I thought you'd be pleased. You've hated having to keep an eye on the place. Now you won't have to."

Kate swallowed her resentment. Jon was right. She had hated the time and attention she'd had to divert from her own life. But it had been Ethan's dream, and she'd been trying to keep it alive for him. "Garrett didn't even call me."

"Maybe he tried and you weren't home to answer. You really need to get a new phone with an answering system that works." Jon dropped his hands and stepped back. "Is that coffee I smell brewing? Pour me some and I'll tell you about Ty."

Kate bit back the frustrated retort that rose to her lips and turned to pour Jon a cup of coffee. She never drank the stuff this late in the day, but he seemed to thrive on it and she'd made a pot just for him. She set the steaming mug on the table and sat down again.

"To start with . . ." Jon resumed his seat across from her and pulled the mug his way. "Ty is more than qualified. And I know you'll like him. He's been a Food Service Specialist for most of his Navy career. He's been in charge of serving up mess for several hundred hungry sailors aboard a destroyer most recently, but his wife is tired of holding down the fort every time he gets deployed. She wants him to stay ashore, so he's getting out."

"Oh, good! A military guy. My employees will love it." Kate didn't know why she was being so ornery. Anyone who could take that monkey off her back should be more than welcome at Ethan's Ribs. And it wasn't like Garrett was selling the place. Just hiring a manager. Something she'd been considering for months.

"You'll like him. I promise." Jon grinned. "He's as laid back as they come, military or not. I never met a sailor who didn't get along with him, nor a subordinate who didn't like working under him."

Kate closed her eyes and willed the last fragments of her resentment into submission. Garrett was a smart man. And surely Ethan would have approved.

"Okay, so tell me about Ty."

THE MAN WHO walked into Ethan's Ribs two weeks later wasn't what Kate had been expecting. For one thing, he was the biggest man she'd ever met. Not big, like a linebacker or a tackle, but tall. Taller than Jon or any of her brothers. He could have played for the NBA if he were any good at basketball. He had broad shoulders, a broad back and muscles under the clingy polo shirt that belonged on the cover of *Men's Fitness*.

He grinned at her, his teeth gleamingly white in a face the color of dark-roast coffee. "Ty Halloway, ma'am." He stuck out his hand.

Kate's hand disappeared into his. Thankfully, he didn't crush it.

"Welcome to Ethan's Ribs, Mr. Halloway. Jon Canfield told me I was going to like you. I hope you'll enjoy working here. I know I'll enjoy *not* working here." After she'd had time to get used to Garrett's high handedness, she'd given in to the relief of not having to balance two jobs at the same time she was bringing up two girls as a single parent.

"Please, just call me Ty, ma'am." Ty's voice was deep and mellow. It was the kind of voice that would always be heard without his ever having to raise it.

"Call me Kate, and I'll show you around."

Garrett had filled Ty in on the history of the rib joint Ethan had poured his soul into, so Kate just focused on acquainting Ty with the physical plant before the first employees began arriving.

The building wasn't new, and the kitchen had not been laid out with the spacious open designs of a modern establishment. Kate hoped Ty wouldn't find the narrow passages and cramped space too constricting. He seemed okay in spite of his size, moving easily through the place as Kate explained things. Maybe the galleys on a destroyer were just as confining?

"Good morning, Miss Kate," the first arrival said as he grabbed an apron off a hook by the door and tied it around his waist. "You must be Mr. Halloway." The newcomer extended his hand toward Ty.

"Just Ty," Ty said, taking the man's hand.

"Ty. This is Earl." Kate cleared her throat and made the hasty, belated introduction. "He's been with us from the start. He's in charge of the secret recipe for the rib sauce."

The morning passed quickly as Kate introduced each new arrival by name and specialty, and by the time the doors were due to open at eleven, it felt like Ty had been there for weeks already. The kitchen hummed with unusually efficient activity, and the scent of barbequed ribs filled the air. Not wanting to cramp Ty's style or undermine his new authority, Kate said her goodbyes and stepped out into the parking lot.

"Hi, Miss Kate," a busboy called as he hurried toward the door. "I hear we have a new boss today. I hope he doesn't make me walk the plank if I mess up."

"I think that only happens on pirate ships, Paul. But you'd better get inside and introduce yourself before the craziness starts."

Paul touched his fingers to the brim of his Tarheels ball cap and disappeared into the kitchen.

Kate hurried toward her minivan. She was already late for her hair appointment. Not that Jacqui would mind. Having her best friend for a hairdresser had its advantages.

A few minutes later, Kate strode into Jacqui's small but busy salon. Cora, another of Jacqui's stylists, had the police chief in her chair as she trimmed his close-cropped gray hair. A woman Kate knew as summer folk was getting her nails done and chatting amiably with the manicurist. Jacqui stood by her chair with her fists on her hips.

"Hi, Chief," Kate said as she took her seat.

Don Atkins nodded a greeting.

Cora swatted him playfully on the shoulder. "You want me to clip your ear for you?"

Atkins mumbled an apology and faced frontward again.

"What's he like?" Jacqui asked as she swirled the cape around Kate's shoulders.

"What's who like?"

Jacqui leaned close and lowered her voice. "What's the new guy at Ethan's Ribs like?"

"Oh, him."

"Yeah him." Jacqui chortled as she wound a strip of paper about Kate's neck and snapped the cape shut. "Is he a looker? He's ex-Navy right? Bet he's pretty buff."

"Jacqueline Paget, you are a happily married woman."

"Just because I'm on a diet doesn't mean I can't read the menu." Jacqui ran her fingers through Kate's blonde curls, lifting them out to the sides, then letting them spring back into place. "What are we doing today?"

"Just the usual." Kate chuckled. "Does Mark know you check out all the new guys in town?"

"Mark thinks it's cute." Jacqui grinned. "So what's he like?"

"He's married, for starters. He's got a wife and two boys. But he is pretty buff. And very tall. Tallest man I've ever met. I thought he was going to be like a bull in a china shop in that cluttered little kitchen, but he's incredibly graceful for his size."

"But do you *like* him?" Jacqui pursed her lips as she trimmed around Kate's face. Kate liked her hair easy to keep, so Jacqui sloped the bangs into the sides, leaving it longer toward the back. All Kate had to do was towel dry and brush and her natural curls took care of the rest.

"I do."

"You sound like you aren't quite sure."

"No, really. I do like him. It's just . . . I don't know. The biggest thing I feel about having Ty take over running the place is relief. Once I got over being irritated that Garrett didn't bother to consult me, anyway. But still . . ."

"It's like another goodbye to Ethan, isn't it?" Jacqui set her scissors and comb on the workstation and bent to give Kate a hug.

"I guess that's the best way to put it. Kate returned Jacqui's hug, then squared her shoulders. "Ethan's Ribs was his legacy. It was his passion and my rescue."

When she'd had such a horrible first pregnancy and nearly died giving birth to Jenny, Ethan had brought her home to Tide's Way to recover. Away from the hustle of her demanding job on the newspaper, she'd been able to regain her health and strength in spite of being a new mother. And all the while Ethan had been working his tail off to transform a run-down restaurant into a rib shack that would draw rave reviews and support his new family.

"As I was leaving, I couldn't help remembering the early years when I worked alongside him with Jenny gurgling happily in her infant seat. I was never in charge of anything, but I helped out where I could. Waiting tables when any of the wait staff called in sick, running dishes through the dishwasher, chopping vegetables, stirring pots of sauce, and keeping the books. They were good years. Except I didn't know it at the time.

"Then Becca came along. That was a surprise since neither of us had any plans to take the chance of my surviving pregnancy a second time. But when carrying Becca turned out to be a piece of cake, Ethan swore it was the fresh salt air of Tide's Way and the pace of life away from the city."

He might have been right. But her hankering to return to the excitement of working for a big city newspaper had never really died in spite of all the good memories Tide's Way represented.

"I get why you're kind of nostalgic today. It's like saying goodbye to an era. Not just losing Ethan, but everything else. Like getting through your first Christmas without him. Valentine's day with no valentine. Having Becca's First Holy Communion without her dad there or Jenny starting Junior High. Maybe it's time you thought about getting on with your life, instead of always looking back."

"Oh, I'm sure I'll get weepy when I watch the girls toss their graduation hats in the air and Ethan's not there to help celebrate. And I know I'm going to cry when he's not there to walk them down the aisle. But maybe you're right. Maybe it's time to let go of what was and learn how to be me again."

Chapter 9

JON WAITED BY his cruiser as Kate's brother Will pulled around the circular drive in front of the Jolee Mansion and came to a stop. Jon had asked Will to meet him here as back-up should Jon run into any criminal element he wasn't expecting. Partly because Will had a history of patrolling this place back when he'd served as a motorcycle trooper for the State Police and partly because his wife was on the Historical Society and had a key to the mansion.

"I'm surprised you're with JJ on this second-chance house project," Jon said as Will came to stand beside him on the overgrown lawn staring up at the historic façade.

Will turned his head in Jon's direction with his brows lifted.

"Kate is definitely not in favor," Jon said. "I'm betting Bree isn't either, considering she's on the committee to save Jolee and make it a historic showplace. I'm surprised they haven't ostracized you."

"There was a pretty heated discussion over the dinner table on Sunday." Will shrugged. "I wasn't completely outnumbered though. Jake and Dad are tentatively in favor. Philip was all for it. Turns out JJ had already talked to Ben and Jake about helping to find employment for the young men she hopes to house here. My mother wasn't too pleased with either of them. I think Kate and Bree were close to convincing her to join the Save Jolee Committee."

"Sounds like a battle of the sexes."

"Pretty much. Except for Meg."

"Might have guessed she'd buck the trend. Joining the Marines wasn't exactly the sort of thing the women in your family go in for."

"She married into the family after she became a Marine." Will chuckled and started walking up the weedy bricked path to the veranda with Jon following. "Why are we here, exactly?"

"An anonymous call reported squatters setting up camp. Atkins sent me to check it out. Allison doesn't go anywhere with me if she can avoid it, and I thought having back up from a state trooper I just happen to know might be smart. Besides, I thought I'd pick your brain about JJ's scheme."

"Well, I'm glad you called. I'm enjoying my new career path teaching at the academy and the occasional stint in hostage negotiation, but it's good to get out of the classroom and back into the real world for a change."

After Will's marriage to Brianna Reagan, he'd given up what she considered to be a dangerous job, riding a motorcycle and hunting down bad guys. Considering how often cops were getting ambushed these days, maybe her fears were justified, but she'd already lost her first husband to a Taliban sniper. Letting herself fall in love with another man wearing a uniform and a gun had been hard for her.

Will fitted the old key into the ancient lock and turned. "Needs a little WD-40 I think. Or maybe a whole new lock." Eventually the tumblers moved, but the door stuck tight in the jambs.

Jon put his shoulder to the door and pushed. With a grudging creak, it swung in.

"If JJ gets her way about this second-chance project, one of the first things we can get these guys busy doing is fixing the place up."

"Providing any of them know how to wield a hammer." Will stepped into the impressively high-ceilinged foyer behind Jon, and then both men stopped, listening to the quiet of the place and on the alert for squatters.

The mansion had the distinctive smell of old houses that hadn't been occupied for years, but it had lost none of its majesty. To the left a high archway opened into the parlor. To the right another archway opened into a formal dining room with a dust-coated chandelier and no furniture.

"Are you sure your informant said there were squatters *in* the mansion?" Will asked after several minutes of utter silence.

"That's what I was told. But how they would have gotten in without leaving signs of entry, I don't know. Unless that old myth about a secret tunnel actually has legs." Jon glanced back at the door that had clearly been locked and showed no signs of tampering.

"Might as well do a thorough check now that we're here," Will said. "It'll keep me off the desk and feeling like I'm still a cop for a little longer."

"Maybe it was just a disgruntled citizen who opposes JJ and thought calling in false alarms would put a spoke in her wheel," Jon muttered as he led the way through the massive, high-ceilinged rooms of the downstairs.

They checked all the window latches, then made their way up the wide curving staircase to the second floor. Dust was everywhere, but all of it undisturbed.

Half of the third floor was a warren of tiny rooms where the indoor slaves had once shared tight quarters. The other half had been the nursery.

"It's an oven up here without any AC," Jon said as he pulled a handkerchief out of his pocket to wipe his sweating brow. "I feel bad for the kids and the servants who had to live up here."

Will stood in the middle of the nursery's main room, pulled his hat off and ran his fingers through his Cameron-blond hair. The same pale color that Jon so loved on Kate. Maybe there was some Nordic heritage along with the Scots.

"Amen to that," Will agreed as he looked around. "Doesn't look like anyone's been anywhere inside the house in spite of your mystery caller." Suddenly he cocked his head. "Do you hear that?"

"Yeah," Jon replied as he hurried to the window overlooking the front drive.

A group of people had gathered on the untidy lawn and appeared to be arguing about something. Both men headed for the stairs.

As Jon burst from the house, a cacophony of angry voices rose from the milling throng of casually but cleanly-dressed men. It was impossible to see who was at the center of the disagreement. He took the stairs three at a time with Will right behind him.

"Take it easy." Jon forced his way into the crowd. "Calm down." He took an elbow to the chest, but ignored it as he wove his way to the source of the conflict. "Step back. Please."

He put his hand on the butt of his baton in case he had to pull it out in a hurry.

JJ! Figures! The diminutive woman stood at the center of the arguing men, obviously intimidated but refusing to back down. Some of the men crowding in on her with angry shouts were townsfolk, but some were out-of-towners Jon had seen at the recent town meeting.

Just as he reached the center, a woman yelped. Two unknown men backed up quickly, looking guiltily toward JJ. JJ staggered. Will caught and steadied her.

"Miss Jennifer. Are you hurt?" Will shielded the woman with his bulk as he inquired into her status.

JJ shook her head. "I'm okay, but Kate—" She turned away from Will and gestured behind her.

Jon gasped.

Blood trickled from a gash just visible below Kate's hairline.

"Back off!" he bellowed at the crowd. "Just back the hell off." He turned his attention to Kate. "Who did this?" He pushed Kate's hair aside to see how bad the cut was.

"I'm fine." Kate batted his hand away.

"I don't know where you came from, but I'm thankful you're here now." JJ sounded shaken, but she lifted her jaw and glared at the crowd of angry men who were now being corralled by Will.

"You're bleeding," Jon tried again to assess the extent of Kate's injury.

"I said I'm fine," Kate's blue eyes glittered with defiance. Then she abruptly turned ashen and slumped.

KATE OPENED HER eyes to a pair of worried faces peering down at her. Jon was on his knees dabbing at her forehead with a square of gauze. JJ crouched at her other side. She started to sit up.

"The EMTs are on the way." JJ restrained her.

"I don't need the EMTs." Kate made another effort to sit up.

Jon shook his head. "Yeah, you do. Just stay put until they at least check you out."

Kate sat up quickly before Jon or JJ could restrain her again. Her head spun and she blinked to ward off the dizziness.

"C'mon, Kate. It's okay to take a break from being Wonder Woman." Jon eased her back onto a jacket someone had spread on the ground for her. This time she didn't fight their advice.

The whine of sirens grew louder as a rescue vehicle roared up the long gravel drive and pulled to a stop.

"What's Will doing here?" Kate caught sight of her brother speaking to a chastened-looking group of men.

"I asked him to come," Jon said.

Kate would have demanded an explanation except Hank Benson had trotted over with his First-In Bag and taken JJ's place.

Hank examined her wound, and then taped a fresh square of gauze over it. He crushed a small pouch between his palms before wrapping it in a length of cloth and placing it on top of the gauze. He slipped a cuff around her arm and drew out a small penlight that he flashed into her eyes. She blinked at the sudden brightness.

Hank tucked his thumb across his pinky and held his hand up in front of her face. "How many fingers do I have up?"

"Three," she answered absently. Why would Jon ask Will to come to the meeting with JJ? For that matter, why was Jon at the meeting? He hadn't been invited. That she knew of, anyway. Of course, neither had the protesters from out of town. How had any of them known about the meeting between JJ and the representatives from the planning board and the town council? She'd only known about it because Bree told her, and Bree heard it from Tony Jenkins, who was on the Planning Board.

Then Hank began to slip a collar around her neck.

"I don't need that," Kate protested, pushing it away.

"Standard procedure," he replied patiently.

"Well, I'm not your standard patient and I don't need it, Hank. I didn't fall, and I didn't hurt my neck. I just got whacked by a clipboard. I don't need a neck brace." She sat up in defiance. Lucky for her, the dizziness didn't make a return appearance.

Jon left her side for a moment and joined Will who was talking to the knot of men while Hank finished examining her. A moment later Will headed in her direction while Jon spoke to the man Kate was pretty sure was the one who had hit her.

"Do you feel nauseated?" Hank pulled the cuff off and rolled it up.

"No," Kate said without stopping to consider the question.

Hank sat back on his heels and glanced up at Will, who had come to stand beside him.

"I'd like to take her to the ER just to get checked out by a doctor," the EMT said. "They'll probably release her, but just to be on the safe side, they'll want to do a scan, and she might need a stitch or two."

"You can explain all this to *me*, Hank," Kate said testily. "I'm my own boss and my brother doesn't make decisions for me."

Hank repeated his suggestion to her. She shrugged. Chances were neither Will nor Jon would give her a chance to object in spite of her insistence on being self-sufficient.

Hank began gathering up his equipment. He handed her the ice pack and directed her to keep it on the wound. "It will reduce the bruising," he explained. "And there'll be less soreness tomorrow."

Jon returned and squatted next to her. "What do you want me to do about the gentleman who hit you?"

"You're making too much out of this." Kate replied. "And I'm not pressing charges if that's what you're asking. The guy didn't mean to hit me. He was just trying to get JJ's attention and I got in the way."

"What were you doing here in the first place?" Will glanced at Jon, then at Kate, waiting for an answer.

"I was getting a story. A story you two interrupted, I might add. A story I don't have the end of thanks to you."

Will held his hands up palms facing her and stepped back a pace. "Don't blame me, Sis. You were the one who passed out."

"We can discuss it later." Jon's tone was gentle but all business. He checked his watch. "Will's going to the ER with you. I'll go catch the girls when they get off the bus. Call me. Please?"

His demeanor was that of a calm professional, but there had been something more personal on his face when their gazes met in the middle of the pushing and shoving mob. And in the last moments before she lost consciousness she'd seen concern replaced by alarm. He wasn't trying to be bossy. He was just worried about her. He'd always been a little overprotective, even when they were kids, long before he became a cop. She should be thankful for his concern.

She nodded. Will helped her to her feet and walked her toward the yawning doors of the rescue truck. He held up her purse and her notebook.

"I got your gear, and I locked your van. I'll come back and get it later. You really need to get a new car. I almost didn't get the window rolled up."

"That's what Jon keeps telling me, but I haven't won the lottery yet."

Will chuckled as Hank helped her into the back of the waiting ambulance and directed her to sit on the folded gurney. He and Will climbed aboard and sat opposite her.

Riding in the back of an ambulance when you weren't seriously injured was embarrassing, but at least they weren't running the lights and sirens.

"So, what was the big story you were supposed to be getting?"

Chapter 10

KATE WAS TRYING to convince Jon she did not need a babysitter when the doorbell rang. Before she could get off the couch to answer it, her mother walked in. Jon got to his feet.

"Mom! What are you doing here?"

Sandy Cameron dropped her purse on the overstuffed chair and hurried to give Kate a hug. She bent down to inspect the bandage on Kate's head. "Will thought it might be good for someone to be here tonight. Just in case."

Kate sighed. She wasn't going to get out of being coddled. She turned to Jon. "I guess that lets you off the hook. Thanks for watching out for the girls and feeding them supper."

Jon gave Sandy a hug and tossed a salute in Kate's direction. "Call if you need anything. I'll see myself out." He strode toward the kitchen. His voice faded as he bid the girls goodbye and let himself out the back door.

"So!" Sandy plopped onto the couch next to Kate. "What's this I hear about you being involved in a protest?"

"I wasn't in a protest, Mom. I was just covering a meeting between JJ and a couple of the guys responsible for issuing building and use permits. I was supposed to be covering the story. Things got a little out of hand."

Sandy tipped her head. "A little?"

"It was supposed to just be JJ, Tony Jenkins and Lyle Beecham. JJ acts like her idea is a done deal. I thought it seemed kind of underhanded arranging a meeting with a

71

member of the planning board and the building inspector and that rat contractor Harold Lee Byrd."

"Which one of them hit you?" Sandy's jaw came forward as if she was ready to do battle on her baby's behalf.

"None of them. I don't know the guy who hit me. I only saw him once before this at the town meeting. But he didn't try to hit me, anyway. It was an accident. He had this clipboard he was waving in JJ's direction. I got in the way."

"A clipboard? And that was enough to send you to the hospital?"

"Everyone overreacted," Kate sighed.

"You were unconscious." Sandy shot back. "I don't think anyone overreacted."

"Mom, trust me. I'm fine. I got a scan. And a couple stitches. I'm fine. You really don't have to stay the night, either. I don't know what Will told you, but— Or was it Jon who called?"

"It was Will. He said the doctor just told him to keep an eye on you for twenty-four hours. But even if you are fine, Dad's gone up to Raleigh overnight so I'd just as soon not go home to an empty house. Why don't we make it a girls' night? We can make up a batch of popcorn and watch a movie in our jammies."

Without waiting for an answer, she got to her feet and headed to the kitchen where the girls were still working on cleaning up the supper dishes. Their enthusiastic greeting for their grandmother made Kate smile. They loved having a movie night with their grandmother because that always ended with ice cream sundaes. Truth be told, Kate enjoyed a relaxing evening doing absolutely nothing but enjoying time with her girls. And her mom, too. Even without the ice cream.

"I THOUGHT TONY Jenkins was on the committee to save Jolee," Sandy said when she returned from tucking the girls into bed and joined Kate in the living room.

Kate looked up from her notes. "He is. But he's also on the town planning board. He probably got wind of JJ's meeting with the developer and decided volunteering to be the liaison would keep him in the loop."

"That would be the loop that wants to sell off the fallow fields to that shyster Harold Lee Byrd and turn the mansion into some kind of halfway house for criminals?" Sandy settled into the overstuffed chair opposite the couch and crossed her legs.

"The same."

"So, those out-of-town guys weren't protestors."

"Who said they were protestors?" That would certainly explain the sudden violence.

"Will thought they might be. He and Jon were only up there because Jon had an anonymous tip that there were trespassers camping out inside the mansion. Which they didn't find any sign of, by the way. But except for Tony, Beecham and Byrd, neither Jon nor Will knew any of the men in the group. When questioned, they were all from out of town. Out of state, for that matter."

"Well, if that was a protest, I have no idea what they were protesting. None of them said anything. They just listened. Except that guy who managed to clobber me with his clipboard. He kept calling JJ's name and peppering her with questions about who she planned to put in the house. She was ignoring him, which is why he got a little rowdy."

Sandy snorted. "That's what you call a little rowdy?" She pointed at Kate's bandaged head.

"Did you know JJ spent half a year away from home, right in the middle of the season the year she was supposed to make her debut?" Kate was tired of talking about her injury. "I discovered she was chosen to be one of the American debutantes at the annual Christmas ball in

London, but she didn't go." There was a chance her mother might even remember that long-ago year. Not that she'd been a debutante, but she had lived in Tide's Way at the time.

Sandy frowned at the change of subject. "I didn't know that. But why is it of interest now?"

"I've been looking into JJ. I was trying to figure out who this mysterious Matthew is."

"The young man she was talking about at the town meeting?"

"Yeah. That one. She seemed awfully invested in him. I thought maybe it was someone she was related to. But she never married, so there are no kids and no grandkids. And she was an only child, so no nephews. I got to wondering about that odd gap in her life. Seemed strange she would skip the big ball in London, unless . . . maybe she got pregnant."

Sandy sat up, looking shocked. "I don't think—"

"Her parents would never have let her keep the baby, of course, but what if this Matthew she talked about was her son? And he was put up for adoption, but JJ knew where he was and followed his life over the years? Or maybe she only went looking for him recently and discovered what had happened to him. That would be a really good reason she's so set on this second-chance house deal."

"Even if that were all true, and it's really nothing more than your imagination running away with you, why does that have anything to do with what happened today?"

"Nothing really. But it might be important to understanding JJ's interest in the scheme."

"I think it's none of your business."

"Of course, it's my business. I'm a journalist. Digging up all the dirt is part of my job."

"I'm disappointed in you." Sandy got up and began gathering up the dirty ice cream bowls.

"Why?" Kate scrambled off the couch and followed her mother into the kitchen. She never wanted to disappoint either of her parents, and it hurt to hear her mother say that.

Sandy Cameron placed the bowls in the dishwasher and shut the door. Then she turned, leaned against the counter and faced Kate.

"You're just guessing at a long-ago possibility. If it were true and JJ had a son she was not allowed to keep, don't you think that would have been painful enough without some overeager reporter digging it all up all these many years later?"

"It's what reporters do," Kate argued.

"But for what purpose? To enlighten or to embarrass?" Sandy bustled around Kate's kitchen straightening things out.

"But if it has some bearing on the plans she has for the Jolee Mansion, don't the people of this town have a right to know that?"

"Kate, I'm on your side as far as using the Jolee Mansion for anything but a historical showplace, but report on the story based on the merits and possible repercussions. You don't have to ruin someone's reputation."

Her mother was right. Her mother was always right. But still . . . Kate was trying to make her mark in a demanding world with a twenty-four-seven news cycle.

"What does Jon think?" Sandy folded the dishtowel and placed it on the rack.

"Jon? About the Jolee project?"

"No, about your suppositions regarding JJ?"

"I haven't asked him."

Sandy turned off the light and closed the gap. She put her arms about Kate and pulled her into a hug. "Maybe you should. That's what best friends are for." She stepped back and rested her hands on Kate's shoulders. "Are you ready for bed? I'm supposed to check you out and tuck you in."

Chapter 11

"MOM! MOM! THERE'S a big moving van down the street. We're getting new neighbors." Becca came running into the kitchen, panting either from excitement or having run full tilt to pass on the news. "And Uncle Garrett is here."

Garrett Shaw followed Becca into the kitchen with Jenny right behind him.

Kate dropped the laundry she was folding and hurried to give her brother-in-law a hug. Although a few inches taller and definitely more muscular, the arms that folded her into his embrace reminded her so forcefully of Ethan that her eyes grew suddenly moist.

She blinked to dispel the unexpected emotion. "I didn't know you were going to be in town."

"Neither did I," Garrett said releasing her. "But I was able to get a few days leave to come down and see how Ty was doing at Ethan's Ribs and help him get his family moved in."

"Can I get you some coffee or something?" Kate hadn't seen Garrett since his wedding seven months earlier. He looked as fit as always, and the gray around the temples made him look distinguished. "Marriage looks good on you. Where's Lacey?"

"Lacey's up the street helping Samari harass the movers." Garrett laughed. "A cup of coffee would be excellent. I was hoping we could take you and the girls out to dinner tonight."

"Mom, they don't have any girls," Becca lamented. "Just boys."

"But Tyrell is nice," Jenny offered.

"You're just saying that because he noticed you," Becca stuck her tongue out at Jenny. She rolled her eyes in her mother's direction. "Mom, Natalie wants to know if I can sleep over tonight."

Kate put her hands to either side of her head. "What happened to my quiet Saturday? Yes, Becca, you can sleep over at Natalie's, but not until we get back from dinner with your uncle."

"I'm going back to help," Jenny said as she headed for the door.

"Don't get in the—"

Kate's warning went unheeded as Jenny flew out the door. This kid Tyrell must be quite a draw. Jenny was growing up way too fast.

Kate reached for a mug and poured a cup of coffee for Garrett.

"What happened to you?" Garrett, leaning against the counter, accepted the mug and gestured to Kate's bandaged forehead.

Kate explained about the scene at the Jolee Mansion the day before.

"A halfway house, huh? That's bound to stir up trouble in a town like this."

Not wanting to get into it with another man who might take up the opposing point of view, Kate changed the subject.

"So, how's Lacey enjoying being a Navy Commander's wife?"

While Garrett described just how well Lacey had taken to the life of a military wife and become an eager and active part of the community, Kate retrieved her laundry and finished folding it.

"How's Ty fitting in at the restaurant?" Garrett asked.

"It feels like he's been there forever. And it's only been a couple weeks. So, I guess you could say he's fitting in just fine. But I kind of wish you'd asked first before you just up and hired him."

Garrett raised his eyebrows. A look so much like Ethan's when she'd said something to surprise him that it made her heart lurch.

"It came up unexpectedly. Lacey and I went to a retirement party for a man I used to serve under. Ty and his wife, Samari, were there as well. While the ladies were off powdering their noses or whatever it is you women do when you go to the head in pairs, Ty and I got to talking about careers. He told me he wasn't going to re-up because Samari was tired of being a single parent most of the time and having to move every few years. I asked him if he had anything in mind, and he hadn't gotten that far in his planning. I guess he was just going to enjoy a few weeks of nothing before deciding on a second career.

"Anyway, long story short. I knew you were having a hard time keeping an eye on Ethan's Ribs and working your own job. Never mind being a single parent now. Ty's Navy rating made him a perfect fit for the job. So, I offered it to him." Garrett shrugged "Sorry. I didn't mean to leave you out of it."

"That's what Jon said."

"I guess you should have heard it from me first, but honestly, I thought you'd be relieved."

"I am. After I got over my snit." She smiled at her brother-in-law. He was a good-hearted man. A lot like Ethan had been. Except he was an officer, used to giving orders and not having to consult with others about decisions he'd made.

"I came down today to help with the move and spend the afternoon at the rib shack checking in on Ty, so I suppose I'd better get a move on. I'll pick you and the girls up around six. That work for you? I'm assuming you'll want anything *but* ribs. Right?"

"I'll walk up with you." Kate put Garrett's empty mug in the sink and followed him to the door. "You can introduce me to the rest of the family."

Kate had seen the For Sale sign go up just three doors down from her home and the Sold sticker added less than a week later, but she'd had no idea her new manager was the buyer. Today the house was a hive of activity. A huge moving van sat in front with ramps from both the side and rear doors. Two spectacularly muscled men sporting shirts emblazoned with *Two Men with a Truck* across their chests were carefully guiding a piano down the side ramp. Jon, in jeans and an old Marine Corps T-shirt, had two hands bracing the leading edge, and a petite, dark-haired woman was firing off a series of warnings and directions that no one was paying any attention to.

As Kate and Garrett approached the house, Ty Halloway came out the front door.

"Hey, Boss!" Ty saluted Garrett, with a broad white grin splitting his face. "And Bossette." He tossed a salute in Kate's direction as well.

"You can knock off the salutes," Garrett said. "You're a civilian now."

"Let me introduce my wife," Ty said, turning to the small woman still trying to direct the movers.

"See what I mean?" Garrett whispered in Kate's ear as Ty managed to grab his wife's hand and drag her away from the men moving the piano up the walkway.

"Kate, this is Samari. Sam, the other of my new bosses, Kate Shaw." Ty made the introduction.

"I'm so happy to meet you, finally. Ty's thrilled to be taking over such a popular place and telling me I'm going to love living in Tide's Way." The pretty woman wrapped her arms about Kate in a quick, eager hug. "And those are my boys." She pointed to two strapping teenagers lugging boxes. Sam didn't look old enough to be their mom. She must have been tougher than she looked, though, to be mom and dad to two active growing boys while her husband went to sea on a regular basis. What must it be like to be surrounded every day by so much robust masculinity?

"Tyrell! Christo!" Sam snapped her fingers.

The two boys set down the boxes they had been carrying and immediately trotted across the lawn to their mother's side. They towered over her. "Yes, ma'am," they said in unison.

"Mrs. Shaw is your dad's new boss. Kate, this is Tyrell Junior," she pointed to the shorter one. "And Christo." She nodded at the older boy.

"Nice to meet you, ma'am." Both boys nodded their heads in Kate's direction. Well brought up Navy brats. They'd get along just fine in Tide's Way. It was easy to see why Jenny, eager to grow up and have boys notice her, was enchanted. They were a handsome mix of their dad's dark skin and engaging smile and their mother's creamy Caribbean coloring. Both were extremely well developed for still being in their teens. Just the sort of young men who would melt any eager young girl's heart.

Where was Jenny, anyway?

The boys nodded once again and headed back to their boxes. Jenny emerged from the house with her aunt Lacey and turned an about face to follow the boys back inside. Kate would have to keep an eye on Jenny.

A man with a sturdily encased laptop showed up to ask Sam a question, and the introductions were over. About an hour later, Garrett and Ty took off to get Ethan's Ribs open for the day. The bulk of the big items had been unloaded and the movers were finishing up under Sam's mostly ignored supervision. After she'd offered Samari and the boys some lunch and been turned down, Kate gathered up a reluctant Jenny and headed home.

Jon fell into step beside them. "How's the head today?" He reached out to touch the bandage lightly, his eyes full of concern. "No dizziness? You look a little beat."

"That's just from helping to move boxes. I'm out of shape."

His gaze traveled down her body and slowly returned to her face. The concern in his eyes turned to something else. "You look in fine shape to me."

"If I didn't know better, I'd think you were flirting with me." Thankfully, Jenny had skipped ahead and missed this bit of dialog. Otherwise there would surely have been even more eye-rolling than Becca had displayed earlier over Jenny's interest in the new boy on the block.

Jon placed a hand on his sweat-soaked chest and assumed an air of crushed feelings.

"I pay you a compliment and you treat it with disdain."

Kate's heart was suddenly filled with a warmth that hadn't been there just moments before. She swallowed hard and tried to get things back to normal.

"It was good to see Garrett again. And Lacey. We're going out for dinner. Want to come along?" She was babbling. And why on earth had she invited Jon to join them?

He shook his head. "I wish I could, but I'm on duty tonight. I traded with Allison so I could take in Becca's game tomorrow."

They arrived at the gate to her front walk and stopped.

"How's Ty working out?"

"I hate to admit it, but you were right. I like him. Ethan would have liked him, too. The staff all love him." She sighed. "And much as I resented Garrett's high-handedness in hiring him without consulting me, I'm really glad he's here."

Jon glanced at his watch. "Gotta get a move on. Be sure to get some rest this afternoon." He touched her forehead and pushed a tumbled curl back behind her ear. "Take care of yourself."

Before Kate could think how to respond to his concern and the tumult his touch churned up in her gut, he'd turned and loped off up the hill toward his own house. She watched him go while her heart continued to beat with an odd, anxious rhythm. Some of the feelings she was experiencing around Jon lately confused her. Instead of the same close feelings of friendship she'd had for him ever since she could remember these feelings were more intense. When he smiled at her, her heart beat a little faster, and when he touched her, an electric hum surged through her veins. But Jon was just a friend. Wasn't he?

Chapter 12

"DIDN'T EXPECT TO see you here. Becca twist your arm?" Becca's friend Natalie Cole's dad gave Jon a playful punch to the shoulder as he stepped up beside him on the sidelines of the soccer field.

"Assaulting an officer is a punishable offense," Jon joked back. "Yeah, Becca did a little twisting. But she didn't have to try too hard. I enjoy watching the girls play."

"You know, if you ever consider coaching, I heard the girls need a new assistant coach."

Jon glanced down at the shorter man. "Sounds like fun, but I'm not sure I could work it around my schedule."

"I guess being a small-town cop does tend to get you called out unexpectedly now and then. You'd be in kind of a fix if the parents dropped them all off for practice some afternoon and left, then you had to leave in a hurry."

"I can think of worse things, but it would be awkward. How come you don't volunteer?"

"Pretty much the only thing I know about soccer is that you have to kick it into the goal to score." Natalie's father laughed at his ignorance.

"You could learn. Kids this age, it isn't all that complicated."

Cole wagged his eyebrows. "Okay, so I prefer being a couch potato. At most a cheerleader."

Jon turned back to the soccer field as the play swerved toward their side of the field.

"Go, Natalie!" Jon shouted as Cole's daughter took off for the goal with unchallenged possession of the ball.

"That's my girl!" Cole shouted as the ball zipped past the goalie and into the net.

A time-out was called and a moment later Becca and Natalie skidded to a halt in front of the men. Cole handed each girl a bottle of water. "Nice goal, sweetie." He gave his daughter a high five.

"I'm going to get the next one," Becca boasted.

"Of course, you are." Cole high-fived her as well and a moment later both girls ran back onto the field.

"What do you think of JJ's plan for the Jolee Mansion?" Cole asked as the action flowed to the other end of the field.

Jon lifted his shoulders and let them drop with a shake of his head. "I'm in favor of creating a second chance home for the men JJ wants to help. Statistics show it works. But I'm not sure how I feel about it happening at the Jolee place. Just not for the same reasons most townsfolk are against it."

"Oh?" Cole gave him a glance before returning his gaze to the gaggle of girls moving back in their direction.

"A lot of history in that old house. Seems a shame to discard it just to turn it into a moneymaker instead of a drain on the town budget."

"That's what my wife thinks. I made the mistake of playing devil's advocate when the subject first came up. Didn't get any nookie for a week."

Jon laughed. "That'll teach you to—"

Cheering erupted, and Becca came tearing down the field dribbing the ball with surprising skill. Jon broke off to shout out his encouragement. A moment later, one of the girls on the other team grabbed a fistful of Becca's jersey, then stuck her leg out and deliberately tripped her. Becca went sprawling.

Jon's heart lurched, but Becca scrambled back to her feet, obviously unhurt, and was sprinting after the girl who'd stolen the ball. A referee held a yellow card aloft and a whistle screeched. Play broke off while a discussion ensued.

"Well, that stinks." Cole grunted.

"She'll get another chance. At least she's not hurt." Jon was pleased that Becca had not retaliated. She was a good sport, and he was proud of her.

But Becca didn't get another chance.

Before the first half was over, the skies darkened ominously. Just before the rain began, alarming jags of lightning ripped across the sky and the decision was made to call the game. Everyone scrambled for their cars.

"Max is going to be so scared," Becca said as Jon pulled out of the lot. "He hates thunder and lightning."

"We'll be home in just a couple minutes," Jon assured her. "We can keep Max company. At least he won't be scared alone."

He had to cycle the wipers into their fastest speed because the rain was coming down in buckets. Even seeing the road clearly more than ten or fifteen feet ahead was iffy. After several more minutes of white-knuckle driving, they pulled into Kate's driveway. Jon would have remained in the car a while to see if the rain would let up, but Becca was anxious about the dog so that wasn't an option.

"Reach into the back and grab my umbrella," he told the girl.

She unclipped her seatbelt and draped herself over the seat, stretching to reach the umbrella that had rolled to the very rear of the cargo area. She turned, clawed her way back into the rear seat and handed Jon the umbrella.

Even with the umbrella, Jon managed to get wet just getting it open, but a moment later both he and Becca hurried up the back stairs huddled under it, trying to stay as dry as possible.

Max didn't greet them at the door with his tail wagging as he usually did.

"He's probably under Mom's desk." Becca shucked her cleats and headed for Kate's little office.

Jon followed after removing his own shoes. Becca was sitting on the floor with Max's head in her lap crooning softly to the dog. Jon joined her on the floor.

"I'll stay with Max. You run up to your room and put on some dry clothes. Then we'll make us a snack."

Jon took Becca's place easing Max's head onto his own lap. He ran his hand over the dog's silky coat and told him everything was going to be all right. The rain drumming at the windows seemed to be lessening, but still the lightning crackled followed swiftly by deafening booms.

CRACK! BOOM!

Max yelped, and Jon cringed at the unbelievably close rumble of thunder.

A loud ripping, crashing sound was followed by Becca's scream. Jon scrambled to his feet and ran for the stairs. Max followed so closely his claws scraped at the back of Jon's heels.

Jon's heart nearly stopped as he reached the top of the stairs. An enormous limb, maybe even part of the whole tree had come crashing down on the roof, smashing its way through the shallow attic and into the hallway.

"Becca!" Jon screamed above the cacophony.

There was no answer. His heart lodged in his throat.

He darted into the first door on his left. Becca's room seemed untouched, but she cowered in the corner with terror in her eyes. He knelt beside her and wrapped his arms around her. She clung, trembling. Max joined her.

Rain was spilling in on the hall floor from the hole in the roof. They had to get out of here. And now. He had no idea just how severe the damage was or if it would get worse.

"Becca. We need to get back downstairs and out of the house."

She nodded but didn't release her grip. He pulled her arms from around his waist and put them around his neck instead. "Hold on tight," he warned as he stood and started for the door. Max hustled after them.

When they reached the kitchen, Jon asked Becca if she had any shoes downstairs other than her cleats. She nodded and he set her on her feet to go after them. He put his own shoes back on, found Max's leash and snapped it onto his collar.

He had no idea how bad things might get, but coming back into the house until the extent of the damage could be assessed wouldn't be safe. He left Becca tying her shoes with the dog huddled against her side while he headed back to Kate's office. He knew she worked on a laptop rather than a desk model and he might as well grab it in case rain got as far down as the first floor.

It was open on her desk and plugged in. He disconnected the cord, wound it up and shoved it in his pocket, then closed the laptop and headed back to the kitchen.

"I got Max's food and dish," Becca said holding up a shopping tote with the telltale bulge of a large-sized dog dish.

"Good thinking." He led the way to the kitchen door and they stepped out onto the porch.

"You hold the umbrella," he told the girl trading her tote for the umbrella. He set the tote and the laptop on the corner of the counter and swung her onto one hip. Then, because Max was panting with panic, he scooped the sixty-pound dog up under his other arm and headed for the car. Another dash back to grab the laptop and Max's gear and shut the door. When they were all safely inside it, Becca pointed through the windshield toward the back yard.

Jon's gaze followed her pointing finger.

The enormous live oak that once had shaded most of Kate's back yard was split right down the middle. One half still stood pointing brokenly at the dripping sky. The other lay diagonally across the roof of Kate's house. The shallow hip-style roof was caved completely in on itself.

Jon looked up at the sky and prayed for the rain to stop before the damage could get worse. Then he pulled out his phone and called Kate.

"YOU CAN STAY here tonight," Jon told Kate as they stood on Jon's deck surveying the damage to her house.

"But we have no clothes. Or even a toothbrush."

"We have Max's bowl and food."

Kate looked at him to see if he was kidding. The remark seemed so out of place.

"And your computer and Becca's favorite stuffed animal."

"But—" her shoulders sagged. She could go out to the island to her parents' place, but shock had her spinning her wheels with indecision. How could so much devastation happen so quickly?

The rain had stopped as abruptly as it had begun, and Jon had called Kate's brother Jake, who was a contractor. Men were scrambling over her roof stretching an enormous tarp over it in the fast dwindling light. Becca, over her fright but exhausted by the day's events, was asleep on Jon's couch while Jenny was comfortably ensconced in Jon's recliner with her nose stuck in a book about dolphins. Kate couldn't think what to do next.

"Look, Kate. Stay here for tonight or the next day or two, at least. I'll go down and get what you need. Give me a list and tell me where to find it. Tomorrow you can start worrying about what to do next. Jake has a roofing guy headed over to take a look, and if you're right here, you'll be handy to talk with the guy. You'll have a better idea how long it will be before it's safe to return to the house. Jake said he'd come by to check things out and make sure there's nothing more than just damage to the roof. You'll want to talk to both of them."

Jon made a valid point. She would want to be on site when the men went through her house assessing the damage and discussing what to do about it even though her mom would welcome her and had plenty of room.

"It just seems like I'm leaning on you too much lately."

"Lean all you want. I'm good."

"You're sure?"

He put a hand on her shoulder and turned her toward him. "I know you're a strong woman, Kate, but you've been through a lot. It's okay to let your friends help you out once in a while."

Kate had the most insane urge to press her face into his chest and wrap her arms about his waist. It would feel so good to just let go and let someone else be strong for a change. It would feel so good to let Jon hug her until the jittery disbelief subsided.

As if he were reading her mind, his arms closed around her and pulled her close. He rested his cheek on the top of her head and tightened the embrace. He rocked her slightly and held her until the Jell-O that was her stomach stopped quivering. He felt good.

Too good.

Reluctantly, she let go and stepped back.

"Thank you," Jon said in a soft, almost whispery voice.

"Thank me?" She shook her head at him. "For what?"

"For letting me be there for you."

Chapter 13

KATE FELT VERY alone and vulnerable as she stood beside the broken trunk of the live oak tree in her backyard waiting for Jake. Last night she'd had Jon's strong arms around her when the magnitude of the storm damage turned her knees to jelly and left her brain numb with shock. In the clear light of day, it looked even worse.

Her brother, wearing a bright blue hard hat bearing his company's logo, strode across the littered lawn in her direction. "It's going to take a while. There's a lot more than the damage you can see from here."

Kate looked up at her brother as her heart fell. "How *much* more than what I can see?"

Jake shoved his fingers into the tops of his front pockets as he glanced down at her. "Structural damage to the northeast side of the house itself. Except for the closet that backs up to Becca's room, your bedroom is almost completely trashed. The main bathroom will need rebuilding as well. The girls' rooms look okay, but the ceilings probably have water damage that will require work. I can get a crew started on the outside wall next week once the adjuster has been by to get his report for the insurance company put together. I've got a roofing guy who can start next week, too. But there will be some permitting issues to bring things up to current code. Once the roof and main supporting walls are done, we can get started on the master bedroom and both bathrooms. At least a month. Probably a lot longer."

Kate's heart did a nosedive at Jake's assessment. "A month? Or more?"

Jake pulled one hand out of his pocket, put an arm around Kate and gave her a side hug. "We'll get it all put back together. I promise. It will be even better than before, but it's going to take a while."

Kate stared at her house without really seeing it. The last year without Ethan had been hard. Harder than she'd ever imagined, but she'd gotten through it. One day at a time, one week after another, until finally there had been light at the end of the tunnel. And now this.

"It should be mostly covered by insurance. What's your deductible?" Whatever else Jake had said she hadn't heard, but the word insurance caught her attention.

"I—I'm not sure." The deductible was just one more blow to her just-barely-staying-afloat finances.

"We can't get started until the adjuster comes so you need to call them if you haven't already. Like today."

"Can I go inside?" She'd need the file with relevant policy numbers and coverage information.

Jake stared at the house for a bit, then down at her. "I'd rather you didn't."

"I need to get the insurance file. And a few other things. Like clothes and stuff. And there's food in the fridge. I can't just leave it all there to spoil."

Jake shrugged. "Wait here."

He jogged around the side of the house and disappeared. A minute later, he reappeared carrying a second blue helmet.

"Put this on. It won't keep you from getting crushed if something big caves in, but it'll protect your head from loose stuff that falls, which is more likely. And stay with me. If I tell you to get out, I mean get out. Right this minute. Not after you've grabbed a couple more things. Got it?"

Kate nodded and headed for the back door.

The kitchen looked like nothing had happened. The whole first floor, in fact. Maybe they could camp in the downstairs while the upstairs was being repaired. At least once the roof was done.

"Couldn't we just live down here until the upstairs gets fixed?" She gestured to the undisturbed spaces.

"No, you can't. Even if there wasn't the possibility of unexpected collapses, it's going to get very messy with sawdust and disturbed dirt. Go out to Mom's. She'll be thrilled to have you."

"And try to organize my life like I was thirteen again." Kate loved her mother, but living with her was going to be a trial.

"It's only for a month," Jake said, heading for the stairs.

"I thought you said probably a lot longer." Kate followed him.

He shrugged and continued to lead the way.

"Where do you keep your suitcases?" he asked as he disappeared around the corner.

"In the closet at the end of the hall, past Becca's room." Kate hesitated at the turn in the stairs, not sure what she'd see once she turned the corner. Not sure she wanted to see how bad it was.

"Change your mind?" Jake asked.

Kate shook her head and took the last three stairs. She sucked in a breath of shock. Jon had described the tree slicing across the hallway, but that hadn't prepared her for the sight. Or the sudden realization of how easily Becca could have been right at that place at the wrong time and been crushed.

"My baby," she whispered as the enormity of Becca's near miss overwhelmed her.

"God was watching out for her." Jake seemed to understand what was flashing through Kate's head.

As she ducked under the tree Jake, handed her the first of the three suitcases he'd pulled from the closet.

"Tell me what you need from your room. You can pack the girls' stuff."

The idea of her brother pawing through her clothing wasn't a welcome thought, but crawling under the trunk of the tree to get into her room was even less appealing. She rattled off a list of basics and watched as he wriggled his tall frame under the tree.

It didn't take long to empty as much of Becca's closet and dresser as would fit into the big rolling suitcase. Jenny's room appeared as untouched as Becca's, and in another ten minutes she had Jenny's stuff packed. She rolled both suitcases out into the hallway and met Jake scrambling back to his feet, dragging her suitcase with a bulging tote slung over his shoulder.

"I dumped the stuff from your medicine cabinet in while I was at it. Anything else we need up here?"

Kate shook her head. There were probably half a dozen things she needed that she'd remember once she was settled in at her mother's house, but at the moment her mind was a blank.

Back in the kitchen, Jake began hauling perishable food out of the fridge. "The power's still on and should stay on for the most part. Should I leave the stuff in the freezer?" he asked.

"I can come back for it later. I just need to collect the insurance file and some other stuff from my office."

She hurried to her office and stopped on the threshold, her brain still scrambled with shock and indecision. What did she need? *Insurance files. Right.* She pulled out the file drawer and riffled through it.

"What's taking so long?" Jake called out from the kitchen.

"Just another minute," Kate called back as she pulled out another drawer and began shoving more files into her messenger bag. When that was full, she snagged a crate with a collection of old magazines, dumped them into the easy chair, and filled the empty crate with her work notebooks.

Jake stuck his head inside the doorway.

"Everything's in my truck since you left your van up at Jon's. I grabbed Max's bed, too. And the jackets and rain gear in the back hall."

Kate took one last look around her office. "I guess that's it, then."

Jake hoisted the crate and headed for the kitchen. Kate followed with her messenger bag over her shoulder and the gut-deep feeling that this was somehow a turning point in her life. There had been so many turning points in her life that she'd never seen coming. Decisions that had been made without a lot of time for debate. Here was another one.

JON HADN'T THOUGHT he'd beat Kate home, but there was still no sign of her when he pulled into his driveway. Jake's truck pulled in right behind him.

"Hey, Jake. What's the word?"

Jake shook his head. "Fixable, but it'll take longer than Kate's patience is likely to last."

"Kate's patience?" Jon wondered what that was supposed to mean.

"With Mom." Jake muttered as he began unloading gear from the back of his truck. "Is Kate's van unlocked? I thought she'd beat me up the hill, but she's probably standing out back glaring at her house as if she could miraculously put everything back just by wishing for it. I'd take this stuff out to the island for her, but I've gotta get home to watch the kids. Zoe has to go out to a meeting tonight."

The van was locked. "Zoe's probably standing in my front hall tapping her toe and wondering where I am," Jake muttered as he piled Kate's belongings beside the van.

"Catch you later." Jake handed the crate to Jon and climbed into his truck. A moment later he was driving down High Street toward town.

Jon shifted the weight of the crate onto his hip. It was already getting dark. Where was Kate, anyway? He looked at the deepening gloom. She didn't have to move out to the island tonight. Or at all for that matter.

Becca appeared at his side. "My stuff." She grabbed the rolling duffle with her initials embroidered on the side and began hauling it toward the house, bellowing for her sister as she went. Jon didn't stop her.

"I'M NOT GOING to hold you captive, but really, Kate. It's not an imposition. I'd enjoy having you and the girls stay here as long as you need." Jon leaned his hips against the counter and folded his arms across his chest. "We've been best friends since I pulled you around in a wagon. It's what best friends do."

"But my parents have more than enough room."

Jon snorted. "They may have plenty of room, but I know you. I know you love your mom, but you'll be on each other's nerves inside of a week. Never mind a month or three. Your mom will hover and worry and you'll be fixing to tear your hair out."

Kate stared back at him, her expression blank.

"Mom?" Becca called from some distant part of the house. A moment later, her footsteps pounded down the stairs and she arrived, breathless, in the kitchen. "I got everything unpacked."

"What do you mean, you have everything unpacked?" Kate asked, looking confused.

"Uncle Jon carried my suitcase upstairs for me, and I put everything away. I even hung my uniforms up, and you didn't even have to ask me." Becca was obviously pleased with herself. "I'm going to put Max's bed in my room and show him where it is." She left the kitchen as fast as she'd come in.

Kate glanced at Jon. "This is a conspiracy."

"I just figured . . ." Jon shrugged. "You should have come up with Jake if you had other plans."

"I got an important phone call. I figured I could take it and walk up and still get here about the same time. I didn't think he'd just dump my stuff and leave."

"He had to get home to watch Molly and the twins because Zoe was going to a meeting."

Kate sagged into a chair, suddenly looking totally overwhelmed.

She did her best to smile up at him. "Keeping that promise to Ethan didn't include letting us move in and take over your house, you know. Your quiet bachelor lifestyle won't survive a week."

Jon laughed. "It didn't last a day. Jenny has already made herself at home in my den, too. But she says she needs her violin, and I didn't see it in Jake's truck."

Kate surged to her feet. "Oh, my God! I forgot all about it."

"I've still got time before I have to go back to work. I'll run down and get it. It's on that table by the couch in the living room, right?"

"The case is under the table along with her music." She slumped back into the chair as if the weight of the world were bearing down on her. "I'll try not to get used to having you at my beck and call."

"Be right back." On his way to the door he bent down and whispered, "Beck and call all you want." Then he kissed the top of her head and left.

As he loped down the hill, he wondered if he was being smart. He wanted her in his house, but his motives weren't entirely altruistic. Maybe it would be better if she spent the next few months on the island learning to cope with her mother's hovering. Better for both of them. But the invitation had been issued, and he wasn't going to take it back. Having her share his home for the next few months was probably the closest he'd ever get to feeling like they were family again, the way he had when he was a teenager after his mother died and he'd practically lived at the Cameron house. When he'd been falling in love with her and watching her fall in love with Ethan.

The violin was right where Kate had told him he'd find it. He scooped it up along with the music and glanced around to make sure he wasn't missing anything before heading back the way he'd come. As he crossed the kitchen floor, his shoe caught something and sent it tinkling across the tile. Whatever it was, came to rest under the edge of a cabinet. He bent to pick it up.

Her lighthouse bell! The one he'd bought her that last glorious summer before Ethan became a part of her life. Where had it come from now? He closed his fingers around the bell and stood there remembering.

That month-long camping trip his dad had taken him on along with the Cameron boys and Kate. They'd explored the outer banks from one end to the other. One of the last stops had been Hatteras Light, and he'd purchased the little bell with a lighthouse on it for Kate. He opened his hand and studied the bell with a faded pink ribbon looped through the top, amazed that she still had it after all these years.

He dropped it in his pocket and headed for the door.

She was still sitting where he'd left her when he strode back into his house and set Jenny's instrument and music on the table. He held out his hand.

"I brought you something else."

Kate extended her hand, palm up, and he dropped the bell into it.

"My guardian bell!"

"I found it on the floor. Not sure how it got there, but maybe the tree falling rattled it loose. Or all those men tromping around on the roof last night." He glanced at his watch. "I've got to get going, but there's pizza in the freezer if you don't feel like fixing anything. I put your stuff in the fridge."

He turned to the shelf mounted by his back door and waved his key fob at it. The decorative support beneath the shelf opened to reveal his service pistols. He lifted one out of the molded case, checked it and dropped it into his holster, then flipped the drop-down case back into place.

"Wow, that's ingenious." Kate appeared at his side.

"I thought so." He snapped the holster. "There's another in my bedroom. I installed them after the first time Becca and Jenny slept over. They're responsible girls, but I didn't want to leave my guns unsecured." Accidents happened, and he'd never forgive himself if anything happened to Kate's babies.

Unexpectedly, Kate wrapped her arms about his neck and kissed him. On the lips. Just as hastily she dropped her arms and backed away. His heart raced at the suddenness of it.

"That was—that was really thoughtful."

He swallowed hard. "Just part of the job." But that kiss hadn't been part of it.

She looked like she was going to say something else but changed her mind. What was she thinking? He reached for his patrol cap sitting on top of the shelf and plopped it on his head.

"I . . . put your stuff in the only room the girls left unclaimed." Hoping she'd be making use of the room but more afraid he'd end up carrying her bags back down to her car.

"Jon . . . I . . ."

"Yes?"

She shook her head slightly. "Nothing. Just, thanks. For everything."

He smiled at her, willing himself not to make the mistake of kissing her back and finishing whatever she'd started. "Make yourself at home and don't wait up. I'll probably be late."

Then he stepped out and shut the door behind him.

Kate looked down at the little bell still clutched in her hand.

Jon had given her that bell when they were what? Fifteen maybe? To remember a fantastic summer camping trip his dad had taken them all on. They'd gone four-wheeling to see the wild horses on Currituck and checked out the Wright brothers' plane at Kitty Hawk. They'd run around the beautiful white sand beaches during the day and had campfires by night. And on their last day they'd all climbed Hatteras Lighthouse. Jon had purchased the little bell in the gift shop with his share of the money his dad had handed each of them to buy something with.

There'd been a little velvet bag once with a legend about guardian bells.

She'd hung it in her dorm at college, and none of the dire things her mother had warned her about going to school in New York City had happened to her. She'd hung it by the door in her first apartment, and it had been her talisman when she was in labor for Jenny. It had been a difficult pregnancy, and she'd nearly died giving birth, but she'd been clutching that little bell in her hand and lived. She'd tied a pink ribbon through the loop and hung it in her kitchen window when Ethan brought her back to Tide's Way. Perhaps it had been on duty yesterday when the tree fell, keeping both Jon and Becca safe.

Closing her fingers around it, she pressed her fist to her chest. She touched the fingertips of her other hand against her lips. Lips that had touched Jon's for just a millisecond and left her heart racing . . .

It was a kiss that was supposed to be a heartfelt thank-you, but it had felt like so much more.

Chapter 14

JON WAS WAITING for the coffeemaker to finish brewing when Kate slipped into the kitchen on bare feet and sleep-mussed hair. She looked adorable and he wanted to give her a hug. And maybe prompt another kiss like the one she'd given him yesterday. For his entire tour last night, he'd thought about that unexpected kiss. He hadn't handled it well. He'd been taken off guard and just stood there, his heart pounding, trying to decide if he should take advantage or let it go and pretend it was nothing.

Years ago, when they were barely twelve, he'd kissed her while they were hiding together, waiting for Ben to find them in a game of fifty-two scatter. It had been the first time he'd kissed a girl, and he was pretty sure it had been her first kiss, too. That kiss had been fleeting. And awkward. She'd backed away from him in haste just like she had last night. He'd been afraid for weeks that he'd somehow breached some unseen boundary of their friendship.

So maybe it was just as well he hadn't made a move last night. He might be in love with her, but her friendship was something he never wanted to jeopardize. He couldn't imagine his life without her in it and if friendship was all they ever shared, that was better than gambling on more and losing everything.

"Good morning. You sleep okay?" How mundane could he make it?

She stretched, causing the neckline of her robe to part half way down to her waist. Jon whipped back to the coffeemaker to keep himself from staring at the enticing curve of partially exposed breast.

"Where are Becca and Jenny?" Kate joined him at the counter.

He reached for a second mug, still careful to avoid looking at her. "I walked down to the bus with them, and they're on their way to school."

"Jon—about last night. I didn't mean to make things awkward."

A pang of regret ripped through him. He finally turned to look at her. She'd adjusted the robe. Thank God. No point in pretending to misunderstand. "You didn't make anything awkward. We're still friends if that's what you're worried about."

"Thanks. I decided you were right us about going to Mom's. If you're really sure it's okay, we'll stay here. Unless something changes."

The coffeemaker was done gurgling, so he poured two mugs and handed one to her. "You're welcome for as long as you need. You want some breakfast? I ate with the girls, but there's still some batter left. Becca was disappointed I didn't have her favorite cereal, so I made it up to her with pancakes."

"I don't do breakfast," Kate said as she wandered over to the table and sat down.

"Can't even interest you in a slice of toast?"

"You don't have to wait on me, Jon. If you do, then I *am* going to feel awkward."

He brought his own mug to the table and sat down opposite her.

They sipped their coffee in companionable silence for a while and then began talking about little things. She asked what his schedule was like in the coming days. He asked about hers. As he sat there watching her drink her coffee with both hands wrapped around her mug, he was overwhelmed with the wish that this could be how his life would always be.

He reached across the table and lifted the wisp of hair covering the cut on her forehead. She'd left off the bandage this morning.

"It looks good. Except for the bruise. It's turned to an ugly shade of yellowish green.

"Thanks for the confidence boost." She touched it carefully with her fingertip. "It doesn't hurt. Much." She glanced out the window, then back directly at him. "I'm sorry I was rude to you that day. I said some things I shouldn't have said. I hope you're not upset with me for not pressing charges."

The cop in him knew she'd been right about not pursuing it. The incident hadn't been malicious. Just an accident. It had been the man in him, the man who happened to love her but had no right to do anything about it, that wanted to punish the guy.

He shook his head. "The guy was sorry enough as it was. But I hope . . ."

"You hope what?"

"I was going to say I hope you won't get into the middle of any more confrontations, but that would be a waste of breath. You're like a dog with a bone when you're on the trail of a story."

She beamed at him, obviously pleased with his analogy. Probably pleased he wasn't going to lecture her again, either.

"That's what a good journalist does." She sat back in her chair and looked at him with a question lurking in her eyes.

"What?"

"What do you mean, what?" she replied.

"You're wanting to ask me something, so spit it out." It wasn't like her to beat around the bush.

"You said you were off duty tomorrow night."

"I am. What do you need?"

She hesitated again. Then sighed. "Would you mind watching the girls?"

"Overnight?" Where was she planning to go now?

"Yes," she replied without enlightening him.

"Care to share where you're headed?"

"Savannah. My friend Kim is helping me with something. She called me last night and asked if I could come down."

She clearly didn't want to tell him what she was up to. She might figure he'd object. He might very well object, whether he had a right to do so or not, but it bothered him that she didn't tell him. Once upon a time they'd shared everything. Well, maybe not everything, but she'd never been this secretive before. Not with him.

"Sure. No problem."

"Thanks. I have to call the insurance company and see how soon they can have someone out here." As she got to her feet and bent to grab her mug, the robe parted again.

This time Jon was sure there was nothing under it. He swallowed but couldn't tear his gaze away quickly enough.

Kate grabbed the front of her robe and blushed. Then she whirled and left the room in a rush.

Since she'd noticed his reaction, maybe she'd be a little more careful in the days ahead. If not, he was destined to become a very frustrated man with a lot of cold showers in his immediate future.

He got up to put his mug in the dishwasher. A second wave of longing hit him when he noticed the little guardian bell now hanging in his window over his kitchen sink.

He must have seen it over the years. He'd been in and out of her house hundreds of times. But until he'd found it on the floor and picked it up, he hadn't thought about it. Or about the day he'd given it to her.

Last night it had surprised him that she still had his boyish gift all these years later. But this morning, considering she'd taken the time to hang the little bell in his window, even temporarily, the question popped into his mind: How important was the little guardian bell? How important was *he*?

"I THINK THIS is it," Kim, Kate's college roommate and former fellow intern with the New York paper back in the day, said as Kate inched her van down a street lined with stately old homes. Kim now working for the *Savannah Tribune*, and was the first person Kate called when she uncovered the fact that Miss Jennifer Jones had been absent from the debutante scene for several months and was thought to have been living with relations in Savannah. Except Kate had learned that JJ had no relations in Savannah—then or now.

Kate pulled over in front of a tall Victorian-era home separated from the sidewalk by a wrought-iron fence and about six feet of lawn fringed with flowering shrubs. She peered across her friend's lap to look up at the tall, ornate façade. What must it have been like to come here, scared and alone and pregnant? Savannah was a beautiful city, but that wouldn't have mattered much to a young girl hiding away so no one would ever learn of her disgrace.

"The kid who lives here now inherited it from his aunt. The aunt bought it after Belinda House closed its doors in 1985."

"I wonder who Belinda was?" Kate wound her window down and reached out to open the door.

"You need to get that fixed," Kim said as she opened her own door.

"I need a whole new car. Or at least new to me. This one's as old as Jenny, almost."

"I couldn't find anything about why it was called Belinda House," Kim said as Kate joined her on the sidewalk. "Just that it opened in 1908 and closed in 1985. The lady you mentioned, if she did come here, must have been one of the last. The kid—his name is Tom Espinosa, by the way, and he's not really a kid. He's twenty-something. He said there are boxes of stuff in the attic that were there when his aunt bought the place but she never bothered to go through them." Kim glanced at Kate with her eyes full of laughter. "He gets first dibs on any money we find, but since he's leaving the key in the planter, he wouldn't know if we found any money anyway."

"How do you know this guy?"

"He works at the *Tribune*. He told me about the house when his aunt first passed and he moved in. He said there were tales about its being a brothel, but his aunt insisted it had been a home for wayward girls, not prostitutes. So, when you called asking about maternity homes for unwed mothers thirty years or so ago, I asked him if that's what his aunt meant by wayward girls. That's when he told me about the stuff in the attic and said we were free to look through it."

The gate creaked when Kim opened it. "Tom needs to spray some WD-40 on that gate."

"Maybe he always goes in the back door." A driveway ran down the side of the house to a tiny garage at the back of the property. That's the door Kate would use if she lived here.

Kim turned a full circle on the porch, shrugged and headed back down the stairs. "Guess you're right. There aren't any planters up there. "

They went back through the gate and down the driveway. Sure enough, the back porch had a large, garishly painted planter overflowing with petunias. The key wasn't even out of sight. Kim grabbed it and thrust it into the deadbolt.

"I feel like I'm breaking and entering or something," Kate said as they stepped inside.

"Can't be breaking when you have a key and the owner's permission." Kim set the key on the corner of the kitchen counter.

Tom was neat for a young guy with no wife. The kitchen was out of date but spotless. The floors creaked when they crossed the kitchen and headed for the front of the house.

The stairs were broad and gracious, widening into a curve at the foot. Kate could imagine a woman of some bygone era making an entrance as she descended the last few stairs in a floor length gown belled out with layers of crinolines and petticoats.

Kate loved old houses. She loved the carved woodwork and handsome cabinetry. This house was about the same era as Jon's and had many of the same elements. "It sure is a beautiful old house."

"Tom's been fixing it up, or so he says. He must have started with his bedroom though, since it doesn't look like anything's been updated down here."

Kim led the way up the stairs. The first room off the landing appeared to be the master bedroom. Kim stuck her head in, and Kate peered over her shoulder.

"Wow!" Tom's efforts were obvious in the master bedroom. The wallpaper had been stripped and the walls painted teal on the north and east sides, beige on the other two. The bed had no frame, just a puffy navy blue comforter stretched across the king-sized expanse. "He appears to be a minimalist, too," Kate commented. A single dark wood dresser was the only furnishing besides the bed.

Kim laughed. "He's a bachelor. All he needs is a bed. A big one to bring his conquests home to. I'm surprised he doesn't have a mirror mounted on the ceiling. Come on. I've got things I need to do today."

They moved past the master bedroom and followed the hall to the end where a hatch with a short length of rope dangling from it gave entrance to the attic. Kim pulled the cord, and a whole panel swung down. The stairs were stiff when Kate tried to unfold them and it took both women to get the steps in place.

"I can see why his aunt didn't get up there," Kate observed. "If she was elderly she probably didn't dare try."

"I hope there aren't any spiders. Maybe I should go back downstairs and look for a broom."

Kate laughed. "I can't believe you're afraid of a few spiders. I've seen you take on critters twice your size."

"I don't care for spider webs in my hair." Kim peered into the shadowy attic.

"Tom said the boxes were up here, right? To know that, he'd have had to go up there, and he probably already knocked all the webs down."

"Go ahead if you want. I'm going back for a broom." Kim headed back down the hall.

Kate started up the folding stairs. There were probably dozens of the busy little critters up there, but she didn't run into any of their creations on the stairs. The attic was large with plenty of headroom between the floor and the rafters. It smelled dusty and old. The boxes Tom had given them permission to search were stacked next to the chimney in the center.

Above her head a string dangled from a bare bulb affixed to the collar tie. She pulled it, and a surprisingly bright light flooded the space. It was going to take all afternoon to go through these boxes if they all contained paperwork.

Luckily or not, depending on what you were looking for, the first four boxes had nothing but clothing in them. Interesting to wonder about the era they came from, but not what she was hunting for. Another box held antique oil lamps and another old magazines. Maybe this was a wasted trip.

"The man doesn't own a broom," Kim complained as her head appeared in the opening. "He's got this electric thing. But I guess you didn't run into any webs anyway, huh?"

She joined Kate and began at the other end of the row of boxes.

"Hey! Mardi Gras in Savannah!" Kim held a garish purple mask on a stick to cover her eyes. "Complete with beads." She held up a fistful of multi-colored beads in her other hand.

"The dresses to go with it are in those boxes. I wonder what Tom's going to do with all this stuff when we report back."

"As long as it's not money or worth selling for same, he probably doesn't care if we cart it off with us."

Kate lifted the lid off the top box in the next stack and chortled in triumph. "This is going to take a while."

The box held old files. She held her breath as she lifted out the first folder and riffled through it. "And they definitely belonged to an organization called Belinda House, but this one's just old bills." She set it aside and lifted out a stack of file folders. Kim joined her and grabbed another fistful.

"This one is tax stuff," Kim said, tossing it aside. "And this one, too." She began dropping the files one at a time on the floor by her feet. "All tax stuff."

The second box on the stack was a total mishmash of papers: Old advertisements with shopping lists penciled on the reverse sides, clippings from newspapers, paperwork for long defunct appliances, menus from local restaurants. "I should have asked Tom if he has a recycle bin," Kim complained as she finished going through that box and began on another.

Deflated that all the paperwork had turned out to be so disappointing, Kate squatted by the bottom box, lifted the lid and peeked in expecting more of the same. Suddenly, hope surged anew. "This one looks like correspondence." She reached in and lifted part of the pile. Postcards and envelopes addressed in faded, old handwriting. The date on the one on top was 1921. The letter below that was dated 1933. There was a sepia-colored post card from a strangely named town in Maine postmarked 1912.

Kim brushed her bangs off her face and sighed. "What a bust! No records of guests, babies born or anything juicy." She slumped onto an old cane-backed chair. "But it was worth a shot, anyway."

Kate stopped what she was doing. "You think Tom would mind if I took this box back to the hotel to go through?"

Kim shrugged. "Don't know why not. Just so long as you remember the rule about money."

They put all the old files back into their boxes, straightened the stacks of memorabilia and old junk, then made their way back to the first floor. Kate left a thank-you note and a twenty-dollar bill on Tom's spotless counter. "Should be good for a pizza and beer."

They locked the door behind them and dropped the key back into the planter.

Kate shoved the box of old correspondence in the back of her van and climbed into the driver's seat. "I hope you've got time for supper. There might be nothing in this box of letters, but we've still got some catching up to do."

Chapter 15

"WAS YOUR TRIP successful?" Jon asked when Jenny handed over the phone.

"Not so far," Kate admitted. "But it was nice seeing Kim again. I haven't seen her in ages. How did your day go? I mean with the girls and all? And what's this with Jenny and Tyrell?"

"There was an unplanned meeting of the Kids Who Care after supper." It was a youth group Jon was involved in at St Theresa's, dedicated to serving the community. "A couple of the members knew of several older folks, one of them needing a walker just to get around, with lots of storm debris littering their yards, and the kids thought we should organize a clean-up for this weekend. I figured it would be okay to take Jenny and Becca with me. Becca hung with me and Jenny hung with Tyrell. I'd say her evening went just fine."

Kate hadn't known that her new manager at Ethan's Ribs and his family were members of St Theresa's and already diving into the activities there. Or that Jenny was developing a crush on their youngest son. It was scary how quickly Jenny was growing into a young woman and noticing boys. She was still just a kid.

"I thought the group was just for teenagers."

"Technically," Jon agreed. "But anyone willing to work is always welcome to tag along. I'm sorry if you think I shouldn't have taken them."

"No! I didn't mean that. I just . . . I was just thinking how Jenny's into boys all of a sudden."

"Tyrell's a good kid. I wouldn't worry." He hesitated, then, "Sooo . . . what time will you be home tomorrow?"

"I have to take Jenny to violin practice at four."

"No need to rush. I'll make a run by home when they get off the bus and get them started on their homework. I can get Jenny to violin if you still aren't back yet."

"Becca has soccer practice after school. She gets dropped off at her friend's house and goes to soccer with her. Just remind her to take the bag with her soccer shorts, cleats and shin guards I left on the bench by the back door to school in the morning."

"I'll have to install one of those whiteboard calendars just to keep track of all your schedules. You made it sound simple this morning."

"I'll be home in time. Don't worry about it."

"Well . . ." Jon hesitated. "We miss you. Drive safely coming home."

"I always do."

The line clicked, and Kate felt a little let down. She and Jon had always been able to chat about anything and everything. Back when they were kids, they'd sit on the beach at night and talk. Even after she met Ethan, she and Jon still used to hang out and talk endlessly. Over the years, that hadn't changed, except during her time in New York and his hitch in the Marines. Even after they were all back in Tide's Way again, she married to Ethan with two babies and he recovering from the end of a relationship, they'd always enjoyed each other's conversation and company. But tonight felt different.

He'd been all business once she'd caught up with the girls' day's events and he'd been given back his phone.

Maybe kissing him had been a mistake in spite of his assurances. She hadn't meant anything by it. At least not when she'd impulsively given into the urge. It hadn't been that kind of kiss. Just because it had left her with a racing heart and the wish that she'd made something more of it didn't mean Jon welcomed such familiarity.

Then there was the problem of her wardrobe malfunction that morning that had left Jon gaping at her nearly naked breasts. It wasn't his fault. He was a normal, healthy male after all. But if the momentary incident had embarrassed her, God only knew what he'd felt. The initial embarrassment that had flushed her face when she caught him staring down her half-open robe had turned into something else as she'd fled the kitchen. Maybe she needed to be more careful about how she dressed or didn't dress around him. For both their sakes.

Jacqui would tell her that her problem was that she needed to get a man in her life again. But the desire to start dating and meeting new men just wasn't there. She had her girls and Jon's friendship. She didn't need a new man in her life to complicate things.

She gave herself a shake and pulled the lid off the box of correspondence.

The old letters sounded so formal. Nothing like correspondence today. Of course, hardly anyone ever wrote letters on paper today. Email and texts had taken over, and proper grammar had given way to abbreviated everything. Manners were different, too. These letters were testimonials to a far more elegant time.

Most of the letters said nothing at all about the reason why the girls were living in this place back then, but a few did allude to the reality of pregnancy. One couple in particular mentioned it.

A boy named Edwin had written letters overflowing with love and concern for a girl named Doris. He constantly apologized for her condition and frequently offered to marry her if her parents would allow it. Kate wondered if Edwin and Doris ever had a chance to make a life together. It felt a little voyeuristic, reading about their affair in Edwin's letters, but they were probably long since dead. His eloquent words told of his anguish and guilt, and there was no doubt he loved her very much. His letters also indicated that her parents had no idea he knew where she was or that he was writing to her and receiving letters in return. How sad to think they might never have had a chance to make a go of it together.

The postcard from the strange town in Maine was one of a dozen from the parents of a girl named Lucy. Sent from places all over the northeast, they must have traveled while Lucy lived out her penance in Savannah.

Kate lifted out the last bundle of letters. They were addressed to Miss Jennifer Jones. Kate sucked in a breath of astonishment.

Pay dirt!

KATE SAT ON her mother's front porch overlooking the Atlantic Ocean with a tall glass of sweet tea on the table beside her.

The morning had been awkward all over again. Waking up in Jon's guest bedroom, followed by the sudden awareness that he slept on the other side of the wall, had put her heart into high gear. She'd dreamt about him just before waking. Dreamt about kissing him again and doing a lot more than just kissing.

Last night, she'd been later getting home than she'd anticipated, and Jon had ended up taking more time out of his day to drive Jenny to violin lessons and pick Becca up from practice. He was in the midst of preparing supper for them when she walked in.

Conversation had been lively during supper. Becca especially seemed to blossom under the attention of a man caring enough to show interest in her thoughts and activities. But Jenny had been animated as well, talking about Tyrell. Jon had sent a conspiratorial wink Kate's way. But then the girls had gone off to watch their favorite program on the television and the conversation had lagged. Just as it had the previous night over the phone.

Waking her girls and making breakfast for them in Jon's kitchen hadn't felt the least bit awkward until Jon walked in with his hair spiked from sleep. She'd blushed because of the vivid dream that had nothing to do with their strained conversation before they'd gone their separate ways to bed. He'd just raised his eyebrows at her and turned to pour himself a cup of coffee, which he'd taken with him when he'd returned to his room to get dressed. Ten minutes later he'd been gearing up to leave for work.

He'd ruffled the girls' hair on his way by and headed for the door. He waved his fob at the gun safe, holstered his weapon and let himself out, hesitating only long enough to say, "It'll be another long day. See you tonight. Or maybe not." Then he was gone.

Was he avoiding her?

Her mother appeared with a plate of her famous pecan praline shortbread bars interrupting Kate's uncomfortable thoughts. She set them on the table between the two rockers and folded herself into the chair opposite Kate's.

"You and the girls should move out here while your house is being repaired."

"I was going to. At least I would have if the whole matter hadn't been taken out of my hands." Kate shrugged apologetically. Jon was right about her mother hovering and worrying, but Kate could have managed. Would have managed. Somehow. And she didn't want to hurt her mother's feelings.

"I guess I was in shock that first night. Jon was there with Becca when it happened, and he called me. By the time I got back, Becca was asleep on his couch. Jake's guys were putting a tarp over the mess and I just couldn't think straight. It was just—just easier to let the guys handle it."

Kate's mother reached out to slide her hand over the back of Kate's head. "That I can understand. I'd have been a basket case, too. I'm glad Jon was there for you."

That makes two of us. Three if I include Becca.

"But you know you are always welcome here. I can see where it would be handy to be right next door to keep an eye on the repairs. But just so you know."

"I know, Mom. And thanks. If we start to crowd Jon's life too much, we'll pack up and head on over." *If I start to crowd his life too much.* Kate grabbed a shortbread cookie and watched the waves rolling in on the beach. Could Jacqui be right about Kate's needing a man in her life again? Was she beginning to feel things between her and Jon that weren't there? Was the unaccustomed intimacy of living under his roof responsible for the things she was feeling and creating the awkwardness between them?

"Jon's always looked out for you. I guess it doesn't surprise me he'd step in and take care of things now." Her mother sipped her tea and pushed her chair into a gentle rock.

Now the awkwardness included her mother's observations. Kate needed to change the subject.

She took a quick breath and plunged in to her real reason for coming out to visit her mother this afternoon. To pick her brain about JJ. "How long have you known JJ?"

Sandy Cameron glanced at Kate with her brows raised. "JJ? Why?"

"You knew her back when she was a debutante?"

Sandy frowned, her lips pursed as she thought. "I didn't know her personally. I was never in the debutant crowd. Besides, by the time she would have been making her debut, I had five busy little kids. Jake would have been about four, I guess. Two very different worlds. But I saw her photo in the paper now and then. She was very pretty and had lots of men courting her. I wonder why she never married?"

"What do you think of this?" Kate handed her mother the birth certificate she'd found in one of the envelopes addressed to Miss Jennifer Jones. "Did you ever hear of a man named Adam Lancaster?"

"Everyone's heard of Adam Lancaster. Why do you ask"

Kate reached across the small table separating their chairs and traced her finger under one of the names on the paper her mother held but hadn't yet looked at.

Sandy Cameron gasped and looked at Kate with shocked eyes.

"Where did you get this?"

"In an attic in Savannah."

"This is private information."

Kate shrugged. "So, who's Adam Lancaster?" she prompted.

"He's dead now, but Adam Lancaster was old enough to be JJ's father. He was a friend of her father's, in fact. And the senior senator from North Carolina before he died in the late nineties. But back in—" She stopped to look at the paper she held. "In 1983 he'd have been in the North Carolina House of Representatives. He had a wife and three daughters. One of them JJ's age. Oh, my word! What a scandal. I wonder how JJ's parents managed to keep it hushed up."

"I think this baby grew up to be the man named Matthew that JJ wants to start a Second Chance House because of. No one knows who this Matthew is or where he lives or anything about him. No one knew she was talking about her own son."

Sandy sank back into her seat, still absorbing the scandalous implications. "That would certainly explain why JJ is so dedicated to making this project happen."

"I almost feel sorry enough to agree with her plan. Almost." Kate emphasized. "But I still don't like the idea of men who've been in prison coming to live in Tide's Way. Walking the streets our kids play on and go to and from school on. We don't know these men. They might be dangerous."

"Her parents must have forced her to give her son up for adoption," Sandy mused, ignoring Kate's remark.

Kate shrugged. "They could have forced her to have an abortion."

Sandy frowned. "Her parents were pretty conservative. They'd never have considered abortion."

"Well, either way . . ."

"I can't imagine having to give a child of mine away." Sandy reached out to put her hand over Kate's. "Every single one of you is more precious to me than words. It would break my heart."

"Maybe it broke JJ's, too. She was only fifteen." Kate at fifteen had been such a tomboy she'd barely even noticed boys as anything other than playmates. Until Jon had brought Ethan home from school one day. If she and Ethan had become intimate and she'd discovered she was pregnant, she was sure she'd have done what her brother Jake had done when he'd gotten his high school sweetheart pregnant. Kate would have gotten married if Ethan had been willing. She would have kept her baby in spite of how it impacted her and Ethan's lives. But JJ wouldn't have had that option. Adam Lancaster already had a wife and kids, and he would have been ruined if he'd admitted his paternity.

"Her father could have pressed charges against this Adam Lancaster guy. It would have been considered statutory rape. Even if he was a friend of the family. But then, maybe JJ refused to tell her parents who the father was. That would explain how his name never got dragged through the mud."

"It would have been the scandal of the century," Sandy muttered, still sounding profoundly shocked.

"So, if this Matthew is the same young man JJ was talking about at the town meeting, then it seems like whatever family he ended up in didn't turn out so great."

"It's not always the parent's fault when kids get into trouble," Sandy reminded her. "Or maybe something happened to his adoptive parents. You know Gabe Hunter who helps train dogs for K9 work at your brother Ben's place?"

"Yeah, what's Gabe got to do with Matthew?"

"Well, nothing directly. But I wondered if you knew Gabe's story?"

Kate shrugged. She'd met Gabe a few times but didn't really know him.

"His parents died when he was around twelve. He came to live with his grandmother in an apartment in Wilmington. But his grandmother was pretty ill and Gabe was left on his own most of the time. He was hanging out with a street gang when Officer Brady got involved."

"The same Officer Brady I did a story on last year?" Kate interrupted. "The guy who was spearheading a drive to provide a Thanksgiving feast for a lot of folk who couldn't afford to buy a turkey or any of the other stuff we all take for granted on the holiday?"

"That Jerry Brady," Sandy agreed.

"When I interviewed him, they were at the VFW hall assembling boxes with turkeys and all the fixin's to hand out the following day. I went back for the big giveaway, and there were a bunch of kids helping out who all called Brady Dad. Two of the kids were black, one was Asian and one Hispanic. All boys. He said they were his foster kids. Gabe was there, but I didn't hear his story."

"If it hadn't been for Brady, I think Gabe could have ended up like Matthew. Or worse. But Brady gave him a hand up. Offered him a job to start with and a home in the end. Brady was the reason Gabe ended up at the academy and became a police officer.

"But think about all the kids who don't have a Jerry Brady to step in when they're treading that fine line between normal kid stuff and getting drawn into a life of crime. All most of them need is a chance. And that's what JJ wants to give them. It really doesn't matter what her motivation is."

"You sound like you agree with her," Kate cut in. She was having a hard time believing her mother had been won over to JJ's project.

"I didn't at first. But then I talked to Will. And your father."

"But Mom, the people this second-chance place would be for are criminals."

Sandy frowned at her. "They're just boys."

"Boys to you maybe, but they're men. Possibly dangerous men."

She glanced at her watch and jumped to her feet.

"Look at the time. I have to get going. I've got a deadline and I haven't even started writing the article yet. And no, it's not about JJ and Matthew." At least not this time.

Her mother followed her to the stairs leading down to the driveway. "Just be careful what you write. Don't go ruining someone's whole life just to get a scoop. Why don't you ask JJ for an interview? Find out more about the facts, both about Matthew and about her vision for Jolee? Maybe you'll see the project in a new light."

Kate skipped down the stairs. "My idea exactly." She waved and dashed around to the driver's side of her ancient van.

She sensed her mother's disapproval, and it made her squirm. In her gut, she knew telling the whole story would hurt JJ and maybe others. Like Adam Lancaster's children and grandchildren. And possibly this mysterious Matthew. But wasn't it a journalist's job to uncover the facts and present them to the people who had a right to know them? To make a difference?

Finding Matthew's birth certificate had been an unbelievable break. Someone's carelessness with those letters had been her bonus. She'd be careful to get all the facts, and she'd even give JJ a chance to explain. But the story would be the scoop of her life. How could she not tell it?

Chapter 16

JON SAT ON the hassock with Becca's stuffed Dalmatian draped across his lap while he sewed the toy's ear back into place. Becca knelt by Jon's knees watching the surgical repairs to her favorite stuffed animal. Kate watched the operation from her place on the couch. He was so patient with her girls. And loving in ways even Ethan had not been. Warmth grew in Kate's heart as she contemplated the two heads bent over their task.

Jon tied off the end and cut the thread. "There. Good as new. But I think he needs a bath." He placed the well-loved toy in Becca's waiting arms.

"Dogs don't like baths. Max hates it when we give him a bath."

"Well, maybe we can wait for tomorrow to bathe Peterkins. He'd be too wet to sleep with if we washed him tonight. Besides, it's off to bed with you now, or your mom's going to get after me for keeping you up so late."

Becca jumped to her feet and wrapped her arms about Jon's neck, dog and all. "I love you bunches and bunches." She turned and hurried over to give Kate a goodnight kiss, then bolted for the stairs.

Kate's heart ached at the tableau she'd just witnessed. Becca had always been partial to Jon. He was her godfather, and an honorary uncle, but in the year since Ethan's death Jon had become even more than that.

Especially while Kate was dealing with her own grief and a life turned on its head, Jon had been there, helping to fill the hole in Becca's heart. Kate would always be thankful he was the kind of man he was, the kind of man who liked kids and listened to their worries and shared their triumphs. He would always be that way for Becca no matter how many kids he might someday have of his own.

It was a good thing that the awkwardness that had come between her and Jon in the last couple days didn't extend to her daughters, but she felt oddly left out. She crossed the room and sat down on the couch opposite him.

"You're so good with Becca. With both my girls. You'd be a wonderful dad. How come you never married and had a family of your own?" Her chest constricted with the thought of Jon surrounded by a wife and kids.

"I never found anyone I could imagine spending the rest of my life with." Jon gazed directly at her across the few feet of space that separated them, but his expression gave nothing away.

"You've never met anyone you thought was special? Someone you could dig?" He was a handsome man, personable, reliable and good at just about everything he chose to do. A woman would be blessed to have a husband like him. It seemed impossible no one had ever captured his fancy, or at least tried to. "Not even Candy?"

"Candy was fun, but I never wanted to tie the knot or make kids with her."

"How come?"

Jon's sea green gaze suddenly burned with an intensity so strong it seared her insides. Had he given his heart to someone and had it trashed? He'd never said anything to her, and she was his best friend. Or thought she was.

"I did fall in love once. A long time ago." A frown creased his brow.

Jealousy crashed through Kate. She had no right to feel such an emotion, but there was no other name for the crushing feeling. She owed him the same unstinting support and encouragement he'd always given her. She didn't need to go all possessive on him.

"What happened?" She almost reached out to touch him but folded her arms across her chest instead.

His mouth quirked up at the corner.

"She married my high school buddy."

The implication sank in slowly.

Her throat felt tight, and her eyes smarted.

"I couldn't marry someone else when my heart still belonged to her."

She gaped at him, her heart racing. *He's talking about me. All this time and I never had a clue.* The humming in her ears grew deafening. "And now?" The words squeaked out of lungs that seemed to have forgotten how to function.

The green gaze grew darker. "I can't remember ever not loving you, Kate. You're not the kind of woman a man ever really stops wanting. At least not this man."

Jon is in love with me? Her chest constricted. Jon had loved her even before he brought Ethan into her life. *He wants me.*

"But you never—"

Before she could finish her sentence, he slipped a hand behind her head and drew her toward him until his mouth was so close to hers that his breath felt warm on her lips.

"So, I'm telling you now," he whispered.

The kiss was tender, yet fierce. An outpouring of emotion bottled up for a lifetime. Kate melted into him as the heat of his passion flowed into her, and she responded with a longing that astonished her. He drew away slowly, his lips lingering on hers until he sucked in a shuddering breath and broke the connection.

"I haven't got the right to ask anything of you, but I'm not sorry for kissing you. If I'd been better at my job, Ethan would—"

She pressed a shaking finger against his lips and shook her head.

"Don't. Don't say it."

He brushed her cheek with the back of his fingers. "I *am* sorry I made you cry."

He stood and walked out of the room.

Until he'd brushed them away, she hadn't been aware of the tears on her cheeks. And for the life of her, she didn't know why she was crying. She had just been kissed like she'd never been kissed in her life by a man she thought the world of. A man who just moments before had admitted to loving her for as long as he could remember. Why was she crying?

She buried her head in her arms. Her lips still tingled with the sensation of his mouth on hers. The emotion blazing in his eyes when he'd told her how he felt still burned her insides. Suddenly lots of other little things fell into place. The zing of excitement whenever they had touched unexpectedly in recent months. The unexplained jealousy. Her instinctive turning to him for help and the comfort of his sheltering embrace when life overwhelmed her. Even the odd awkwardness of the last few days and the dreams filled with yearning need.

She'd been in love with Ethan. Head over heels in love when she'd been seventeen. And she'd loved him until the day he'd died. She'd grieved and still felt his loss. But Jon had always been there. He'd been there before Ethan, and she'd loved him then, too. Just not the way she'd loved Ethan.

It was hard to put her finger on when friendship had begun to be something more, but the rightness of it made her heart swell.

She lifted her head at the silence that had settled around her. How long had she been sitting here marveling at the breathless wonder of what had just happened? She turned to check the clock on Jon's mantle. Eleven-thirty. A long time.

Max wandered in and placed his muzzle on her knee, his dark eyes peering up at her, his eyebrows twitching, reminding her he still needed to go out. She got up and walked him to the back door. With her arms wrapped about herself to ward off the evening chill, she watched the dog wander about the yard sniffing carefully before finding a place to pee.

When he came back in, he wagged perfunctorily and headed for the stairs. Presumably to find his bed next to Becca's. Or more likely to get up on Becca's bed and curl up next to her.

Kate locked the door and turned out the lights. She'd intended to work on her story, but her mind was too full of Jon to concentrate. She drifted about the darkened house a bit longer before deciding to take herself to bed.

At the top of the stairs, Jon's door was closed. She hesitated but then went on to her own room just down the hall. She closed her door and leaned against it.

Even now her lips recalled the way his kiss felt. Her heart beat at its normal pace, but it felt fuller. Would the awkwardness still be there between them come morning? Maybe it would be worse. Maybe she should do something to make sure it was not? But what?

JON LAY ON his back, his arms folded behind his head staring into the dark. Had he blown everything to hell and back by giving in to the overwhelming need to kiss Kate? Maybe he shouldn't have declared himself at all.

A soft knock caused him to suck in a startled breath. Before he could move, the door opened and Kate stood there, silhouetted by the light in the hall.

"Are you still awake?"

He sat up and swung his feet to the floor.

She shut the door with a soft click and came to stand in front of him. He started to stand, but she put a hand on his shoulder and pressed him back down.

"I heard somewhere that loving means never having to say you're sorry," Kate said.

"It's from an old movie, but it's not that simple." Was she sorry he'd kissed her? Was he supposed to be apologizing?

Her thighs pressed against his knees as she leaned closer, her eyes on a level with his. Her silky pajamas covered more than his boxers, but not by much. His brain might not know how he should be reacting to her presence here in his bedroom after what had gone down earlier, but his body sure didn't have any doubts. What did she want from him? What was she expecting? He wasn't a saint.

Her eyes glimmered, and she seemed to be struggling to decide what to say. She cleared her throat twice before replying.

"We both seem to be carrying around a lot of guilt. Maybe it's time we let it go. Your second-guessing yourself won't bring Ethan back, and my being sorry won't erase the argument he and I had, but hanging onto the guilt might mean missing out on something else. Maybe something that was always meant to be."

He cupped her cheek with one hand and brushed his thumb over her lips. "What are you trying to say?"

"I think . . . I think I'm falling in love with my best friend."

"You think?" His startled heart felt like it was trying to make an escape.

"I *am* falling in love with you."

He couldn't have heard right. "Say again?" His chest felt tight and his voice sounded funny.

She leaned her forehead against his. "I'm falling in love with you."

"Kate," he breathed her name in disbelief. "Oh, Kate."

She toppled him onto his back and climbed onto the bed beside him. Then she curled against his side and laid her head in the curve of his shoulder.

He combed his fingers through her curls. She had to hear the God-awful drumming his heart was making. Did she have a clue how turned on he was? The woman he had loved and lusted after for most of his life was sprawled nearly on top of him with very little clothing on and had just uttered words he'd never expected to hear. He wanted to take her so badly it hurt.

"Kate? I don't think—"

She shook her head, brushing his chin with her curls. "Don't think. Just be. Just . . . hold me. Please?"

He pulled his feet onto the bed and rolled onto his side, pulling her against him and tucking her head beneath his chin. She wanted him to hold her, only now she'd know everything. He'd chosen to share his feelings. Now he couldn't hide his lust.

Her body molded itself to his, the softness and scent of her invading his entire being. She didn't say anything as she skimmed her fingers rhythmically back and forth over his bare chest. His body hummed like a plucked guitar string, and his thoughts were a total jumble. God only knew what was going on in Kate's head.

Kate listened to the rapid thumping of Jon's heart as her fingers brushed through the curls on his chest. It felt so right to be here with him like this. Even just two days ago, she'd have been aghast. But tonight everything had changed.

She closed her eyes and said a little prayer, asking Ethan for permission to love Jon. Ethan would understand. He was probably grinning down at them now with that lopsided grin that had always made her heart do a little jig wondering why they were being so chaste and not getting it on.

"It's okay, honey. I'm good with this. Now you be good to him."

126

Ethan's voice in Kate's head startled her. Had she fallen asleep? Had she been dreaming?

I made him promise to take care of you, and he kept it. Now it's his turn.

Kate's heart lurched. The voice was so real. So Ethan. But the aroused man molding his body to hers was Jon. And she wasn't asleep.

Ethan? She whispered in her soul. But he was gone. If he'd ever been there in the first place.

"Jon?"

"Hmmm?"

She pushed her head away from his shoulder and looked up into his face. The fierce green blaze wasn't visible in this light, but she could imagine it. Jon did everything with passion. He put his heart and soul into caring for others, from his job to his volunteer work with teens. To Becca and Jenny. To her.

"What?" he asked again.

"I want . . ." It came out breathless and barely audible. "I want you to kiss me again."

His hand trembled as it cradled the side of her face. "If I kiss you now, it won't stop at just kissing." His voice sounded husky and uncertain.

"I know," she murmured as anticipation blossomed. She trailed her fingers down over his toned abs and beyond to let him know she was well aware of how things would go next. If he kissed her.

He groaned softly and rolled up onto one elbow. "Oh, Kate . . ." His voice trailed off as he lowered his head and brought his mouth down on hers.

It started out gentle and a little hesitant just like before. But then his hunger showed. From somewhere deep inside her, an answering need rose to meet his. The kiss became more urgent, more passionate, more desperate.

Jon slid his hand beneath the silky barrier of her pajama top and caressed her breasts with the same hungry passion of his kisses. His other hand cupped her butt, pressing her firmly against his arousal.

"Jon," she gasped breathlessly before things got to the point that speaking wasn't possible any more. "Just so you know . . . I've got an IUD."

"Outstanding," he rumbled as he began removing her clothing. "Because I don't have any condoms. I don't know what I was thinking."

That made her laugh, and the drive to hurry eased. Like she'd given him any reason to plan for such a necessity. She relaxed into the pillows and let him finish undressing her. Then he removed his boxers and tossed them onto the floor.

"You are so beautiful," he murmured as his gaze swept over her and then returned to her face. "So beautiful."

He moved into the space between her thighs, and with his weight supported on his elbows, he framed her face with both hands. He kissed her again, lingeringly, lovingly, and far less urgently. "I want to make this the best night of your life."

Chapter 17

WHEN JON HAD woken this morning, Kate had been curled into him like two spoons in a drawer and the glow of loving her and being loved by her made the day seem bright and full of sunshine even though the sun hadn't come up yet. He'd savored the sweet scent of her overlaid with their lovemaking and been hard all over again. He'd kissed the back of her neck and caressed the swell of her breast with his thumb, hoping she'd wake up as turned on and eager as he was. Then his phone had vibrated on the table beside his bed.

Slipping quickly from the bed, he'd managed to get into his uniform without waking her, but couldn't resist one last kiss before leaving her asleep in his bed.

Now, here he was, faced with an angry woman and a disillusioned teenager. Not how he'd wanted to start this day at all.

The boy's mother went back into her trailer and slammed the door in her son's face.

"I suppose you're going to arrest *me* now." Aaron Cavaleri's shoulders slumped. He looked defeated, disappointed and hurt.

"Have you had any breakfast?" Jon asked the boy.

Aaron looked surprised at the question. Then jerked his head in a negative.

"Neither have I. So why not let's go get something to eat. And talk."

"Sure. Why not. It's better than going directly to jail without passing go." A hint of arrogance tried to cover the boy's vulnerability. "Do I hafta ride in back?"

In answer Jon opened the passenger door of his cruiser and waited for Aaron to climb in. Then he shut the door and walked around and slid into the driver's seat.

"How long has this been going on?" Jon asked as he popped an instant ice pack and handed it to the kid.

Aaron gingerly applied the pack to his bruised cheek. "I'm not sure what you mean."

"I mean your mother hitting you."

"She's just pissed that I called the cops when her boyfriend started slapping her around. Why does she let him do it? My father would never have treated my mother like that."

Jon started the car and pulled out of the beaten dirt driveway as he considered his answer. In truth, Aaron's father had mistreated Aaron's mother. Until his death, Sheila Cavaleri's husband had gone on periodic benders, come home mean drunk, and should have gone to prison except that Sheila would never press charges. The only respite Jon had been able to give her and her young son was to lock Bryson up until he sobered up and went home contrite and promising to change. Aaron had been nine when his father crashed his truck and put an end to it, so the boy was clearly in denial about that truth. Choosing to remember only the good things about his dad. Jon couldn't really blame him.

"It's a cycle that's hard to break, and it's rooted in your mom's lack of self-esteem." Putting it in terms a sixteen-year-old would be able to grasp wasn't the hard part. Helping Aaron deal with it was.

"But my mom's beautiful and smart. She shouldn't feel like that."

Jon pulled into the parking lot of Joel's Diner and turned off the engine. "You know she's smart and beautiful, and I know it. So does most of Tide's Way. But sometimes life has a way of turning things around in a person's mind. Most of all, your mom needs to feel loved. Lonny Ward fills that need in spite of the way he treats her."

"I love her," Aaron shot back.

"I know you do. And that's a good thing. But it's not the same as the love between a man and a woman."

Aaron turned his head away and stared out the window.

Jon waited.

"We gonna eat or not?" Aaron tossed the ice pack on the floor and started to get out. Jon sighed and followed him into the diner.

Margie cruised by as soon as Jon and Aaron had seated themselves at a booth in the far corner. She dropped a couple menus on the table. "Be back in a jiff."

Aaron bent his attention to the menu, and then, when Margie returned with two steaming mugs of coffee, ordered the Joel's Breakfast Special. Jon ordered scrambled eggs and grits.

"How are things going at school?" he asked after Margie had bustled off with their order.

Aaron shrugged. "Okay." He dumped three packets of sugar into his coffee.

"You playing any sports?"

By the time Aaron had rehashed the latest football game, their breakfast arrived. The kid ate like he hadn't eaten in days, but Jon figured that was just his age, not a sign of actual deprivation.

Aaron was a good kid in a bad situation, but he seemed to be coping relatively well. At least until this morning. The bruising on his cheek wasn't as bad as it could have been. It was mostly the bruise to his soul that Jon worried about. He'd seen Aaron in church, knew he was an acolyte and had another support system there. Unfortunately, he had no other family besides his mom.

"There's a group at church could use a guy like you."

Aaron looked up but kept eating.

"It's called Kids Who Care."

"Why would I care, exactly?"

"You care about your mom. Enough to call for help even though it got you slapped around."

Aaron shrugged and folded the last strip of bacon into his mouth.

"We're having a clean-up day on Saturday."

"What are you cleaning up?" Aaron mopped up the syrup with the last bite of his waffle.

"Debris that got blown down in that storm last week for a few elderly folk who can't do it for themselves."

Aaron shrugged noncommittally.

"Everyone will come back to my place." Jon hesitated. Maybe going back to the church would work out better considering his current home situation. "Or maybe back to the fellowship hall, and we'll have pizza and a meeting to plan our next effort. We'd love to have you."

"You're a slow eater," Aaron said, wiping his mouth on a napkin and pushing his empty plate away. He didn't comment on Jon's invitation.

"I like to taste my food going down."

"I missed my bus. And I haven't got my books."

"That I can fix," Jon replied, shoveling in the last of his eggs. He tossed two bills on the table. "If we get a move on, you'll only miss homeroom."

After running by Aaron's house and asking Sheila to hand over Aaron's backpack, Jon pulled up to the front entrance of the high school. He pulled out two cards and scribbled a note on the back of one for the school office. "Keep the other one. If you need anything, call me on my cell. It'll be just between you and me. Nothing official."

Aaron took the cards, studied the note, then tucked the second card into his pocket. "Thanks Officer Canfield." He slid out of the car and stood. "Thanks for breakfast, too. And for . . . well, for everything else, like not arresting me for knocking the bastard down."

"Try not to do it too often. And I'm serious. If you need anything, or just want to talk call me."

Aaron patted his pocket where he'd tucked Jon's extra card. "Gotta go." He shut the door and took the steps to the front door three at a time.

Jon pulled away from the curb wishing there was more he could do for the boy. Something more substantial than just a pep talk and a breakfast. Sheila Cavaleri had raised a fine son in spite of her own problems. From the few brief moments he'd spoken to her when he asked for the backpack, he knew Aaron would be welcomed home again at the end of the day. Nothing would be said about the morning's events, and life would go on without anything changing.

Unlike his own life, which had taken an abrupt one-hundred-eighty the night before. A grin spread across his face at the memory of Kate's asking him to kiss her again, followed by a night that had exceeded anything his imagination had ever dreamed up. He felt happier than he had ever felt in his life.

He glanced at the clock on the dash. Kate would be up by now. Probably getting the girls off to school unless they'd left already. He waited until he pulled into the lot behind the town hall where the cramped police quarters were housed. Then he pulled out his phone and punched in her number.

"SOMETHING'S DIFFERENT ABOUT you today," Jacqui said as Kate seated herself in the beautician's chair.

"I'm homeless."

"You told me that already. Oh, my God. I can't even imagine!" Jacqui closed her eyes and shuddered. "How bad is it?"

"Bad enough so I can't stay there until Jake gets it repaired."

"You're out on the island at your mom's?"

Kate shook her head.

"So, the rumors are true." Jacqui snickered.

Kate jerked around to look at her friend and hairdresser. "What rumors?"

"That you're shacking up with the local cop." Jacqui grinned. "Of course, I didn't believe the gossip, but—oh my God, you are! Aren't you?"

The heat in Kate's cheeks was a dead giveaway. What had felt so right last night had nothing to do with sordid rumors. She'd been living in Jon's house for over a week, but there hadn't been anything more than that until last night. But Tide's Way was a small town. People made assumptions. And they talked.

Jacqui excused herself long enough to turn the open sign over and lock her door. She came back and plopped down into the chair next to Kate's. "Tell me all. I'm your BFF. I need details."

Jon was Kate's best friend forever. And much as she loved Jacqui, there were some details she wasn't going to hear.

"Moving in with Jon seemed like the best plan when my house got trashed. He reminded me how much my mother would hover and drive me crazy. He was right, of course. Mom would have. Besides, it's easier for the girls to be on their regular bus route and they can still play with their friends in the neighborhood."

"And you can get it on with the most eligible bachelor in Tide's Way. I know a few ladies who are going to be devastated."

"Jacqui, stop." Kate couldn't help laughing at her friend's earthy delight, to say nothing of the bubbly feeling of happiness she'd woken with that kept tugging her mouth into a grin.

"He's always had a thing for you."

"How do you know that?"

"I've always known. Jon better never play poker because his face gives him away. You were just so dazzled when Ethan burst into your life, you never noticed. And since Ethan's death, Jon's been like a bear with a cub. Talk about hovering!"

Come to think of it, he had hovered. He just didn't yammer at her the way her mother did. But he always seemed to be there when things went wrong. Like the night of the town meeting when he materialized at her side as two men on the verge of fisticuffs knocked her down. Like the afternoon at Jolee when she'd gotten clocked by a lousy clipboard and then fainted after declaring she was fine.

"It's in his genes to be protective. It's what makes him a good cop."

Jacqui shook her head at Kate. "He loves you, Kate. I hope you aren't going to end up breaking his heart."

"Why would I want to break his heart?"

"I don't know. Guilt about Ethan's death? The crazy idea you don't have a right to a happy life with someone else?"

"Ethan gave me permission to fall in love with Jon." The admission surprised Kate.

It surprised Jacqui even more. "Ethan did what?"

"I know this is going to sound crazy, but I heard him in my head. And he told me it was okay."

"My aunt wouldn't say it was crazy. She talks to my mother all the time, and Mom's been gone for twelve years. They were less than a year apart in age, and they never did anything without the other. Except for getting married, I mean."

"Well, Ethan never talked to me before." His voice had sounded so real, she couldn't shake the feeling he'd been watching. Maybe that should bother her, but it didn't. "When

I realized I was falling in love with Jon . . . I guess I was having some doubts about it. I heard Ethan. In my head. I could even picture him grinning when he said it."

Jacqui launched herself off her chair and gave Kate a hug. "I'm so happy for you. You deserve it. And Jon does too."

"Ethan said that, too."

"My aunt would love to hear that story."

Kate gasped. "You can't tell her. You can't tell anyone. They'll think I've gone over the edge."

"My aunt wouldn't. But I won't tell." Jacqui made a zipping gesture in front of her mouth. Then she picked up her shears and got back to business. "Just a trim, this time, right?"

"Just a trim," Kate agreed.

She needed to have a talk with the girls. Before the whole town knew.

KATE'S SATURDAY DIDN'T go as planned. Having the whole day to be with her girls and have a discussion about her changed relationship with Jon got shot down when Kate got a call from her boss about a fund-raising event he wanted her to cover in Wilmington. Becca was invited to spend the day with her best friend, and Jon offered to take Jenny along on the Kids Who Care clean-up day.

It was a perfect day for a walk to raise money for Alzheimer's research, and she'd done her best to talk to lots of folks with different stories to tell so her article would be interesting. The story was done and submitted, but she was late.

The sounds of energetic young voices wafted from the open church hall doors as Kate parked her aging van and hurried across the parking lot to join the after-work pizza party.

Kate glanced around the big room looking for Jon among the clusters of laughing teenagers and chaperoning adults.

136

Apparently the party was over. Dozens of pizza boxes lay empty on the equally empty tables.

"Hey, Kate." Jon came up from behind her and circled her with his arms. His voice sent a thrill of warm excitement down her spine.

"Looks like I missed supper, too," she said turning to face him.

He planted a kiss on her upturned lips, surprising her with the public display of affection that was obviously so much more than just friendship. Then he winked.

"Doesn't take long to miss out with this crowd. They worked up an appetite this afternoon. Jenny seemed to enjoy herself. Maybe she'll join us officially when her birthday rolls around."

"Speaking of Jenny, where is she?" Had she seen the intimate greeting from Jon?

Jon pointed across the room to a bunch of kids gathered around someone who was apparently seated in the center of the group playing a guitar. Kate stretched up onto her toes but still couldn't see her daughter.

"She's being swept off her pretty little feet by your new restaurant manager's son, who has musical ability as well as charm."

"I hope she didn't make a pest of herself."

"She worked hard. I've another new kid who showed up today, so I kept Jenny and Aaron with me and sent the others out with my assistant dads to supervise. Aaron's a nice kid, but he's sixteen. Apparently too old for Jenny to have a crush on."

"Jenny's not old enough to have a crush on anyone," Kate said, with a hint of outrage in her voice that she tried to tamp down.

Jon just raised his eyebrows at her, but before she could say anything more, his phone buzzed. He snatched it off his belt and checked the screen.

"Canfield here." He answered the call in a clipped professional voice. Then, after listening for several minutes, "I'm on my way."

"Sorry," he said to Kate. "I invited you to stop by, but now I have to leave."

"I understand. I'll stay and help picks up." She waved her hand in the direction of the empty boxes and rubbish bins overflowing with paper plates and cups.

"That's part of the job for my assistants, filling in when I get called away unexpectedly. Don't feel like you have to help, but would you mind driving Aaron home?"

"Which one is Aaron?"

Jon pointed to a tall lanky kid who was already beginning to collect pizza boxes. He held up a finger indicating he wanted her to wait a moment, then crossed the room to speak to the young man. Aaron glanced in Kate's direction and nodded. Then Jon tagged one of the fathers and spoke briefly to him before striding back to her.

"Wait up for me?" He touched her shoulder.

Of course she'd wait up for him. Without waiting for him to make the first move, she tiptoed to place a kiss on his half smiling lips. The hand resting on her shoulder swooped around to pull her in closer.

"I could get used to this." He kissed her again. Then he let her go and turned toward the door.

Chapter 18

KATE SAT ON the bed while Jenny arranged her new uniforms in her borrowed closet and Becca collected discarded tags and dropped them into a plastic bag.

Jon's behavior at the church hall still warmed Kate's insides. His unabashed display, not caring who might take notice as he claimed her lips before hurrying off to respond to an urgent call. Apparently, he wasn't making the mistake of keeping his feelings to himself this time around. He was announcing it, staking his claim.

Ethan had never been overly demonstrative. He hadn't even liked holding hands, and after their more carefree high school days, wouldn't have been caught kissing her in public, either. Somehow she knew Jon's easy display of affection wasn't just because it was all so new between them. He would always be like this. It still surprised her that he'd loved her for so long and never once given himself away. How hard it must have been for him to watch helplessly while she fell in love with Ethan and left him behind.

"I don't know why I can't go to Stewart Junior High like Madison," Jenny complained, dragging Kate's attention back to the project at hand. Madison Avery lived on the next street over and was Jenny's best friend. "Then I could wear what I want."

Kate felt strongly about the quality of the curriculum at St. Theresa's K-eight, and she had explained her reasons before. Besides, tonight she had another discussion that couldn't wait any longer. She just couldn't figure out where to begin.

Jenny straightened the collars of her uniform shirts. Finicky beyond her usual. Perhaps something was on her mind, too?

"Mom?" Her back to Kate. "Are you and Uncle Jon in love?"

Or perhaps she was reading Kate's mind?

"Yes," she answered without beating around the bush.

Jenny turned to face her. "Are you going to get married?"

Whoa! That was a little fast. From a couple nights of passion to a lifetime commitment? Not that Jenny had any idea what had gone on in Jon's bed. Kate hoped.

"I don't know."

"That would be the best thing ever." Becca plopped down onto the bed beside Kate. "Then we could live with Uncle Jon even after our house gets fixed."

Kate wrapped her arm about Becca and reached for Jenny's hand. "I've only known I feel that way about Uncle Jon for just a very little while. Usually people take time to get to know each other before they decide to get married."

"But you've known him forever. You knew him even before you knew Daddy." It sounded like an accusation. As if Jenny wasn't in favor of replacing her father. Yet. Or maybe ever.

"I have known him for a long time, but he was my best friend. I was in love with your father and I never felt that way about Uncle Jon while your father was here."

"But now that Daddy's gone . . ." Jenny's voice faded away. She swallowed hard. "Now that Daddy's gone, that changed?"

Kate nodded. "Not right away." Not until she'd begun to notice him as an attractive man. Until his presence set her skin to tingling, and the sight of him made her heart jump.

"But you still love Daddy. Right?"

"I'll always love your daddy. He will always live in my heart and be part of my memories. Part of our family memories."

"So why do you need another husband?"

Becca's head jerked from Jenny to Kate as if she were watching a Ping-Pong game. Clearly there was no doubt in her mind that adding Jon to the family was an excellent idea. She didn't share Jenny's reservations about replacing the man in their family.

"Jenny," Kate said as she drew her daughter closer. "nothing has been said about marriage. Maybe nothing will ever be said. I just don't know. But however things work out between Jon and me, do you think your daddy would want me to be lonely all the rest of my life?"

Jenny stared at her toes and shrugged.

"He wouldn't. I know he wouldn't." Becca jumped in with conviction. "He would want me to have two daddies. He would want Uncle Jon to take care of us."

Suddenly there were tears rolling down Jenny's cheeks. Kate pulled her onto her knee and hugged her. Becca wrapped her arms about both Kate and Jenny, and they clung to each other while Jenny's outburst ran its course.

"I miss Daddy," Jenny hiccoughed as she freed one arm to wipe her face.

"I know you do, sweetheart. I do, too."

"Me, too," Becca added. Then she jumped up and ran to pull a tissue from the box on the bedside table. She handed it to Jenny. "I'm sorry I made you cry."

Jenny wiped her eyes with the tissue and slid off Kate's lap. "I guess it would be okay."

"What would be okay?"

"I guess it would be okay if you married Uncle Jon." She squared her shoulders. I think Daddy would be okay with it." *I'm okay with it*. Ethan's imagined words.

"Thank you." Jenny was so like her father. "Right now that hasn't even come up. Maybe it will. Maybe not. But I appreciate your approval if it does." Not that Jon wouldn't be all for it. He'd loved her that way forever. If she went out and suggested it right now, he'd be on the phone before she finished proposing, making an appointment with the town clerk to get a marriage license. For her, loving Jon was too new, too fragile. She needed time to let it settle into her being.

"I'm going to tell Uncle Jon he can be my new daddy." Becca was already half way to the door.

"Becca. No." Kate looked at her sternly.

Becca halted and looked back, her young face clouded with confusion.

"That's something Uncle Jon and I need to discuss first. I promise you will be the very first to know, but for now, I don't want you to say anything to him. Or to anyone else."

Becca pouted.

"Promise me you will keep this conversation to yourself?"

For a moment, Becca looked mutinous, but then she drew an X across her chest. "Cross my heart promise. But we can still live here, right?"

"We can't exactly go home right now," Jenny reminded her.

"Not until Uncle Jake says it's safe," Kate agreed. "For now, we will be staying here. And right now, it's your bedtime. Go say goodnight to Uncle Jon and remember your promise."

Becca skipped out of the room.

Kate stood and gave Jenny another hug. "Do you want me to come back to tuck you in?"

"I'm too big to get tucked in." Jenny gave her mother another squeeze before releasing her and beginning her getting-ready-for-bed ritual.

Kate retreated to her own room to remove her work clothes, and since it was already late, put on her pajamas and a robe. When Becca had had time enough to finish her nightly routine, Kate crossed the hall to tuck her baby in.

Becca would have been horrified to think of herself as a baby, but Kate was going to cherish every moment of her growing up. And as long as her youngest baby still liked being tucked in, Kate planned to enjoy it.

Afterward, she blew Jenny a kiss from the doorway and headed downstairs to the living room.

In the archway to the spacious room with a big, flat-screen television mounted over a gas fireplace, Kate hesitated. Jon sat at one end of the couch with a beer in one hand, watching Sunday night football. A warm feeling puddled in her stomach as she considered what it would be like to always find him waiting for her like this.

He'd been waiting for her most of his life. The thought was humbling. And he'd have waited forever had an unspeakable accident not ripped Ethan from her life.

She crossed the room and ruffled her fingers through his hair as she passed by. Jon glanced up at her as she rounded the couch and plopped down next to him. He welcomed her with a smile and slid is hand along the back of the couch, then let it drop onto her shoulder and pulled her against his side. With a sigh, she laid her head on his shoulder and surrendered to the wonderful feeling of being wanted and loved. His love was so unexpected. Totally undeserved, yet so generously given.

"Sounded like you were having a serious conversation up there. Girl talk?"

"Jenny asked about us."

"What did you tell her?" He sounded suddenly uncertain.

"She wanted to know if we were in love."

His brows rose, but he said nothing.

"I told her yes."

Jon tipped her face up with two fingers and covered her mouth with his.

"I hope you don't get called out again tonight," she murmured when he finally drew away, leaving them both breathless.

"That makes two of us," he replied as he parted her robe and slipped his hand inside.

Kate hadn't fooled around on the living room couch since she was a newlywed. Doing it now, doing it with Jon, was a total turn-on. Until she remembered the girls. She pushed Jon's hand away and pulled her robe together.

"We might get caught." Would Jenny be so generous about finding her mother half naked and in a shockingly shameless embrace with Jon? Not likely.

Jon caressed her cheek with one knuckle and looked sheepish. "Good point. We could go to bed early."

"What about the game?"

He shrugged. "It's only football." He fumbled for the remote and shut the television off. "I'd rather spend my time playing with you. I've got a lot of catching up to do."

HE PLAYED HER like a master. As if he'd had years to learn all the ways to pleasure her best. Kate sprawled against the pillows on Jon's bed, totally sated and languidly happy. Jon, on his back beside her, reached for her hand, pulled it to his mouth and kissed the backs of her fingers.

"I love you, Kate."

"I love you, too." She made the effort and rolled onto her side.

He turned his head looking a little surprised. Then a grin spread across his face. "Not just you *think* you're falling in love?"

"I don't deserve you."

He ran his fingers through her hair pushing it back behind her ear. "You deserve every good thing that comes your way. I'm just glad you decided it's okay to let me into your heart and maybe into your life."

She pushed herself onto one elbow so she could look down at him. "You've always been good. You're almost too good to be true." She paused and made a face. "I can't think of a single bad thing you've ever done. Unless it's the time you sailed a glow-in-the-dark Frisbee across the road just as a car came by and scared the crap out of the driver."

He chuckled, then sobered again. "I've had my moments. Mostly no one knows about them."

"Like what?" She settled in with her head on his shoulder.

"If I tell you, you won't respect me anymore."

"Yeah, I will." She toyed with the soft mat of curls on his chest.

"I almost got expelled in high school."

Kate sat up fast and twisted to look down at him. "You didn't!"

"I did. I could have done jail time, too, if the principal had been a hard-liner."

"What on earth did you do? And how come you never told me?"

"I wasn't very proud of it after the fact. The fewer people who knew, the better. Including my dad."

The idea of Jon's doing anything that could have landed him in jail boggled the mind. "What on earth did you do?"

"If you lie back down so I can wrap my arms around you, then I'll share my youthful indiscretion."

As she squirmed back into his embrace, her breasts dragged across his chest. He sucked in a short breath and rolled one nipple between his fingers. "You sure you want to know about my misdeeds? A second round would be a lot more fun."

She grabbed the busy hand and placed it on the small of her back. "Tell all."

He sighed. "A bunch of us spray-painted the school mascot on the back wall of the school the night before we hosted the annual game against our arch rival."

"That's all?" Kate snorted. "Here I was thinking you'd done something really heinous."

"It was the sheer size of the paint job. Covered the entire outside wall of the gym. Damages would have put the charges beyond mere misdemeanor."

"How did you get caught?"

"We didn't."

"So how did you get in trouble then?"

"There was a new kid at school. He had a record for spraying graffiti on public property in Charlotte where he came from. Everyone just assumed it was him, and if I didn't confess, he would have gotten in big trouble."

Kate gave Jon's middle a squeeze. "That kinda makes you a hero."

Jon barked out a laugh. "Definitely not a hero. But my coming forward and confessing bought me some goodwill with the Monsignor. Instead of reporting it to the police and my dad, he made me clean it off. Then I had to do a hundred hours of community service. My buddies helped me do the cleaning because I didn't rat them out, but I spent the next few months praying my dad would never find out or the punishment would have been even worse."

"Was Ethan one of the buddies involved?"

Jon hesitated. Then she felt him move his head on the pillow. Ethan had let Jon take the blame. It had been a boys' prank, but Jon had been the man among them.

She tipped her head back and stretched to kiss his jaw. "Well, that still makes you pretty darned perfect in my eyes."

"How about if I told you I went AWOL in Italy? If my commanding officer had found out, I'd have spent time in the brig repenting."

She shook her head. "Still not counting it."

After a long pause, he said in a hesitant voice. "I got roaring drunk the night you got married. Stinking, falling-down drunk. Your brothers had to put me to bed, and I was so hung over the next day when I had to report back to Lejeune, it's a wonder my CO didn't make me ruck up and go for a ten-mile run in full gear."

She'd never even seen him even a little tipsy, and it was hard to picture him totally smashed. There was a lot of him to put to bed, even for men as big as her brothers. "Considering what I know now, I guess I could forgive you for a lot more than just having too much to drink."

"It won't happen again. Even if—" He suddenly pulled his arm out from under her and sat up.

Kate jerked back in surprise. "Jon?"

He got to his feet and crossed to the window where he stood, silhouetted against the vague light of a waning moon with his arms folded across his chest.

Kate waited to see if he would come back to bed. Something was bothering him. Something he maybe didn't want to share with her?

Not one to retreat from difficult scenes, she climbed out of bed and followed him.

"Jon?" She touched him on the shoulder.

"Hmm?" He didn't look at her.

"What's wrong?" Confusion and doubt raged in her breast. Had she said something? Or was it just the memory of her marriage to Ethan?

He turned to face her then, dropping his arms, but not touching her. "I promised your husband I'd watch out for you. That didn't include poaching. But that's what I want, Kate. I want you for myself. I want to be the guy you marry the next time around. Is that wrong?"

She wanted to touch him, but he was still stiffly unapproachable. As if he'd erected a barrier between them, in spite of the fact that they were both naked. "It's not wrong, Jon."

"Yeah?" His voice was harsh. "I wonder what Ethan would think now. Some friend I turned out to be. Screwing his wife the first chance I get."

"I'm not his wife anymore. I'm his widow. And he wouldn't think less of you. I know he wouldn't. I told Jenny the same thing."

"You told Jenny what?" His voice went up on the last word. He glanced at the bed and back at her.

Kate shook her head. "Not about that. She just asked if we were in love and when I said yes, she wanted to know if we were getting married."

He swallowed. "Are we?"

"I told her most people take a while to get to know each other first."

"But we already know each other."

"That's what she said."

Abruptly Jon swept her into his embrace. "I'm sorry. It's harder to banish this guilty feeling than just saying it. I want you so bad, but I keep getting this awful feeling I shouldn't."

Kate wrapped her arms about his waist and hugged him. "I asked Jenny if she thought Ethan would want me to be lonely for the rest of my life. She thought about it. Then she cried because she was missing Ethan. But in the end, she decided her father would understand."

"Well, he better understand all of it because I'm taking you back to bed, and I'm not going to be virtuous about it."

Long after Jon had fallen asleep, Kate lay awake, thinking about all the years Jon had been virtuous about his love for her. He'd stood aside and watched her fall in love with his best friend. He'd gotten drunk to bury the hurt when she married Ethan. Jon had stood at her side when Becca was christened, promising all the things a godparent promises, probably aching because Becca wasn't his child. In the end, he'd helped her bury Ethan, held her when she wept, and stood by the promise he'd made to take care of her with no thought to himself or what he wanted or needed.

And she hadn't answered his question.

Chapter 19

JON SAT AT the kitchen table staring out the window at nothing in particular while he drank his coffee. He'd been ridiculously disappointed when he woke alone in his bed. He'd have been the first to agree that for the girls' sake it was better that Kate returned to her own room before they woke up. But he'd still felt bereft to find her gone.

A slight shuffle caught his attention, and he turned just as Jenny came into the kitchen. She crossed the room and dropped an impossibly loaded backpack on the bench by the back door. She went to the refrigerator and took out a jug of milk.

"Good morning, Jenny."

"Morning," she muttered as she reached for the Cheerios.

"I made some cinnamon rolls." Jon pointed to the pan on the stove.

"My father liked Cheerios." She filled a bowl, added milk and put the jug back in the refrigerator.

"You can have both," Jon offered. "Or not. You're up early."

She slid into the breakfast nook opposite Jon without comment. For someone who had given Kate permission to move on with her life last night, Jenny seemed a little resentful this morning. He didn't really blame her. Her father had been gone barely more than a year, and it had been a hard year for her. Hard for all of them, but Jenny and

149

Ethan had shared an especially close bond. He'd need to be patient with her.

"Have you made any plans to celebrate your birthday yet?"

She looked up at him, her eyebrows peaking as if she were surprised that he remembered her birthday was just a few days away. "I was supposed to have a party."

"Was?"

"I haven't got a house to have a party in right now."

"Have it here."

She slitted her eyes at him. "Here?"

"Why not here?"

"I didn't think you would want a bunch of kids messing up your house."

"Jenny, I've had kids messing up my house on a regular basis for a while now. I'd be fine with you having your friends over for a party."

"What kids?" Again the attack mode.

"The kids we worked with yesterday cleaning up yards. Usually we meet in the church fellowship center, but occasionally I invite them all here for a pizza party or a movie night."

"How come you got involved with a bunch of kids? It's not like you have any of your own."

"Kids Who Care was my idea." He'd started the group after Candy had left and his life had seemed sadly empty. Living with Candy and her teenage son for three years, Jon had discovered how much he enjoyed spending time with young people.

She nodded and shoveled in another mouthful of Cheerios. Jon sipped his coffee considering.

"You know, in a little over a hundred and twenty hours, you'll be a teenager. You could become an official member."

She wagged her head. "Maybe." Then she went back to eating.

"Jenny?"

She looked up again.

"I hope you know you can tell me if something's bothering you. I'm a good listener."

She nodded.

"Please, be honest with me. I know your mom talked to you about us, and I don't blame you if you have some resentment about it. I'll understand. I just want you to know I care about your feelings, too. They are as important to me as your mom's."

She blinked rapidly.

He reached across the table and touched her cheek lightly. "I love you, Jenny. I've loved you since you were just a few hours old and your daddy put you into my arms. You were the first newborn baby I'd ever held. He was so proud of you, and I was so afraid I was going to break you somehow. But I didn't drop you then, and I don't ever want to do anything to hurt you now. I hope you know that."

She hiccoughed and looked back at her empty bowl. She nodded briefly. When she lifted her head again, the incipient tears were gone, but her smile was a bit wobbly.

"So I can tell my friends the party is on after all?"

"You can definitely tell your friends the party is on. Can I come?"

That brought a smile. "I think you better be there. I invited a few boys and they might get a little crazy."

In a rush, Becca swooped into the kitchen, dropped her backpack next to Jenny's, gave Jon an enthusiastic hug and went to the stove to sniff the cinnamon buns. "Are these for us?"

"I made them to be eaten." He gave Becca permission, but kept his eyes on Jenny. "Let me know if there's anything I can help with for Saturday."

"Thanks," Jenny said as she slid out of the breakfast nook.

"What did I miss?" Kate asked as she came into the kitchen wearing a ridiculous pair of slippers that looked like rabbits.

"Uncle Jon said I can still have my party," Jenny answered as she hoisted her backpack onto her slender shoulders. "Come on, Becca. We'll miss our bus."

Kate lifted her eyebrows. "You sure?"

"Of course, he's sure," Jenny answered quickly. She probably expected him to change his mind if her mother started describing the event. Or maybe she was just making sure he made good on his promises now that she'd given him permission to court her mother.

Becca grabbed her backpack and followed her sister to the door, still licking her sticky fingers.

When the door shut behind the girls and quiet returned to the kitchen, Jon patted his thigh and invited Kate to sit.

"Are we still on?"

She crossed the room and sat, wrapped her arms about his neck and tipped her forehead against his. "Of course, we're still on.

"I don't want to push," but he was pushing and he knew it. He just couldn't help wanting some kind of assurance that the last few days hadn't been a fluke. He wanted the right to wake up every morning and find her still in his bed, even with the girls sleeping across the hall. "I just want to know you're mine."

She leaned away from him. "I don't belong to anyone, Jon."

His heart lurched.

"We know each other about as well as any two people ever can. Well, almost," she added. "But I'm still my own person."

"I know. And I admire the person you are. I'm proud of you and your achievements, and I promise, I'll be your biggest cheerleader. Forever. I guess that's what I'm asking.

For the right to be with you . . . forever. I just put it wrong. I'm not good with words like you are."

She eyed him with an inscrutable blue gaze. "Is that a proposal?"

"Do you want it to be?" He held his breath. It was too soon. Way too soon. He should have waited.

Kate leaned in and put her head on his shoulder. He could no longer see her face or the expressions flitting across it.

If she tells me no, I don't think I can take it.

"It just seems so . . . so quick. It seems . . ."

He bit his tongue to keep from saying the wrong thing, but his heart was beating a frantic tattoo.

"A week ago you were still my friend."

"I *am* still your friend. I'll always be your friend." That truth could never be changed no matter what her answer was.

"Then you were my lover."

Her desperate, greedy lover.

"And now you want forever."

If he didn't die of heart failure first. His heart felt like it was on the verge of a catastrophic event.

Kate slid off his lap and walked over to the sink to gaze out the window. He could hardly breathe. She touched the little guardian bell with one finger, and it tinkled. After a long, uncomfortable silence, she turned to face him. He still couldn't read her expression. And now he couldn't breathe at all.

"I don't want to make a mistake." She chewed her lower lip. He wanted to kiss it and make her stop talking, but he stayed where he was.

"I don't want to rush into anything and hurt us all if it's the wrong thing."

Jon rarely cried, but he felt like it now.

"Can I think about it?"

THE LITTLE SUNROOM off the main living area was an idea place for Jon to keep an eye on Jenny as she welcomed her guests as they arrived. Kate was somewhere, probably in the kitchen or the dining room setting out the food.

As promised, there were boys, but so far they were behaving in a way that would make their mommas proud. It was actually the girls who surprised him. Or rather it was one particular girl. She seemed older than the other kids. At least she acted that way, strutting around with her chest thrust out, showing off her perky, young breasts, and batting her eyes at any boy who took notice. He'd seen a lot of teenage preening and posturing at Kids Who Care, but nothing as blatant as this girl.

Jon went back to reading his book, trying to concentrate on the words in front of his eyes instead of the babble of young voices coming from the other room and the siren trying to lure the boys into her personal orbit.

"Here you are," Kate said from the doorway.

He put a marker in the book he wasn't really reading and set it aside. "Is there anything I can help with?"

"No." Kate sighed and moved to sit in the rocker by the window. "It's all on autopilot from here on in. Until it's time to break the party up. It was good of you to tell Jenny she could have her friends over."

"Not a problem." He'd do just about anything for Ethan's girls. He'd promised, after all, and riding herd on a bunch of teenage partygoers was a piece of cake.

"Do you believe that Cynthia Abbot?" Kate rolled her eyes.

"The one with the too short cashmere sweater? She must be turning her father's hair gray. Is she in Jenny's class?"

"She's the sister of one of Jenny's classmates. I'm not sure how she got herself invited. I'm just glad Jenny isn't copying her. If Cynthia were my daughter, I'd be considering grounding her until she was eighteen."

Before Jon could respond, a shriek came from the dining room. In an instant Jon was on his feet and headed to see what disaster had caused it.

"You did that on purpose!" Jenny's friend Madison was frantically wiping pizza sauce off the front of her white blouse. She was making a determined effort not to cry, but she was clearly distressed.

"Jeremy bumped me," Cynthia said, turning to the young man in question. He looked confused but didn't dispute Cynthia's claim.

Kate ignored Cynthia and wrapped her arm about Madison's shoulders and whispered in her ear. They disappeared into the kitchen while Jenny rounded on Cynthia.

"That was mean."

Cynthia lifted her nose a little higher. "Baby."

"She's not a baby. You—"

"Jenny?" Jon cut her off before the catfight could escalate. "What about the game you planned to play?"

Jenny leveled a daunting hazel gaze his way but then got his unspoken message.

"Hey, everyone. I got this awesome new game where you get to make things up. The crazier the better. And everyone else has to figure out if you're lying or not. Anyone want to play?"

There was a chorus of assents, and most of the kids followed Jenny into the living room. Only Cynthia and Jeremy were left by the buffet table.

"You don't want to give it a try?" Jon asked.

"It's kid stuff," Cynthia said condescendingly.

"It might be fun," Jeremy said. He turned and headed in the direction of the game that was getting under way.

Cynthia sniffed and followed.

Thank God I'm not her father! There would be no ifs about the grounding until she learned some manners, at the very least. Jon helped himself to a miniature cream puff and ate it while leaning against the door jamb watching Jenny and her friends.

A few minutes later, Kate and Madison reappeared. Madison was wearing a clean blouse and looking a lot happier. Kate left her squeezing in between Jenny and another girl and came to stand by Jon.

"Have I ever mentioned how good you are with kids?"

Jon draped his arm about her shoulders. "I think you did mention it once. And it led to a very pleasant night if I recall."

Kate snaked her arm about his waist and gave him a squeeze. "Maybe it will this time, too."

"I'm always hopeful."

The game had grown raucous with youthful laughter as Jon guided Kate back to the sunroom and suggested a much quieter game of cribbage. She beat the pants off him. Twice. By the time he finally pulled off a win, the party was breaking up and there had been no more fires to put out. Parents began pulling into the driveway, and before long only Madison was left.

Kate headed to the kitchen to start putting away the food. Jon carried platters in from the dining room and brought the kitchen wastebasket back to clean up the tipsy piles of paper plates, plastic tableware and napkins.

Jenny and Madison showed up and began to help.

"Hey, kiddo, it's your birthday. No work for you this time." He took the handful of plates she'd brought in from the living room, then held the bin out for Madison to dump the stack of empty glasses in. "Say goodnight to your mom and go ahead up to your room and do whatever it is girls do when they are supposed to be going to sleep."

Jenny skipped toward the kitchen while Madison disappeared back into the living room.

Jon was rolling up a paper tablecloth when Jenny returned and hovered at his side.

He stopped what he was doing and turned to her. "Did you have a fun party?"

"Thanks." Jenny fidgeted with the hem of her shirt and didn't meet his eyes.

"You're very welcome."

"I just wanted to say . . ." she stopped as if she'd forgotten what she wanted to tell him.

He squatted, balancing on his toes so he was looking up at her downturned face. "You just wanted to say?"

Whatever it was, the words weren't coming. Instead, she launched herself at him, wrapped her arms about his neck and nearly toppled him onto his butt. He put one hand out to steady himself and hugged her with his other arm.

Finally she disengaged herself and squared her shoulders. "I'm sorry about the way I acted the other day."

Jon stood and pulled her into another hug. "It's already forgotten. Except for the part about my invitation to join the Kids Who Care."

"Can Madison join even if she doesn't go to St Theresa's? She's been thirteen for four months already."

"Of course she can."

"Well . . ."

"Happy birthday Jenny."

"It was my best birthday ever." She gave him another quick hug and disappeared around the corner. A moment later both girls were giggling as they climbed the stairs.

Chapter 20

KATE STARED AT her computer screen in the busy newsroom, but the words went unread. It wasn't the distraction of people chatting on phones and working on stories for the next issue, but the busyness in her own mind that had nothing to do with the story she was writing.

In the days since Jon's sort-of proposal, she'd avoided any conversation that might bring them back to that point. They made love each night, but the proposal hadn't been mentioned as if neither of them wanted to be the first to bring it up again. He'd generously told her she could take all the time she needed, but his crushed expression haunted her when they weren't together.

Before he'd declared himself and they'd become lovers, she'd wondered if he'd given his heart to someone and gotten it broken. Now she was doing the breaking. She hadn't meant to hurt him, but a sudden panicky feeling had closed in on her. What if she couldn't love him enough? What if her own selfishness came between them like it had between her and Ethan?

What if all these years he'd silently been in love with her, he'd built her up to be some paragon she could never live up to? What if she married him and turned out to be a disappointment?

She stood abruptly shoving her wheeled chair backward so fast it crashed into the cubicle wall.

"Hey, what gives?" Kevin Greer said from the other side of the wall. His graying head popped up and he peered down at her. "You just discover the biggest scoop of the century, or what?"

"Or what," she answered, grabbing her jacket. "I just remembered something I have to get before the place closes." She snatched her messenger bag and loaded her laptop and notes into it.

Kevin rolled his eyes and disappeared.

As trapped as she'd felt in Jon's kitchen the morning they'd skirted around the idea of marriage, the feeling was worse now. She headed for the stairs and the exit and finally sucked in a steadying breath of air when she stepped out into the parking lot.

What was the matter with her? Falling in love was supposed to be euphoric. Being in love was supposed to erase all doubts. She loved Jon, she realized now, with a passion that was entirely new to her. It wasn't the heady craziness of youth, or even the sublimely free-spirited love of young newlyweds. It was something that had been building for years, that until just recently, she'd never acknowledged or allowed herself to acknowledge. She'd loved Ethan and that had been enough.

But now there was Jon. She might be her own person, but she couldn't ignore Jon's needs. Or his feelings. Not that she wanted to ignore either. But it wasn't just her any more. Four people's lives would be changed by whatever she decided now.

Becca had urged her wholeheartedly. Even Jenny had decided it was acceptable. Maybe it was okay to say yes to whatever Jon was asking. They could always take their time making it happen.

Maybe her doubts were just as unreasonable as her behavior. Jon would never think of her as a disappointment. He'd never expected more than she had to give before. Why would he start now? All he wanted was to be allowed to love her the way a man loves a wife. He didn't want to replace Ethan, with her or with the girls. For them he just wanted to be another adult in their life they could rely on for support, encouragement, love and guidance.

Every day she avoided answering him would just hurt him more and gain her nothing.

If she hurried, she could stop at the grocery store and get the makings for his favorite meal. She didn't have to go through his stomach to get to his heart, but greeting him at the end of the day with a hot meal and a big hug might go a long way to setting the tone for the evening.

As she dashed through the aisles, she kept checking her watch. The chances of beating him home were slim. He wasn't as sanguine about the girls being latchkey kids as she was, and unless he'd been called elsewhere to handle some police problem or another, he'd be home with them already. But he wouldn't have started fixing dinner yet.

She pulled into Jon's driveway and reached for the window toggle, but before she could lower it to unlatch the door, Jon opened it for her.

She gathered up her messenger bag and the groceries and slid from the van.

Jon was still in uniform and wearing a sense of urgency that didn't portend anything good.

"Sorry, I've got to go." He leaned across her arms full of stuff and kissed her briefly. "There's been a bad accident out on seventeen. I'll be home when I can." He shut the door of the van for her, and then hurried to his cruiser.

He backed around, pulled out onto High Street, and headed in the direction of Route 17 without looking back.

JON STILL WASN'T home, and the girls had gone to bed hours ago. Kate had reworked her story about Matthew, but unsatisfied with it and filled with growing worry about Jon, she closed her laptop. She changed into her pajamas, started the gas fireplace and curled up on the end of the couch with a book she'd been meaning to read.

The sound of the cruiser door shutting woke her with a start. She rubbed the sleep from her eyes and waited for Jon to appear.

"You didn't have to wait up." He sank onto the ottoman, weariness etched into his face as well as his movements.

She put a marker in the book that had slipped onto the couch when sleep overtook her and set it aside. "Obviously, I didn't. You look . . ." Awful was the word that came to mind. "Beat."

"I'm sorry. I should have called. I'm—I'm not used to having to report in." His apologetic smile was strained.

"It's okay," she assured him, leaning forward to give him a kiss. He looked so troubled her own heart began to ache.

She got off the couch and walked around behind him so she could massage his shoulders. They were tight as she worked her fingers and thumbs in circles.

"Take your shirt off so I can do this right."

Wordlessly, he tugged his tie free and tossed it on the couch, then unbuttoned the shirt, shrugged out of it and tossed it on top of the tie, followed a moment later by his T-shirt. He braced his hands on his knees as she began methodically massaging the muscles in his neck, then his shoulders and finally down his back.

He groaned as she worked. "You could get a job doing that."

She returned to his neck, running her fingers upward into his hair, then started all over again.

"A cop and two little kids died tonight." His voice was low and full of pain.

Kate immediately moved back to the couch and covered his hands with hers. "I'm so sorry." *Was there anyone from my paper there?* The question hovered on her tongue, but she bit it back. This wasn't about her job or her employer. It was about Jon. If he needed to tell her about it, she was going to put her reporter hat away and be his comforter.

"A county deputy stopped to help a woman with a flat tire. While he was changing the tire, a panel truck rammed into the back of the cruiser, slamming it into the car and pinning the deputy in between. The kids had unbuckled their seatbelts to watch. They were airlifted to New Hanover, but they didn't make it. The deputy was dead at the scene. I just came from informing his wife."

Kate couldn't imagine having to process such a scene. She knelt between Jon's knees and wrapped her arms around him. He dropped his head onto her shoulder, and they sat like that for a long time without speaking.

Was he reliving the scene? Or perhaps reliving the awful job of telling the man's wife?

"I can still hear her," he murmured against her neck.

"Her who?" The deputy's wife?

"The woman who just lost two kids. They were only seven and eight. If they'd been smaller and still in car seats, they might still be alive. The baby was fine."

Kate hugged him while he recounted the keening of the woman as her children were taken out of the car and placed on stretchers. He'd removed the baby from his car seat and brought him to his mother, and she'd clutched him so tight he'd squealed.

"I'm so sorry," Kate said again.

"I'm bushed, and I really need to go to bed," Jon said after a while. "But I'm afraid to go to sleep."

"I'll come with you."

He nodded and got up. "I'll walk Max first."

Kate retrieved his clothing from the couch and headed up the stairs.

As she was arranging his uniform jacket on a hanger, Jon walked up behind her and put his arms about her waist.

"Thanks for being here." He kissed her neck.

"I'm glad I am," she murmured, leaning her head back against his chest.

When his hands slipped under the hem of her pajama top and closed around her breasts, it surprised her. Somehow, sex seemed like the last thing she'd have been interested in if she'd been the one who had gone through what he'd seen this night. But what did she know? Maybe he was seeking reaffirmation of life after such appalling loss.

She forced herself to stop thinking about what had happened earlier and just be there for him, whatever he needed. Very quickly she didn't have to force anything. Jon carried her to the bed, removed her pajamas and stripped off his remaining clothes in record time. With almost no foreplay, he plunged into her, driving hard, seeking whatever it was he was seeking with such desperate need.

She clung to him and gave back as much as she could until he shuddered with release and collapsed on top of her. She held him, murmuring in his ear and running her fingers up and down his sweaty back and then into his hair. This was a hurting, vulnerable side of Jon she had never seen. Not even when he was twelve and his mother had died of breast cancer.

WHEN JON WOKE, the clock beside his bed said four-twenty. Kate slept with her arm draped across his chest and one leg thrown over his. They'd made love . . . if you could call the desperate pounding he'd given her making love. He must have fallen asleep pretty fast because he didn't recall even rolling off. And he hadn't dreamt about the accident as he'd feared. He wasn't sure what had woken him now.

He turned on his side and pulled Kate into the curve of his body. He cupped her breast in his hand, marveling at the wonderful soft fullness of it, but there was no lust in it. Just a lovely, welcome reassurance that she was still there.

He was still so uncertain about where their relationship was going. He'd begun to worry that he'd blown his chances twice. The first time when he'd been sixteen and too unsure of himself to tell her how he felt. And then when he'd told her all too forcefully what he wanted now.

He inhaled the scent of her and relaxed, brushing his thumb over the silky surface of her breast. Nothing would be too great to bear if he could always come home to this. To her.

Chapter 21

"THANKS FOR COVERING for me last night," Allison Jolee said as Jon came into their shared office and dropped into his chair. She went back to whatever she was doing on her computer. Not a word about how sorry she was for the deputy's family or the woman.

Jon had already followed up and been to the hospital to speak to the driver of the panel truck who had lawyered up and wasn't answering any questions.

The lab work showed the guy had not been drinking, but he hadn't had a coherent answer about how he'd managed to ram into the deputy's vehicle with its blue lights flashing, either. Last night he'd mumbled something about what his wife had said, but his wife hadn't been in the truck, which led to Jon's suspicion that he'd been texting his wife. The phone had been in plain sight, and now they were just waiting on a subpoena for the phone records to prove it.

Jon logged in and brought up the accident report to add this morning's information to it. There would be charges and the man might do time, but that didn't bring back two little kids or the deputy. Jon dreaded the funerals, but he'd go.

"My aunt is gaining in the polls," Allison said, interrupting Jon's thoughts.

He looked up at her, shaking his head to clear the images. "Excuse me?"

"My aunt is going to win, you know. And when she does, I'll be your boss."

"If she appoints you chief."

Allison shot a condescending gaze across the small office. "Of course she'll appoint me. She knows how much I want the job."

Not more than I do. Jon left the protest unsaid. He went back to his report.

"You'd better be prepared to ask how high when I tell you to jump else you'll be out of here faster than you can spit."

Jon refused to even look up or answer that spiteful comment. If she got appointed chief, she wouldn't have to fire him. He'd be gone before her first day on the job. Wilmington would probably take him back if they had an opening, but he'd miss the small-town atmosphere. Being a cop in a town like Tide's Way was very different than being a cop in a city. Even one the size of Wilmington. He liked knowing everyone. He especially liked working in a place where cops were still treated with respect. Sure there was risk involved. No law enforcement job was free of risk as last night's accident proved. But Tide's Way was different. He loved the years he'd spent in uniform in the town he'd grown up in.

Allison tried twice more to goad him, but he tuned her out and focused on his report. Finally she gave up and left, snatching up her cap and laptop. Jon's shoulders relaxed.

When his cell phone vibrated in his pocket, he leaned back and fished it out.

Kate!

"Hi, Kate. What's up?"

"I just wanted to know how you were doing today."

"Before or after I heard your voice?" He smiled even though she couldn't see it. The irritation of the last half hour evaporated, and he leaned back in his chair to enjoy the moment, thankful that Allison had chosen to leave before Kate called.

Kate chuckled, her sexy low chuckle that turned him on so easily. "I'm glad I called then."

Jon waited to see if there were another reason she had called. Especially since the preceding week had been so full of mixed messages and last night he hadn't exactly been a thoughtful lover.

"Last night I was going to fix a nice meal so you'd forgive me."

"I've no idea what you think you need to apologize for. I should be the one saying I'm sorry."

"What have you got to be sorry about?" She sounded confused.

"I shouldn't have dumped all that stuff on you, and I definitely shouldn't have made love to you like I was trying to punish somebody."

"Jon, don't. You don't have anything to apologize for. I understood, and it's okay." She hesitated before going on. "Nothing in life is guaranteed, and I was going to tell you I'm not sure what I was waiting for. After I fixed your favorite Chicken Parmesan, and . . . but you had to go out and . . ."

"I hope there are leftovers."

"I have a better plan now."

"Better than Chicken Parm?" Better than making up in bed? Without the specter of a horrific accident taking over his head?

"Becca's been invited to spend the night at Natalie's, and Jenny is sleeping over at Madison's. It's just you and me, so I thought maybe we could pick up some ribs or something and take supper to the beach." Her voice sounded a little breathless as she finished in a rush. What she had to be nervous about, he didn't know. He'd go anywhere she wanted.

"Sounds like my kind of night. I'll make sure I'm not on call if some idiot drinks too much and starts smacking his wife around."

"Is seven too late? I have to cover something JJ's doing this afternoon and file the story before I'm out of here."

"You still want to eat at the beach? It'll be getting dark." Dark would be good for making out. Or were they too old to misbehave at the beach?

"We'll bring candles." Kate laughed and made a smooching sound. "See you back home." The line went silent.

Now what was that all about? What did she mean about guarantees and what had she been thinking she needed forgiveness for? Was she thinking about their current relationship and his proposal, as sloppy and unromantic as it had been, and how she'd been avoiding the subject for days? Somehow continuing as they were didn't sound like Kate. Especially not with her daughters to consider. She'd want to set a good example for them. That left breaking whatever was going on between them off completely, unless . . . And she had said she'd see him at home. And they were going to the beach. Alone. At night. That didn't sound like a goodbye.

His heart picked up the excitement of his thoughts, and suddenly his day looked a lot brighter. Whatever happened with Allison and JJ, as long as Jon had Kate, nothing else was all that important. Her office was in Wilmington. They could meet for lunch now and then if he worked there.

He popped his cap back on his head and started for the door. He stopped long enough to ask Atkins if he could be strictly off duty tonight. Thankfully, his boss was busy with something else and didn't question the request. It was Allison's turn to be on call anyway. He whistled as he headed for his cruiser.

"YOU'RE AWFULLY QUIET." Jon glanced across the console at Kate as they drove across the bridge to the barrier island. The tantalizing odor of barbequed ribs filled the car.

Uncertainty filled Kate's heart. She'd never done anything like this before. She and Ethan had drifted slowly toward the idea of getting married until it was just something they knew they were going to do. Ethan had never made a formal proposal, and neither had she. With Jon, everything had happened so fast. The commitment of marriage had caught her off guard when Jenny had brought it up, and she hadn't known what to say to Jon when he made it clear he was on board with that outcome but hadn't actually proposed.

Jon wouldn't have changed his mind. She had nothing to be apprehensive about, but the butterflies in her stomach kept fluttering.

"I was just thinking about stuff," she answered evasively. If she was going to be the one to bring the subject up again, she didn't want to do it here in the car while he was driving. "Did you have a good day?"

She hadn't had a chance to ask before because by the time she'd gotten home after filing her story, Jon was helping the girls haul their sleeping bags and gear to their friends' homes. While he was gone, she'd changed and filled a cooler with everything they needed to go with the ribs and her proposal. On his return, he'd regaled her with his humorous take on how much the girls felt was absolutely essential for a single night away from home.

"What do you think of JJ's chances to unseat Quinn?" he asked, not answering her question.

"I hate to say it, but I think she's got a good chance. Why?"

"Allison went out of her way to inform me that JJ was going to win and that once she was in the mayor's office, Allison would be appointed as Chief of Police. She was already rubbing my nose in the fact that she'd be my boss. Which isn't going to happen whoever wins."

"You know something I don't?"

"Not really. But I do know there is no way on earth I'd work for that woman. She gets the nod and I'm history."

The car left the paved road and crunched across the sand and gravel parking of Anchor Beach. The lot was empty, which was a good sign. The sun had already set and dark was fast approaching, but dark was good. Kate felt braver in the dark.

Jon grumbled as he lowered the window to open the driver's door. "I don't suppose you'd let me buy you a new car?"

You could give me one for an engagement present, she thought, but didn't say. She wagged her head as if she were considering it.

He reached into the back for the cooler and the ribs and followed her toward the path. Kate tapped the top of the anchor as she passed it. Her brother Philip insisted that old custom brought good luck.

"Someone told me the other day that the Historical Society is pretty sure they know where that anchor came from," Jon remarked as he copied her action.

Kate glanced back at the old-fashioned anchor. It had never occurred to her to wonder what ship it might have come from. Or even if parts of the wreck of it might still lurk in the waters offshore. Clearly history was not her calling. But maybe she should pay more attention to it considering her profession.

"According to Tony Jenkins, it wasn't that long ago. They're looking for proof that it was a merchant ship sunk by a German U-boat in WWII."

Jon continued the story as he spread the old quilt she'd brought on the sand and pinned it down with the cooler, her tote, and his shoes.

Kate dug through the tote and brought out three candles, which she pressed into the sand in front of the quilt.

"You weren't kidding, I see." Jon accepted the lighter she handed him and flicked it to life. Soon three dancing little flames did their best to ward off the gathering dusk.

"I don't kid about ambiance," Kate replied with a nervous chuckle.

Jon lifted one eyebrow at her comment. "The moon won't be ambiance enough? It's due to rise soon."

In some ways their companionship was just as it had always been. Easy and comfortable. But there was something new and exciting racing along just below the surface. It grew as they sat side by side devouring their ribs and laughing over the mess they made. Jon fished the wipes out with his pinky fingers and dropped them on the quilt.

"I used to think your mom's ribs were the best, but Ethan's are even better," he said as he cleaned his hands.

"He started with mom's recipe, but then he embellished. Mom graciously conceded the title of best ribs years ago." Kate mopped her face and hands and dumped the used wipes into the empty ribs sack.

Jon pushed the empty bag and cooler to the side and covered Kate's hand with his. "So . . . you going to tell me why we're here?" His hand was warm and big. He curled his fingers under her palm and ran his thumb across the back of her hand.

"Let's go for a walk. You were right about the moon." She jumped to her feet and pulled him with her.

"It's not like you to beat around the bush, Kate," Jon said as they strolled across the still warm sand.

Kate stopped and made a big deal about looking all around them. "There's no bush here."

"Kate." Jon stopped walking and pulled her around to face him. "What's bothering you? If it's about the way I behaved last night—"

Kate shook her head.

"Is it what I said last week? I can take it back. We can just go back to being—"

Kate covered his mouth with her free hand. "We can't go back, Jon. Not from where we are now. It's not like you aren't . . ." She hesitated trying to decide how to say it. "You're still my best friend. But you're more than that now. You're . . . We're . . . We slept together. There's no going back from that.

She took her hand away from his mouth, but he didn't reply.

"I don't want to go back. I love you, Jon. I love you as a lover, and . . . and—" She broke off entirely as the enormity of what came next rolled over her.

Jon dropped abruptly to one knee. He fumbled in his pocket for a moment and then held out a small white box.

"I didn't do this very well before, but I want to get it right this time. Please? Will you be my wife? I promise—"

"Jon, get up. Please. You don't have to kneel down for me. Not ever."

Even by the eerie light of a nearly full moon, the blank look that came into Jon's eyes was clear. He thought she was getting ready to say no. Hastily she fell onto her own knees, grabbed his head in both hands and pulled his face down to hers. She kissed him quick and hard. Then again more gently. She pulled away and whispered. "Yes."

He tipped his head toward the sky and said, "Thank you."

Is he thanking me or God? Does it matter?

She buried her face in the soft fleece of his vest and wrapped her arms about his waist.

"I love you, Kate," he said into the hair on top of her head. "God, I love you so much. I was afraid you were going to break my heart all over again."

He sank back onto his heels and fumbled again with the little white box. The ring glittered in the moonlight.

When did he go ring shopping?

He lifted her left hand and slid the ring onto her finger. It fit perfectly.

How did he even know what size?

Jon kissed her knuckles and pulled her back into his embrace.

Kate held her hand up and gazed at it over his shoulder. "It's beautiful."

There were three stones. A beautiful marquise cut diamond flanked by two round stones that looked almost black in the moonlight.

"It's actually two rings." Jon reached for her hand and tilted it to show her that the stones on either side were mounted in a guard ring that nestled neatly with the diamond. "They're sapphires. Our birthstones."

"You are the most amazing man."

"I'm glad you think so." He kissed her fingers, then her lips. "I hope you don't believe in long engagements."

Chapter 22

"YOU LOOK PRETTY chipper for such a gray day. Have you found another argument against my project?" JJ asked as Kate joined the small group gathered in front of the Jolee Mansion.

No, but I've found out your secret shame. "I am pretty chipper this morning." Love had a way of turning any day, however gray, into a sparkling new adventure.

"Miss Jones . . ." A man wearing a press badge from a news station out of Raleigh grabbed JJ's attention. "Would you mind joining me over here where we can get the mansion in the background?"

"Excuse me," JJ murmured, then moved to comply.

Kate dragged out her dog-eared notebook and a pen, preparing to record any new tidbits of information JJ might share with the TV news crew. As the reporter introduced JJ and the topic they were covering for the evening news, Kate's mind wandered to the birth certificate in her messenger bag.

JJ was even more eloquent and passionate this morning than she had been at the town meeting. Kate jotted down a note here and there, but she already knew most of the story.

"There has been considerable pushback from those interested in preserving the historic significance of the Jolee Mansion," the interviewer said, switching gears. "How do you propose to overcome some very legitimate objections? Especially the historical ones?"

"The Jolee Mansion is actually not the oldest building in Tide's Way," JJ replied with a smile for the camera. "Most folks have forgotten, or never known that Emmy Lou Davis' antique shop was built about twenty years before the mansion. It was the original Jolee home before Simon Jolee added the acreage, bought slaves and began growing tobacco."

"That house is now a commercial enterprise," the interviewer countered. "Don't you think turning the actual planation mansion into a museum to commemorate and preserve the history of Tide's Way and a long-lost way of life would be a better use of the property than this second-chance project you are proposing?"

JJ launched into a list of plantations in North Carolina that had been turned into historical showplaces and explained why most of them did not support themselves. None of the economic arguments were new, and Kate would have been happy to agree with them if it weren't for Matthew and the cause JJ was championing.

Kate waited patiently for the television segment taping to wind up. JJ had agreed to a private interview afterward. She was in for a shock if she thought Kate was just going to rehash all the previous discussions.

"Thank you for your time, Miss Jones." The interviewer then turned to the camera, gave his personal sign-off and motioned for the taping to stop. Within minutes the three men and one woman had broken down their equipment and packed it into a van with the station logo on the side. Then they were driving down the long row of oaks, leaving a haze of dust behind them.

JJ looked around and then turned to Kate. "Did you wish to interview me right here? Or . . ."

Kate debated. There was nowhere to sit down and be comfortable here, but she couldn't exactly invite herself into JJ's home. "We could go to Joel's."

JJ nodded. "Sounds good. I'll meet you there."

Ten minutes later they were seated in the booth farthest from the door with two heavy ceramic mugs steaming in front of them. The waitress had moved on to flirt with a table full of rowdy construction workers on their mid-morning coffee break.

"I wanted to give equal time to both sides of the debate," Kate began. "But I don't need to rehash anything you already said earlier this morning or at the town meeting. By the way, I didn't know that Emmy Lou's antique store was the original Jolee home. Does Emmy Lou know?"

"Well, of course she does," JJ replied. "She is a descendent of the Jolees."

"Wouldn't that make the shop eligible for listing on the National Register of Historic Places? How did she get permission to run a commercial enterprise?"

JJ smiled. "There are no restrictions on homes so listed, either at the federal or state level. If there were, we wouldn't even be having this discussion because the Jolee Mansion is already listed. But it is not listed as a Historic Landmark. That would be different."

"How would it be different?" Her sister-in-law would know about the difference. Maybe Kate should have asked Bree why no one on the Historical Society had thought to petition for such a listing years ago when the property was first bequeathed to the town.

JJ outlined the differences between the two listings and then returned to the monetary and tax justifications for using the mansion for her project. Kate heard her out even though she'd already done her homework on the financial side of the equation.

"What I would like to know more about, Miss Jones—"

"Please. Just call me JJ. I prefer it to Miss Jones."

"Okay, JJ. Let's talk about your proposal. Why do you think it's a good idea to introduce even petty criminals into our community?"

As JJ began to explain about how giving these men a second chance could make all the difference in the rest of their lives, Jon's explanations echoed in Kate's head. She rubbed her thumb against the back of her very new engagement ring. Would this issue end up coming between them and taking some of the shine off their new relationship?

"But what about the children of Tide's Way?" Kate asked after JJ brought up the veteran's son, accused of statutory rape for having consensual sex with a fifteen-year-old girl even though he'd not known she was a minor and was barely over the age of eighteen himself. "I agree this guy wouldn't be a threat, but where do you draw the line? What about a thirty-year-old peeping tom or someone convicted of indecent exposure. Not many people take that seriously, but it's disturbing for the victims and it can and often does escalate. There are half a dozen elementary school bus stops within a football field or two of the Jolee driveway. It's not safe for our kids if we make it possible for some man to lurk in the trees along Stewart Road waiting for some little kid to get off the bus so he can flash her. Or worse."

"Serious sex offenders would not be considered. The plan is for these men to be employed and paying rent. They'll be so busy re-establishing their credit they won't be lurking anywhere."

JJ continued outlining the vetting process, which Kate had already heard from both her and Jon as well as read in the outline for the project.

Kate decided to get to the point she really wanted to discuss.

"Tell me about Matthew."

If she'd taken JJ off guard, it didn't show in the woman's face or body language. JJ just smiled a slight, sad smile before speaking.

"Matthew was a troubled youth. His mother . . ." JJ hesitated for a fraction of a second. "His mother became ill

177

when Matthew was quite young. His father spent more and more time caring for his wife and less and less time in the rearing of his son. When they moved to be closer to the center where Matthew's mother was being treated, he had to leave all his friends behind and start over. Moving is hard on any kid, but it was harder on Matthew given his home situation. He began hanging out with a group of kids who felt as left out as he did.

"He wasn't a bad boy or a troublemaker, but trouble seemed to find him. At first it was just wild kid stuff, but the law enforcement community labeled him as trouble and kept their eyes on him. Eventually he ended up in prison.

"I think the judge gave him a stiff sentence for a relatively minor offense simply because it was clear to everyone by then that his father had given up trying to govern him. He stopped showing up to bail Matthew out when he was arrested. If he'd been a year older, or had this been thirty years ago, Matthew might have been given the option to enlist in the Army in lieu of jail. But it wasn't, and he had to do his time."

JJ broke off and brought her coffee mug to her lips. Her eyes looked haunted. Kate waited for her to go on, but when it seemed that she wasn't going to, Kate reached into her messenger bag and slid the birth certificate out.

"Even then, things might have been different if his parents hadn't died while he was in prison." JJ picked up the story and Kate folded her hands over the paper she placed face down on the table in front of her.

"He would have had a home to return to. He'd managed to complete his high school education while he was inside, and he probably could have gotten a job at the factory where his father worked. That wasn't the case, however. His mother finally passed away from the cancer she'd been battling for more than ten years, and his father began to drink. The house was sold to pay off the medical bills, so when Mr. Keyes had too much to drink and ran off the road one night, totaling his car and killing himself, there was nothing left for Matthew to come home to. Not even a third-rate apartment with a drunken, heartbroken father."

JJ's story told with such carefully emotionless delivery touched something inside Kate that she hadn't wanted to feel. She wanted to view all these possible men coming to live at Jolee as criminals with no sad past to mitigate who they were now. It was no wonder that JJ felt so passionate about this project. Had she not given her son up for adoption, he might have had a successful career or maybe even have been a lawyer like JJ's father.

The empathy curling in Kate's gut short-circuited her focus on debunking the Second Chance House plan.

"What happened to Matthew?"

"He . . . " JJ pinched her eyes shut. "He took his own life."

Kate sucked in a gasp of horror. The vision of a despondent young man with nothing left to live for putting a gun to his temple screamed through Kate's head. JJ had probably not had any choice about things when she'd given birth to Matthew, but no doubt she'd soothed her personal loss all these years with the promise that she'd given her infant son a better chance at life than she could have provided. Then even that solace had been ripped away from her.

Kate reached across the table and covered JJ's hand with hers. "I'm so sorry."

Suddenly there were tears brimming in JJ's perfectly made-up eyes. She blinked hard to keep them from welling over. "I don't know how you found out. You're going to write about this, aren't you?" The words weren't confrontational. Just resigned. She freed her hand from Kate's and rummaged in her purse for a tissue.

"I was going to," Kate began. "I wanted to stop you from pushing forward with this plan of yours. I was willing to do anything. I—I found this." She pushed the birth certificate across the table and shoved her hands into her lap.

JJ took the paper and unfolded it. Her eyes widened as she realized what she was holding. Her gaze jerked back to Kate's. Then back to the document. It fluttered in JJ's trembling fingers.

"I thought my mother burned it," she said at last.

"It was in a box in an attic in Savannah. The attic of the house you lived in when you were there. Along with these." Kate fished a large manila envelope out of her bag and handed it to JJ. "There are letters from Matthew's father in there. I'm sorry. I read them and I shouldn't have. But I promise you, no one will ever hear about them from me."

"Thank you," JJ mouthed the words, apparently unable to find enough breath to make them audible.

The letters had painted a picture of a young woman very much in love with the older man who had seduced her. A young mother heartbroken about having to give her baby up. And a man, who apparently loved JJ as much as she'd loved him, trapped in a marriage he could not get out of. The scandal would have ruined so many lives had Matthew's birth become public knowledge. It still could, Kate realized. Had she written the article she'd set out to write, that man's daughters would have had their memories of their father tarnished, and they were entirely innocent. The man's wife would be hurt, even if it had been a loveless union. JJ would have had her heart ripped out all over again. The pain and regret she already lived with was beyond Kate's ability to even imagine.

Kate tucked a folded ten-dollar bill under the edge of her mug and stood. "I'm sorry I sprung that on you like that. Maybe another day we can talk again, and you can tell me more about your plans and how you envision them coming to be. I've still got major reservations about this program being in my neighborhood, but I'll try to keep an open mind."

She bent to give JJ a hug and then hurried to the door and her beat-up minivan in the parking lot as if someone were after her. She wasn't sure what she thought or felt anymore. When she'd set up this appointment, she'd been dead set on getting a personal interview with JJ to launch her media campaign to stop Second Chance House from ever happening, even if it meant dredging up an old scandal to do it.

Jon had warned her, but she hadn't listened. This morning JJ had made Matthew real for her. A troubled but very real young man. Once upon a time an infant his mother had loved more than she loved herself. Once a toddler exploring his world under the watchful eyes of adoring adoptive parents. Then a little boy, frightened and friendless, who lost his mother. Maybe if he'd had a place like Second Chance House to come home to after his life spun out of control, his story would have ended entirely differently.

Chapter 23

"WRITER'S BLOCK?" JON murmured in Kate's ear as his hands dropped onto her shoulders.

She jumped in surprise. "How do you do that?"

"Do what?" He kissed her temple and swiveled her chair around to face him.

"Sneak up on me like that? When I try to walk anywhere in this old house without making any sound, the floor squeaks or I stub my toe and swear. You're twice as big as me and the floor never even sighs."

Jon looked down at his stocking feet and shrugged. "I don't know. Just lucky, I guess. And more graceful."

"Graceful?" Kate gaped up at him. "Are you calling me a klutz?"

"You're the one who said you stub your toe and swear. Not very ladylike, either." He grinned.

"You like it when I'm not very ladylike," Kate countered, lifting one bare leg and crossing it over the other, deliberately exposing far more than she would have if they hadn't been alone in Jon's little study with her girls long since in bed.

He put one hand on her knee and slid it slowly down her thigh toward her lap. "Is that an invitation?" He kissed the corner of her mouth.

Excitement curled in Kate's groin, and her breath caught in her throat. She turned her face to exchange the teasing kiss for something more torrid. Jon's fingers teased their way closer, his thumb drawing arousing little circles against the sensitive skin of her inner thigh.

She dropped her leg back to the floor and broke off the kiss. Her breath came in gusty little gasps. "I—I need to talk to you about a few things. Before I forget."

Jon chuckled and reached behind him to grab the extra chair he kept by the door. He lowered himself into it looking so cool it was hard to believe he had just been a hair's-breadth from turning her gambit into something shockingly needy.

"I'm a patient man. What do you want to talk about?"

The most patient man she knew. Look how long he'd waited for her to return his love.

"I want to know more about how you see this Second Chance House happening in Tide's Way without putting anyone in jeopardy."

Jon leaned forward, resting his elbows on his thighs with his hands hanging loosely between his knees. "We've discussed this before. I'm not sure if there's anything I haven't already told you."

"I met with JJ today. She says all the men who would be considered would either be employed or at the very least have a viable interview scheduled before they could move in. But who's going to hire them? What kind of work are they going to find?"

"Jake has promised to take on two new apprentices, for starters. Ben said he could use help with training new rescues at the Royco center. He wants to enlarge his Paws4Vets program. Working with dogs would be a great way for a guy who's just gotten out of prison to find some peace. And that's just in your family."

"So, that's what? Three or four jobs? There's not that much in the way of employment here in Tide's Way, and don't forget there's no public transportation." To say nothing of the fact that her entire family seemed to be on Jon's side of this issue.

"The Ford dealer in Wilmington has promised to donate a nine-passenger van. One guy could drive everyone else to work before taking himself to his job. Some of them can catch rides with people they work with until they can afford to pick up a used car for themselves. Kate, where there's the will, there will always be a way.

"Frank Billington is begging for workers willing to learn the ins and outs of growing and harvesting strawberries. And they could keep them busy in the greenhouses in the winter. Since his stroke, Old Man Billington hasn't been able to do much around the place, and his youngest son is off to college next fall. Write it down, I'll give you the whole list of jobs being offered."

Kate retrieved her notebook and started a new page with Jake and Ben at the top. When Jon was done, the list was a lot longer than Kate had imagined it could be.

"By the way, Ty says there's always a need for help at Ethan's Ribs. Especially when the college kids go back to school."

Kate should have known that. She'd struggled to keep the place staffed during the two years she'd limped along after Ethan was gone. She counted the jobs on her list.

"I thought there were only going to be ten or twelve guys in this Second Chance House. You've just listed more than thirty jobs." Thirty ex-cons in Tide's Way had to be enough to scuttle the project in spite of the growing support it seemed to be gathering.

"That's JJ's plan for Jolee because that's about all the place would hold comfortably unless they turned the bedrooms into bunkrooms, and that wasn't what she envisioned. She doesn't want them to feel they've exchanged one prison for another. She wants them to feel like they have some space of their own, even if it's just a bedroom. But don't forget, once a guy gets his feet under him, he'll want to move on and find his own apartment. And he'd still keep his job if he likes it and everything is going well. Then the next new guy that comes to take his place at Jolee will need employment. It's good to have reserve spots available. Billington will get the first compatible recruits because he needs them the most urgently."

"You make it all sound like it's a done deal."

Jon raised his eyebrows but didn't reply.

"They're ex-cons. They don't belong in Tide's Way."

Jon sighed. "They're not hardened criminals. Just guys down on their luck who happened to be unfortunate enough to run afoul of the law."

Kate shook her head. "I would have thought a cop would be on my side in this."

Jon scooted his chair closer and put his hands on her knees. "I'll always be looking out for you. You know that. And you can always count on me, but there are going to be times we don't agree on everything. That's healthy. It means we both still have thoughts and ideas of our own and the freedom to discuss them. Like now."

"But why Jolee?"

"Tide's Way is just the sort of close-knit community that could offer these young men a new way to view life and support them while they find their way in it. Everyone knows everyone. There would be lots of eyes keeping track of their progress and the kind of concerned and caring people who reach out to anyone who needs a friend."

"But Jolee—" Anger bubbled in Kate's gut. She didn't like the idea, and she wished it would die a natural death. She couldn't ignore JJ's moving story of how Matthew had gone from a decent kid with a dying mom to a man so desperate he'd take his own life, but why did it have to be in Tide's Way? And why was Jon turning this into an argument that could ruin everything?

"I don't want this to come between us, Kate. I just want you to keep an open mind. If the idea of using Jolee disturbs you, then why not make it your mission to find an alternative site?"

JAKE'S WIFE, ZOE, squealed when Kate held out her left hand for inspection. Bree slanted a glance at Jon, then back to the sparkling engagement ring.

"Wow! Jon. You're more romantic than a Hallmark card." Meg, Ben's wife of almost fifteen years and a Marine at that, smirked at Jon. He was too happy to care.

Sandy wrapped her arms around both Jon and Kate in a group hug. "This is the best news I've had all year." She leaned away to look into their faces. "Kate, you are one lucky lady." Then she pulled Jon's head down to her level and kissed him on each cheek. "You've been my unofficial son ever since . . . well . . . for a very long time. I can't tell you how happy this makes me."

"Does that mean I get to call you Mom, now?" He lifted Kate's petite mom off her feet. She slapped him playfully and begged to be put down.

"I'd be honored," she said when he'd set her back on her feet. "Now everybody shoo so I can get dinner on the table."

Kate hung back to help out while Jon stepped onto the deck where her father leaned against the railing watching the gang on the beach. The older kids were tossing a Frisbee back and forth while Kate's oldest brother Philip and the twins kept an eye on the younger kids who were digging industriously in the sand.

"Maybe I should have asked you first," Jon said as he joined Cam at the railing. "I asked your daughter to marry me and she said yes."

Cam looked up, his eyes widening, then blinking hard. Wordlessly, he reached out to pull Jon into an embrace. After a moment, he held Jon away and patted his shoulder. "Well," he said, then cleared his throat. "Well, that's great news. My girl is lucky to have you."

"Hi, Daddy," Kate crossed the deck.

"Hey, honey." Cam folded her into his embrace. "Not that you young folks ever ask for permission anymore, but you've got mine anyway." He kissed her forehead.

"Thanks, Daddy." She held out her hand for another round of inspections. Jake, just joining them on the deck, whistled. Cam's eyebrows rose.

"Nice." Cam said. "The man's got good taste. And smarts. You be good to him."

"Daddy!" Kate protested as she linked her arm through Jon's. When she looked up at him, Jon's insides warmed.

"Kate? Have you had any luck finding an alternative site for Second Chance House?" Jake abruptly changed the subject.

"I keep hoping for something in Wilmington or Jacksonville to show up."

"Why Wilmington or Jacksonville?" Cam frowned.

"Because it's not Tide's Way." Kate's jaw was set and the sparkle in her eyes was no longer a happy one.

Jon sighed. He'd hoped she'd begin to see things differently. He'd been patient enough, trying to explain why it was a good plan and giving her suggestions about where to find facts and information to back it up.

"I don't remember all the particulars, but I bet Mike Kennedy could fill in some of the blanks." Cam seemed to ignore Kate's stubbornness. "Mike is the guy who founded the veterans' shelter in Wilmington based on a place he became familiar with in Boston when he was at Harvard. He was so impressed he came back and started Home Port. Only difference was Mike had money and he purchased his facility outright. But this Boston place was originally leased from the government for a dollar a year. It had been a hospital at one time but had been vacant for years inviting all kinds of trouble. So the government was happy to approve the plan this guy presented to turn it into a veterans shelter."

"What does a veterans shelter in Boston have to do with what JJ wants to start for ex-cons?" Kate grumbled.

"Well, the Jolee place has been vacant and falling into ruin for a while now," Cam answered patiently.

"But—"

"But if it's Jolee you're most concerned about, what about that shut-down factory on the other side of Route 17? It's been vacant a few years. I don't know who owns it, but—"

"I do," Jake interrupted. "But it would take a ton of money to make that place livable. More than JJ has managed to raise so far."

Cam sighed and wagged his head from side to side. "So maybe that place won't work, but there are other places that might. I just thought I'd point that option out. You're the investigative reporter. I bet if you dig around deep enough you'll find something."

"Dinner's on!" Sandy stood in the doorway waving everyone to come in.

"Talk to Mike Kennedy," Cam said as he turned toward his wife.

"Maybe he knows of a big empty building in Wilmington," Kate grumped as she turned to Jon. "It feels like you guys are all ganging up on me."

"We're just trying to help you see the bigger picture."

"I don't like it. I don't really care how many Matthews there are out there just so long as they don't come here."

Jon's chest tightened with frustration, but he refused to argue with her about it. Not here. Not today. Not when they were supposed to be celebrating their engagement.

He bent to kiss her. "Have I told you lately how much I love you?"

"C'mon. Break it up. You heard Mom." Jake laughed, then leaned over the railing, shoved two fingers in his mouth, and whistled loudly. Within minutes a herd of kids pounded up the stairs, Becca and Jenny among them. The rest of Kate's brothers came up behind them, Will and Philip each with a toddler on their shoulders, and Ben with twin girls on each hip.

"You've got enough kids in this family to start a soccer league," Jon muttered into Kate's ear as they followed the crowd inside.

Kate glanced up at him. "I thought you liked kids."

"I do. Just saying." He bent his head and kissed her again. If he lived to be a hundred, he'd never stop wanting to feel her lips beneath his, responding to him. Even when she was upset with him, like she was now. Maybe that angry fire just added to the excitement.

A cacophony of forks tapping water glasses erupted from the vast dining table.

Jon broke away grinning. "I forgot what brats your brothers could be."

Sandy had pushed the piano bench up to the end of the table and indicated that Kate and Jon should share the place of honor for this Sunday's family dinner.

Will and Bree's son Sam was tagged to say grace, and for at least the few moments while he rattled off the standard prayer, relative quiet reigned. Then everyone whooped and began reaching for the steaming platters of roast pork, candied sweet potatoes, several different vegetables and assorted side dishes.

Just as Kate reached for the meat platter, the phone in her pocket began playing *God Gave Me You* by Blake Shelton.

Jake snorted. Will rolled his eyes. Meg grinned.

"Shouldn't that be *my* ring tone?" Jon whispered.

Kate blushed as she fished the phone from her pocket.

"I thought we agreed, no cell phones at the table," Cam said, looking displeased.

"Sorry, Daddy. I forgot to leave it in my purse." Kate glanced at the screen.

"I wonder what JJ could be calling about on Sunday?" Jon murmured as he caught a glimpse of the screen on her cell. Without answering or even looking at him, Kate scrambled to her feet and hurried toward the front hall. As soon as she was out of her father's line of sight, she lifted the phone to her ear.

Kate paced the hallway listening to whatever JJ was saying. It was brief, and a moment later Kate dropped her phone into her purse and hurried back to the dining room.

On her way past him, she bent to kiss her dad's cheek and offer an apology. The rest of the family had turned their attention to Halloween.

"What was all that about?" Jon asked as she slid onto the bench beside him.

"JJ wants me to meet someone, but she didn't say who." Kate shrugged, her brow furrowed.

"Sounds mysterious." He gave the inside of her thigh a teasing squeeze under the table and winked.

She hissed in surprise, then laced her fingers through his and dragged his hand back onto the table. "Later."

"Definitely later," he whispered back. He picked up his knife and began buttering his roll. Life was good. Very, very good.

Chapter 24

IT WAS LATE when they returned to Jon's home on High Street. Becca had fallen asleep, and Jenny was pretty close. Jon hoisted Becca into his arms and carried her toward the house while Kate gathered up her things and urged Jenny to get moving.

After he'd deposited Becca on her bed, removed her shoes and covered her up, Jon headed back downstairs. He shucked his shoes by the door and headed to the kitchen to grab a beer and pour Kate a glass of wine. He didn't bother to turn the television on. Something had been bubbling inside Kate all evening, and he knew she'd be wanting to talk when she came down.

He was halfway through his beer before she walked into the room. She was dressed for bed but was clearly not in the mood to get there any time soon. He sighed and set his beer aside.

"Well?" He looked up when she didn't join him on the couch.

She had her arms folded tightly across her chest, and there was nothing sultry about the look in her eyes. He'd seen her frustrated and upset before. He'd even seen her angry, but this seemed different. It seemed personal and aimed at him.

"You're supposed to be on my side," she said, her voice flat and accusatory.

"I *am* on your side. Always." He patted the couch beside him.

She ignored the invitation. "You're supposed to support me. You always used to. And now that you're going to be my husband, it seems like you should be doubly on my side."

The tension he'd felt in his chest earlier in the day returned with a vengeance.

"If you'd sit down we could talk about whatever is really bothering you."

She didn't move right away but finally flung herself onto the ottoman facing him and just out of reach.

"So, are you going to tell me what I've done so wrong, or do I have to guess?" It had to be about Jolee or the Second Chance project in general, but how she'd gotten to this angry state he had no idea.

"I don't like JJ's plan."

"And that's why you're angry with me?"

"You don't care how I feel." Her voice went up at the end. She swallowed and glanced away.

He leaned forward and reached for her hands, but she moved them out of reach. "Kate, I always care about how you feel." His heart felt like something was sitting on it. "But we aren't always going to agree on everything. It's okay to think differently sometimes. And compromise is always possible if we're willing to talk things out."

She gazed stubbornly away from him.

Feeling like all the happiness he'd suddenly found in the last few weeks was slipping from his grasp, Jon took her chin in his hand and turned her face toward his. There was a lost look in her eyes that sliced into him. "Kate, I love you. You know that."

"Then why won't you support me?"

"You want a yes man? Like a dog that comes when you call and never has a thought of his own?" His voice rose. He took a breath and forced himself to speak calmly. "Is that what you want me to be?"

A tear rolled from the corner of her eye and slipped silently down her cheek, but she didn't answer. That tear should have crushed all his resistance, but for some reason it provoked him to unexpected anger. He let go of her chin and folded his arms across his chest.

"Maybe I should be telling you that you should support me? Maybe I should be angry that you haven't bothered to follow up on any of the information I've given you? You haven't, have you? You just made a snap judgment and you refuse to entertain any facts that might not agree with your point of view."

Suddenly too angry to stay seated, he shot from his chair and paced across the room to the windows and then back again.

"You haven't, have you?" he repeated. "You spent two days digging up a birth certificate so you could humiliate a good woman in the hopes of undermining a very worthwhile project, but you didn't bother to look into any of the facts I gave you in support of why it *is* a good project. You've got blinders on, Kate."

She gaped at him as if he'd slapped her.

That especially should have put a stop to his tirade. He didn't get angry very often, and he didn't know what to do with the emotion now. The best he could do was to keep himself from shouting at her and waking the girls.

"You want me to support you, then do your homework. All of it. Then maybe we can have an intelligent debate."

Kate jumped to her feet and faced him. "Are you implying my argument has no validity? That I'm being stupid?" she bit out between gritted teeth.

"That's not what I said, and you know it." Turmoil churned in his gut, but he didn't know how to reel in the anger at her stubborn refusal to give any other point of view except her own due consideration.

She opened her mouth, but then didn't say anything.

"I think we both need to cool off before this discussion is totally off the rails. Until then, I'm outta here."

He spun on his heel and left the room. He had no idea where he was going, but he didn't care. He just needed to get out of the house so he could breathe again.

He jammed his feet back into his shoes without bothering to untie them, snatched the keys to his cruiser out of the shell and yanked the door open.

"Jon?"

He hesitated, but didn't turn around. Then he let himself out and carefully shut the door behind him.

He didn't look toward the door as he backed his cruiser out of the driveway and turned onto High Street. If she'd followed him to the door, he would have gone back, but if he didn't look, he wouldn't know.

Forcing himself to calm down and drive carefully, he turned toward the waterway. Five minutes later he was crunching into the gravel lot at Anchor Beach. As he climbed out of the vehicle, he realized he'd forgotten his phone. He'd left it on the kitchen counter on vibrate so they wouldn't be interrupted. Maybe that was a good thing. He needed to get a grip. He needed to think. He needed a good long walk to burn off the frustration and anguish.

KATE STOOD IN the kitchen doorway for a long time after the sound of Jon's cruiser faded away. With her fingers pressed to her mouth and her eyes aching with unshed tears, she tried to come to terms with the fact that Jon had just walked out on her.

Her best friend. Her tender lover and husband-to-be had just walked out on her. And it was her fault. Just like it had been her fault the night Ethan had stormed out of the house and never come home. What was wrong with her?

She stood there absorbing the reality of Jon's leaving and trying to piece together the argument that had led up to it.

Her body trembled and her feet grew cold, but she didn't move.

He would come back. It wouldn't be like it had been with Ethan. Jon would be home soon. He'd drive around a while, but it was the middle of the night and there was nowhere to go. He'd come home. He had to.

I'll call and apologize.

She reached for her purse where she'd dumped it on the kitchen counter and stopped. Jon's phone was sitting beside the purse. She sagged down into the old rocker that had belonged to Jon's mother, defeated.

From the rocker, she could see the driveway. She'd see his headlights even before he turned in. She'd driven him from his own home with her stubbornness. This was her fault. She had to apologize. He would be home soon and she would promise to do the research he asked her to do. Once she'd done that, he would listen. Of course he would listen. He was always reasonable, even if she sometimes wasn't.

When the mantle clock in the living room chimed one o'clock, Jon still hadn't returned. Kate was stiff and shivering. Worry gnawed at her insides.

What if something happened to him? It would be all her fault. Again. She got up and walked around the house, going from one window to the next, hoping to see his headlights coming up the hill. But there was nothing. Barely even any moon. The world was just plain dark.

And it was her fault.

Jon had every right to be angry with her. She hadn't done everything she could to check the facts. She'd been distracted by two unexpected assignments at work and hadn't gotten back to this one. She was a reporter, for Pete's sake. It was her job to check facts. It was her job to keep an open mind. Maybe she did have blinders on about this project, but she hadn't been able to get past the fact that JJ wanted to have criminals living in her neighborhood, in her town. And she hadn't wanted to be convinced otherwise.

After several circumnavigations of the house, she subsided onto the couch and pulled the afghan around her. The clock struck two. Jon was still gone.

When the clock struck three, she got up and went to wake her computer up. She began googling the things Jon had wanted her to look up. She didn't bother to take notes. All the arguments he'd offered were there for her to read. She had been wrong. Really wrong.

Jon's mother's little mantle clock struck four as she closed her computer again and returned to the couch.

Jon still hadn't come home.

What if he'd been so angry he'd driven too fast and missed a curve? But wouldn't someone have called her by now? Maybe something had happened to him but no one knew about it yet?

Her body trembled at the possibilities that began parading across her mind.

She must have dozed because she abruptly opened her eyes to a faint gray light creeping in through the sheer curtains. Jon stood across the room at the window, his bulk silhouetted against the coming dawn.

Her heart leapt with relief. She struggled off the couch and hurried to his side.

"Jon?"

He looked down at her over his shoulder. "I'm sorry I walked out like that. You probably worried."

Probably? No probably about it! Anger shoved relief aside. She spun to stand between him and the window. "I was worried sick. It wasn't fair."

"Well, that makes two of us then, doesn't it?"

She jerked back as if he'd slapped her. He was saying she wasn't playing fair either. "I wasn't the one who stormed out of here in the middle of an argument. I wasn't the one who let you down. And I'm not playing fair?"

His jaw tightened, but he didn't say anything.

"I suppose you want us to move out of here and go out to my parents'?"

He cupped her cheek with one large, calloused hand. "No, Kate. I do not want you gone. I want us to fix this. I've waited for you for most of my life. I'm not giving up on us so easily. But right now I have to take a shower and get dressed for work. I'm tired. I'm betting you are, too. Tired is not a good way to be and work through this."

She didn't feel tired. Just confused and hurt.

And guilty. At least he'd come home. This time she had a chance to get things right. She turned her face and kissed his palm.

He groaned and pulled her into his embrace, his cheek pressed against her hair.

Kate slid her arms about his waist. They stood that way without moving or speaking as seconds stretched to minutes. So much still left to say between them. A rift she hadn't seen coming and wanted desperately to fix before it could get any wider.

Just not right now.

Chapter 25

AS JJ USHERED Kate into a living room as elegant as its owner, a dark-skinned man with an unruly crop of black-brown curls rose from a leather upholstered Chesterfield armchair. He was impeccably dressed in creased, gray slacks, polished loafers, and a navy blazer over a crisp white dress shirt and a gray-and-blue striped tie, but the grin on his face seemed at odds with the formal room or his attire. He looked as if he'd have been more at home in jeans with a T-shirt sporting some racy slogan stretched across his impressive chest.

"I'd like you to meet Lucas Trevlyn," JJ said as the man extended his hand toward Kate.

He was at least as tall as Jon with equally broad shoulders and a flat stomach that promised washboard abs beneath the starched white shirt.

"Kate Shaw," JJ informed the man as his big hand enfolded Kate's. The rough callouses were another contradiction with the jacket and tie. Who was this man and why did JJ want her to meet him?

"Pleased to meet you, Ms. Shaw." His voice was as impressive as his physique.

"I know you're probably wondering why I asked you to come here today," JJ said as she gestured to a matching leather armchair and took a seat on the couch facing the chairs across a glass and mahogany coffee table.

Kate sat, and Lucas Trevlyn followed suit.

"I'm always curious. It's part of the job," Kate offered when JJ didn't immediately enlighten her.

Trevlyn crossed one leg over the other and folded his hands atop his knee. He was obviously waiting for JJ to take the lead as well.

"You told me the other day you would like to hear how I envisioned keeping Second Chance House a safe and compatible enterprise here in Tide's Way. Lucas Trevlyn is a part of that plan. Lucas, tell Kate a little of your story and how you see this project going forward."

Lucas looked startled to be called on so quickly. He rolled his shoulders and glanced out the window briefly before turning to Kate.

"I—I'm an ex-con, ma'am." He cleared his throat but didn't elaborate.

So the polished man before her was a veneer. What lay beneath it?

"Lucas, that was a long time ago—"

"But it's part of who I am and part of why I think I can make something of this project that others might not understand."

Kate was tempted to pull her notebook out and start taking notes. But that seemed wrong in this setting somehow. She'd just have to rely on her memory. She waited for Lucas Trevlyn to go on.

"Lucas' history is a lot like Matthew's. With one major exception," JJ added. "He met someone who gave him a chance when he was ready to give up. A police officer as it happens."

"Not Jerry Brady, by any chance?" Brady's name had come up often in discussions about Second Chance House.

Lucas looked from Kate to JJ and back with a frown creasing his forehead.

"Lucas is from Charlotte, and no, not Jerry Brady. Kate, I am counting on anything Lucas might tell you about himself to be off the record unless he tells you he is okay with the information being made public. Is that agreed?"

Kate nodded. No need for the notebook after all.

"I can keep secrets with the best of them, Mr. Trevlyn."

The grin returned to his face, making him look ten years younger. "Please call me Lucas." He pushed his fingers through his curls, leaving them even more disheveled than before. When Kate nodded, the grin disappeared. He glanced down at his big hands and didn't speak for several long moments.

"I was pretty messed up," he began at last. "My teenage years were pretty wild, but not on the wrong side of the law. I had a good, hard-working mom, but my dad took off before I could walk. I had a foot in two camps. My mom was white. My dad was black. I wasn't sure where I belonged or how I should be behaving." That explained the coloring. The slender almost aristocratic nose and the softening of his curls he must have gotten from his mother.

"My troubles really started after I came back from three tours downrange . . . From Iraq and Afghanistan," he explained. "I should have stayed in the Army. I knew my place there. But instead, I got out when my hitch was up. I wanted to go back to being the same kid I'd been when I left. I thought I could leave the nightmares behind and forget the stuff I'd seen. Along the way, I got into a few scrapes. I was more than old enough to know better, but at the time I didn't care. I went from one extreme to another. Obeying every order without question to breaking any law that got between me and whatever I wanted at the moment.

"When I finally ended up doing time, I got drawn into an even more dangerous cycle of misbehavior. I'd been drinking pretty heavily after I got out of the Army, and prison should have dried me out. Instead, I was introduced to drugs. So once I was back on the streets, it became a troubling cycle of more crime to support my new habit. In less than six months, I was back behind bars. I was no innocent, but the things that happened to me that trip weren't pretty. By the time I got shoved back onto the street again with nothing but a few personal items in a trash bag, I was ready to give up. I did give up."

This time when his gaze met Kate's, there was no hint of the engaging smile and a world of hurt was reflected in the warm brown eyes. The man looked like he'd just lost his mother or his best friend to some unspeakable tragedy. The heartbreak was so palpable, Kate felt it in her the pit of her stomach.

"What happened?" She didn't even know this man and she wanted to wrap her arms about him and make the hurt go away.

"Sam Montgomery happened." Lucas sighed, shook his head and pasted an attempted smile on his face. "He was off duty and on his way home when he saw me standing on the wrong side of the guardrail on a bridge over I-77 where I was trying to screw up the courage to end the nightmare my life had become.

"I've had a lot of time to get squared away since then. I've found a place for Christ in my life again, and I believe Sam was sent to me that night for a reason."

A vision from the movie *It's a Wonderful Life* flitted through Kate's head with a far more deadly ending. George Bailey had jumped from a bridge into water that was freezing but not so far down as to kill him before Clarence the angel changed his fate. For Lucas, the drop would have been final.

"Have you figured out what that reason was?"

"Some," he answered quickly. "I went back to school, got my degree and then a master's. I counsel men who've found themselves where I once was. Sometimes I serve as an advocate for teenagers who need someone to speak on their behalf when they get tangled up in the legal system or in foster care. Even if Miss Jones' plan works out, I hope to continue that. Those boys need someone they can trust on their side in a system that feels like it's rigged against them, but I could do a lot more to help guys like me."

Kate glanced at JJ, then back to Lucas. Jon's pleas for her to listen to his view with an open mind tumbled through her thoughts. Another pang of guilt to add to her share of last night's blow up.

"I've been there. I know what it's like to get sucked into a whirlpool with nowhere to go and no one to reach out and haul you back from the point of no return." He sat forward in his seat and made a gesture as if he were offering someone a hand up. "I know I can help these young men not to make the same mistakes I made when I got out the first time. I know what they need in their lives to make it.

"They need structure from outside until they learn how to apply it from inside on their own. They need people they can trust who aren't going to lure them back into the mire they just got free of and won't go reporting them to their parole officer the first time they slip up. They just need a place to go and a fresh start. A job that gives them satisfaction in doing something well and seeing the results both through their own eyes and the eyes of others. Success builds confidence, and confidence is their only sure way out."

The facts Kate had read about recidivism at three in the morning echoed Lucas' words.

Lucas looked at JJ. "I'd like to change the name of your project though. I've been thinking about it. It is a second chance and all that, but I think something that doesn't always remind them where they came from would be more encouraging." Lucas paused for a moment. "Have you ever heard of St. Leonard of Noblac?"

Kate had not. Neither, considering the puzzled look on her face, had JJ. Kate was a practicing Catholic, but she wasn't up on all the many saints the church had canonized over the last two thousand years. She shook her head.

"Is he someone important to you?" JJ asked.

Lucas thrust a finger under beneath his collar and pulled out a silver chain with a pendant on it. "Sam gave it to me," he said as if needing to explain why he wore such a thing. Almost as quickly he tucked it away out of sight again.

"St. Leonard is the patron saint of prisoners. But more than that, the story told of him was that he was granted the right to liberate prisoners he felt were worthy of a second chance. Of course, there are the usual tales of miracles. Prisoners praying for release, invoking his name and having their shackles fall away. But in truth, many of the men he'd had faith in and secured release for came to him when they had nowhere else to go. Eventually the queen bestowed land on him, and those men who stayed with him were sometimes given small plots of their own to cultivate so they could support themselves honestly."

Kate sat back in her chair. "So, you want to call it St Leonard's?"

Lucas tilted his head to the side as he looked at her. "Not *Saint* Leonard's. That might put off guys who feel like God had deserted them, or maybe never had any faith to begin with. But what about Leonard's Place, or Leonard's Promise, or something like that?" Was that a blush creeping up the man's dark cheeks?

JJ nodded. "I'm fine with that, Lucas."

Lucas was an interesting man with an interesting past, but what actual credentials did he possess? Beyond the fact that he was exactly the sort of man Jon had been trying to make her consider.

"What, besides your past experience, do you bring to the table?" Kate asked. "What did you get your advanced degree in, and how do you plan to go about helping these men who are barely more than teenagers?"

"Social work was my major. If I didn't have a record, I might have tried for law school, but I'm actually pretty happy doing what I'm doing." He folded his hands on his knee and relaxed again. "While I was going to school, I was a bouncer in a nightclub. That's where I learned how to handle big, belligerent guys without using violence. With my Army background, I taught self-defense at a YMCA for a few years. Most recently, I've been counseling prisoners who are soon to be released. Helping them get their plans pulled together before they find themselves standing on the outside of the prison fence with nowhere to go."

"It's easy to see why JJ thinks you're a good fit for this job." Kate was a lot more impressed than she'd expected to be. "But do you have any experience managing any kind of establishment? Things like budgets and inventory?" She knew from her experience with Ethan's Ribs that those things didn't come naturally for everyone. At least, they hadn't come easy to her.

"I was a sergeant in the Army, ma'am. Managing personnel and programs comes with the rank." He glanced at JJ, then back to Kate. "Ms. Jones told me you're concerned about the safety of people living in Tide's Way. Kids and, well, just safety in general. I would be running this place with that kind of concern in mind. Having a chance to live an honest life and make a decent future is too rare a gift to waste on men who can't muster the discipline to make the most of the opportunity. They wouldn't be staying long enough to make trouble. And I will personally answer for all of those we bring into the program."

"That's a lot of responsibility for one man to accept." If she'd been at a tipping point to seeing Jon's side of things in the middle of the night, this man, Lucas Trevlyn, had toppled her into Jon's lap.

"I've got broad shoulders." He shrugged the shoulders in question. "I was very good at keeping men in line."

"Are you going to be it?" If this establishment was coming to Tide's Way in spite of all the negative publicity, it could use half a dozen men like Lucas.

"Am I going to be it, what?" He frowned.

"Are you the only employee for Leonard's Place?" She hesitated. "The only one making decisions?"

Lucas glanced at JJ. Was he looking for backup?

"Lucas will be the only employee, yes. But we plan on forming a board who will oversee his activities and the overall planning, running and decision making as well as budget and finances. Some of those who've helped me get this far will be on that board, but we will be adding to it. Members who live here in Tide's Way."

"People who have skin in the game," Lucas interjected. "They'll get final say on who gets to move in, too."

"I wonder if you would be willing to consider serving on that board?" JJ asked, leaning forward and lifting her brows slightly as she posed the question.

"M-me?" Kate sucked in a surprised breath. "You want *me* on your board?" Personal involvement in bringing a project she'd up to now opposed into existence was a leap of faith she wasn't sure she was either ready or qualified for. Her head buzzed. Was this an answer to her impassioned declaration to Jon about wanting to make a difference? Jon would probably say so.

"Why not?" JJ's eyes took on a martial light. "You're invested in Tide's Way. You ask all the right questions about the project. You're smart. And—" she smiled slyly. "If you're on our side, we might get some good publicity."

Chapter 26

THE GIRLS WERE asleep, and Jon was out on the veranda. He hadn't said much all evening. Not that he was the one who needed to make the next move. He'd already apologized for his angry words and storming out of the house.

It was Kate's turn to say she was sorry. Her turn to admit she was just as much at fault. Actually, more at fault. He'd been justified for losing his patience with her. Ever since JJ had proposed the project, he'd been trying to get her to consider the positive aspects, but she'd been so obstinate she hadn't even followed up like a good reporter should.

Instead of digging into JJ's personal life, she should have been reading up on what happens to men and women after they get out of jail. She should have been digging into the facts and telling those stories when she had a chance. She not only hadn't been fair to Jon, she hadn't been fair to her readers or to JJ.

She hung the dishtowel over the rod and turned out the overhead light. Procrastinating wasn't going to make eating crow any easier.

Jon sat in the huge old rocking chair he'd rescued from someone's trash and refinished himself. With his hands folded behind his head, he gazed toward the waterway, his thoughts who knew where. Kate crossed the veranda and stood in front of him. He brought his arms down and spread his thighs to accommodate her standing between them.

"Did you get a chance to take a nap today?" she asked.

"If you count falling asleep in my cruiser while I was having lunch, then yes." He reached for her hands. "Did you?"

She shook her head. After her meeting with JJ and Lucas, she'd done a lot more digging and fact finding. She'd actually located homes just like the one JJ wanted to open and made phone calls to them. She'd been on the phone most of the afternoon.

"We can have this conversation tomorrow," he offered, folding her hands into his as he looked up at her.

Maybe that was what he was hoping for. His eyes looked tired in spite of his nap. And he was probably bracing himself for another round of arguments.

She dropped to her knees so he didn't have to look up at her. She pulled her hands free and placed them on his knees. And cleared her throat. And swallowed. She studied the backs of her hands, pale against the dark blue of his uniform trousers.

"I'm sorry." Her words came out barely more than a whisper.

"Kate—"

"No, don't say anything. I just have to get this said." Her voice was stronger now. She lifted her gaze, but only as far as his chest. "I was wrong. And I'm sorry. I was pigheaded and unfair. You were right about that. I should have listened to you before. I should have looked deeper. I should have talked to people who know a lot more about it than I do. Including you. And I'm sorry." She swallowed again. "I'm especially sorry because I hurt you."

When he didn't say anything, she looked into his face. He was biting his lips together with a wrinkle crowding down on his eyebrows.

"Aren't you going to say anything?"

"You told me not to."

"Are we good?" She held her breath.

Slowly, he bent forward until his forehead rested against hers. "We're good." He cradled her face in both hands and kissed her on the mouth. A gentle kiss. A forgiving kiss. Then he pulled her onto his lap and wrapped his arms around her. "We're more than good."

"DOES THIS MEAN you're calling off your crusade to keep JJ from pursuing the Jolee project?" Jon asked after Kate had told him all about meeting Lucas Trevlyn and what his role would be.

They had come in from the veranda when the rain began and were seated at the kitchen table with steaming mugs in their hands.

"Lucas would make a good salesman, I think."

"You're teetering." Jon took a sip from his mug.

"I think," she said cautiously, "that if anyone could make this work, Lucas is the right man for the job.

"In addition to the homework you said I needed to do, I did a little digging around about Lucas Trevlyn, too. He didn't tell me anything about his time in the Army except that he was a sergeant and was good at keeping men in line. Incidentally, he was a bouncer for a nightclub for a few years, too. But he's got a purple heart and a bronze star and a dozen other commendations. He was deployed to a war zone three times in his six years in the Army."

"Did you find out what when wrong after he got out?"

"He never got a diagnosis, but I'm guessing PTSD. He was self-medicating with alcohol and got a few DUIs and lost his license." Lucas had seemed so self-possessed and confident that morning it was hard to imagine him a drunk with an itch to lash out. "He got into a few brawls. Then he put a guy in the hospital. He said he was trying to find his way back to the kid he was before he joined the military, but I'm thinking he was trying to drown out the nightmares.

"I talked to Meg, too. She said his story sounded like a ton of others she's heard." Meg, Kate's sister-in-law and a Marine veteran, had horrors of her own from Iraq. "She said having a guy like that in charge would change her mind about JJ's project if she wasn't already on board. She's excited about giving these guys a chance to work with dogs, too."

Jon took another drink of his coffee and remained silent. It was a tactic of his, she'd come to realize. If he just listened and didn't comment, she would often talk herself around to his way of thinking. Most of the time. When she wasn't being pigheaded.

"JJ offered me a position on the board."

He set his mug down abruptly. "What did you say?"

"I haven't said. Yet."

"What are you thinking? Yea or nay?"

"I'm thinking I'd like to sleep on it." The prospect of accepting still scared her. Not just serving on the board, but accepting that this might be her call to make a difference. All these years, she'd seen journalism as her calling. And it still was, wasn't it? She needed time to think. "But first I'd like to go to bed and see where that leads. I hear make-up sex is amazing."

KATE STARED UP into the dark. Her body, replete from lovemaking, felt heavy and ready for sleep, but her mind was going a mile a minute. A story had blossomed in her mind as she lay cradled in Jon's embrace listening to his breathing even out into sleep. She didn't want to get up, but she couldn't stop the ideas flashing through her head, either. In her room, there was a pad of paper and pencil beside the bed for just such brainstorms. Of course, if she'd been sleeping alone, there would have been no reason to stay in bed in the first place.

How quickly she'd become accustomed to the sound and feel of Jon sleeping beside her. Not just accustomed to, but lost without it. Maybe he had felt this way for all these years, but for her it was brand new. Last night had felt like forever.

But Lucas' story kept edging into her mind. One minute that deeply hurt look in his dark eyes haunted her. In the next, his amazing story of fighting his way back challenged her preconceived notions of what kind of men ex-cons were apt to be. If it hadn't been for a cop named Sam, Lucas had been sure he would be either dead or locked up permanently. Jon had been so right. If JJ's project could save just one such man, wouldn't that make it worthwhile? Maybe she'd been focused a little too much on kids she knew and the possibilities for harm coming to them and not enough on kids who grew up with nothing but harm. Kids like Lucas and Matthew.

Jon rolled onto his side and wrapped an arm possessively about her waist. Even asleep he established his new claim on her.

She could almost hear his voice in her ear, *If not Jolee, then where?* Her brother had offered a few ideas, but she hadn't been listening then.

Cautiously, so as not to disturb him, Kate lifted Jon's arm and slipped out of his embrace. She found the chair he had tossed their clothing toward earlier, felt around for his T-shirt, scooped it up and tiptoed to the door.

With Jon's T-shirt covering her and a cup of hot tea at her side, she woke her computer up and started searching the real estate ads for buildings for lease in Tide's Way and the surrounding area. She scribbled a few notes and phone numbers in the book she always carried in her purse. Satisfied that she had found everything remotely acceptable and being unable to do anything further until morning, she opened a new file and began typing.

She was tapping away, more than halfway through her story idea, when Jon's arms slipped about her shoulders from behind.

Gasping, she whirled in her chair. "You keep doing that!" It still surprised her how silently he could creep up on her and take her totally off guard.

He nuzzled the side of her neck without answering.

"You should wear that little bell you bought me. Like a cat." She turned all the way around and offered her lips.

"What would be the fun in that?" He chuckled then kissed her.

"What are you doing up in the middle of the night?" he said when he finally ended the kiss.

"I'm doing what you told me to do. Looking for an alternative site."

"Can't it wait until morning? I got lonely."

Kate glanced back at her story. She had the gist of it down. She could figure out how to finish it in the morning. Then she could call Lucas and make an appointment to talk about what she could and couldn't include in her story.

She closed the laptop and laced her arms about Jon's neck. "We're behaving like a pair of horny teenagers."

Jon lifted her into his arms and started for the door. "You make me feel like a horny teenager."

KATE COVERED ALL of JJ's appearances over the next few days, squeezing in trips to view government files and visit real estate sites. With the election just a week away, the pace of her job with the Wilmington paper was as intense as it ever had been in New York. JJ was indefatigable. More than twenty years Kate's senior, she had the energy of a woman half her age. Kate dropped into bed at night so tired that if it hadn't been for the newness of Jon's expert lovemaking, she'd have fallen asleep without much more than a kiss and a mumbled goodnight.

But she'd taken tonight off. Jon had done so much to cover for her over the last couple weeks, but tonight was Halloween. Three days ago she'd come home to find her mother busily sewing a costume for Becca. Vaguely, Kate recalled Becca asking about being a Disney princess for Halloween, but she'd been so intent on the story she was trying to put together and keeping up with JJ, she hadn't given Becca's request a second thought. Her mother was thrilled to be asked to help out, but Kate felt guilty.

Jenny said she was too old to go trick-or-treating and had begged to go to a party at the Halloway's instead. She insisted no one was wearing a costume, but when she came down the stairs, Kate wished they were.

"Whoa!" Jon said as he waved his passkey at the gun safe and holstered his weapon. "Who are you supposed to be? Lily Munster?"

Jenny made a face. "Whoever that is."

"Before her time," Kate muttered to Jon as she took in her daughter's blackened hair and Goth makeup. "I hope that stuff washes out."

Jenny tossed her head. "Of course."

Jon shut the gun safe and scooped his cruiser keys out of the big shell that sat on top of the shelf beside his cap. "Ready to go, Jenny?" He fitted the cap on his head and then stepped over to kiss Kate on the mouth and give Becca a quick hug.

Kate handed her daughter the container with the cupcakes Jenny had made earlier and frosted almost as black as her hair. "You've got your cell with you?"

Jenny rolled her eyes. "Of course."

"If things get out of hand or . . . or anything, call me. I'll come get you." How quickly her daughter was growing up. First no trick-or-treating, now a party with kids mostly older than she was, including Ty's charismatic, musical son. No telling what kind of games would be played. Samari seemed like a responsible woman who'd managed to rear two well-behaved sons while her husband served his country. Surely she could be counted on to keep the party under control.

"Mo-om."

Kate hugged her before she could scoot through the door after Jon. "Have fun, honey. I love you. And you look—super."

"Love you too, Mom. Later." She hurried out, the container of cupcakes clutched to her chest.

Unless he got tied up, Jon planned to swing by the Halloways to pick Jenny up at ten. It was a school night, after all. Otherwise, Kate would have to bundle Becca into the car and go after Jenny herself.

"Well, Belle. You ready?" Kate turned to her younger daughter. What a difference! Only three years apart, yet tonight they barely looked like they were in the same generation. Still in love with Disney princesses, Becca's straight brown hair had been curled into luxurious waves and she wore an elaborate yellow gown that stopped just above her toes.

"Do I look super, too?" Becca spun in a circle making the skirt bell out around her legs.

Kate hugged her younger daughter with a laugh. "You surely do. Your grandmother is a genius, and you are a beautiful princess.

Kate grabbed her own cell phone and two large bowls of candy she would leave out for trick-or-treaters to help themselves since no one would be home. She turned both porch lights on and set one bowl where the kids would be sure to see it. Then she and Becca set off, cutting across Jon's patio, through the wall of poplar trees and into her own backyard.

Her house was dark with scaffolding crawling up the back where Jake's crew was still working on repairs. They would never live in that house again now that she and Jon were planning to be married. Such a short time ago, she couldn't wait. Now she had no desire to return to the home she'd shared with Ethan. The guilt and indecision that had kept her from accepting Jon's proposal that astonishing morning in his kitchen seemed silly now.

She'd never blamed Jon for what had happened to Ethan, but he'd clung to his guilt as much as she'd clung to hers. Pray God he'd been able to let it go just as she had. Maybe Ethan's voice in her head, telling her it was okay, had been a figment of her imagination, but if it hadn't been, she hoped Ethan had talked to Jon, too.

"Why are we stopping here?" Becca asked, pulling Kate from her thoughts as they rounded the front corner of the house and headed for the front stairs.

"We don't want anyone to be disappointed, do we?" She gestured with the remaining bowl of candy.

"Oh! That's a good idea."

Kate unlocked the door and turned on the porch light. Then she set the bowl at the top of the stairs and headed back down.

"Do you think Max will miss us?"

"I thought you said he was sleeping on your bed when you left."

"Oh, yeah. I forgot." Becca took a skipping step and reached for Kate's hand.

WHEN JON FINALLY stepped into his kitchen and locked his gun away, he presumed both girls would be long asleep. Kate probably was, too. He set his hat on the shelf and dropped his keys in the shell, then headed for the living room.

Kate was curled up in his big chair with a book open in her lap. Amazingly, she was still awake. She tipped her head back to accept his kiss as he leaned over the chair.

"Was it a crazy night?" She asked as he sat down on the couch and began to remove his shoes.

"No crazier than Halloween always is. Old Mrs. Griswold called the station three times to complain that the kids were making too much noise. I had to break up a rowdy crowd of teenagers hanging out at the bandstand on the common. Escorted one inebriated father and his kids home, and wrote up a few complaints no one will follow up on tomorrow. Nothing out of the ordinary." He removed his tie and dropped it on the end table. "Come sit with me?" He patted the space next to him on the couch.

He'd had a heart-to-heart talk with Ethan while he cruised around his little town keeping tabs on the holiday shenanigans. Actually, it had been kind of a one-sided conversation because Ethan wasn't in a position to reply. But Jon had laid out all his doubts and guilt and shared with his friend how much he loved Kate and promised to take care of her always. For himself and for Ethan. He wasn't sure he would have been able to divest himself of the guilt so easily if he'd been moving into Kate and Ethan's home, but here was different. Here was *their* place. His and Kate's.

Kate got up and skirted the coffee table to plop down next to him. He wrapped his arm about her and pulled her close. "I love coming home and finding you here."

"I kind of like being here when you get home." She turned her face up for another kiss, and he obliged.

"Jenny has a boyfriend. Did she tell you?" he said when he lifted his head.

Kate jerked out of his arms and gaped at him. "She's just a baby."

Jon wagged his eyebrows. "Not any more. She's discovered boys. You should have seen that coming at her birthday party."

"But she's only thirteen."

"Specifically, she's discovered Tyler Halloway."

"When I was thirteen, I was—" Kate began.

"When you were thirteen you were hanging out with me and your brothers. You were a thorough tomboy. You weren't a very girly girl. Of course, that was what I loved most about you back then." He'd mostly liked having her around. She might not have been into boys yet, but he'd sure been into her.

Kate laughed. "I guess I wasn't, but really, Tyler is her boyfriend? It's not just a one-way crush? And she told you that?"

"Not exactly. But she couldn't stop talking about this paragon of teenage machismo. Let's see if I can remember everything." Jon tapped his forehead.

"She loves his black curls and his blue eyes. She likes that he's taller than most of the boys she knows. He's smart. He plays the guitar. He plays football, and he's on the junior-high team. He speaks three languages, and he's lived in four different countries, not counting the US."

"Amazing. And a little unsettling."

"Apparently he's just as taken with her, too."

Kate relaxed back against Jon's side, contemplating how quickly her little girl was growing up. Discussing the facts of life and purchasing beginner bras had been hard enough. In just another year or two, she'd have to face the reality of dating, curfews and trusting Jenny to make smart decisions about intimacy.

"It's kind of scary."

Jon murmured an agreement.

"I was thinking after you left how big a gap there seemed to be between Jenny, all got up in Goth, and Becca, still happy to be a princess."

"Enjoy it while you still can." Jon cupped her cheek and turned her face to his. "Can we talk about us now for a little bit?"

"Sure." She tipped her head back to see his face better.

"I love blue eyes, too. Your blue eyes, not Tyler's." He kissed one and then the other.

"What about us?" she prompted.

"When are we getting married and making this legal?"

Chapter 27

"CAN WE BE bridesmaids?" Becca asked as soon as Jon called "his girls" together for a family meeting to discuss the possibility of a Christmas wedding. Becca bounced on the ottoman in her eagerness.

"It's not going to be that kind of wedding," Kate answered, glancing at Jon. "Is it?"

Becca stopped bouncing. "What kind of wedding doesn't have bridesmaids with pretty dresses?"

"It will be whatever kind wedding you want," Jon spoke directly to Kate and reached for her hand. She scooted along the couch until her thigh touched his. He lifted his arm and wrapped his fingers around the back of her neck.

"Mom's been married before," Jenny spoke up. It was hard to tell what she was thinking.

"Does that mean you don't get to wear a white dress?" Becca asked frowning.

"It's going to be a small wedding. Just family. And maybe a couple of friends. But I would like you to be my maids of honor. Both of you together."

"Do we get to wear pretty dresses?" Becca asked.

"It's not about dresses," Jenny said a bit impatiently.

"Of course, you get to wear pretty dresses," Kate answered her younger daughter. Then turned to Jenny. "Are you okay with this?" She reached a hand toward Jenny, who stood awkwardly half way behind the ottoman her sister occupied.

Jenny ignored the hand. "I thought it was already a done deal." She looked pointedly at her mother, who was now leaning against him. Then she glanced toward the stairs leading to the bedrooms before looking at Jon with a knowing glimmer in her eyes. The message was clear.

That Kate was now sleeping in his bedroom had not gone unnoticed, and Jenny expected them to tie the knot rather than continue living in sin. Or maybe it was something else. He'd have to ask Kate later. A lot about girls, especially teenage ones, was still a mystery to him.

"Your opinion is important to me," Kate answered patiently.

And so was the example they were setting, which had been Jon's argument for setting a date in the relatively near future.

"Well, I approve, if that's what you're asking, but why wait for Christmas?"

"If not Christmas, then when would be a good time?" Jon asked gently.

"I guess Christmas is all right." She sagged onto the ottoman beside Becca. "Can I invite some of my friends, too?"

"Like Madison?"

Jenny wagged her head. "Well, maybe Madison, but I'd kinda like Tyler to come."

Tyler with the blue eyes and a guitar. Kate tipped her head back to look at Jon over her shoulder. He gave her a told-you-so grin. Maybe he wasn't so clueless about teenage girls after all.

"Maybe your mom will invite his whole family. Ethan's Ribs can live without their manager for a day. Would that be okay?"

Becca bounced off the ottoman and headed for the door. "Natalie is going to be so jealous when I tell her I get to wear a pretty dress and be a maid of honor."

Jenny rolled her eyes. "She's such a baby sometimes."

"She's just excited," Kate defended her youngest daughter.

Jenny got off the ottoman and crossed the room and looked out the window.

"What are we going to do with Daddy's house?"

"What do you think we should do?" Kate asked.

Sell it! The thought shot through Jon's head, but he didn't say it. Ethan had been his friend and he'd more or less gotten over feeling guilty about poaching Ethan's woman, but living in the man's house with said woman was a whole other thing.

Jenny glanced over her shoulder for a moment. "We should sell it and live here. I like this house. I mean, I liked our old house, too, but this one is bigger. And it's higher up so I can see the ocean from my bedroom."

Jon almost let out an exaggerated sigh of relief. He and Kate hadn't discussed this particular detail of their future, but maybe Jenny was unwittingly paving the way for him. Kate stood and crossed the room to join Jenny by the window.

"Maybe someone with little kids will move in, and I can get a baby-sitting job," Jenny suggested hopefully.

Kate wrapped her arms about her daughter and rested her chin on Jenny's head. "You are growing up so fast it scares me sometimes."

"Not me," Jenny said turning to give Kate a hug. "Did you know Tyler is in Uncle Jon's Kids Who Care club?"

JON LEFT WORK in a happy state of mind in spite of the election cloud hanging over his future job prospects. By Christmas, Kate would be his wife. Becca and Jenny were pleased to be a part of it. Becca with bubbling enthusiasm and Jenny more quiet about it but accepting. They'd set the date with Father Frank and sent the announcement to the paper the day after Kate's feature article on Leonard's Place had appeared above the fold on page one.

The article was a masterpiece of well-researched and unbiased journalism and Jon was proud of her. She'd met with Lucas Trevlyn a second time in Wilmington and come home a total convert. Her story had appeared along with photos of the new location Jake had been instrumental in securing and a sidebar about the director JJ had employed. The response had been overwhelmingly positive.

Partly because of the new building since there was still heavy opposition from the Historical Society, especially the Save Jolee Committee who had a bond issue on the upcoming ballot to fund the renovation and preservation of the Jolee Mansion. Partly because many of the fears had been allayed about how the place would be run. Kate seemed surprised every time she got another email or snail mail letter thanking her for the piece and applauding her journalism.

Jon pulled into the driveway beside Kate's rattle-trap minivan. It would please him to give something personal and romantic as a wedding gift, but perhaps it would be more practical to get her a new car. He knew a few things about maintaining vehicles, but he wasn't the mechanic Ethan had been and the repair bills to keep the twelve-year-old heap on the road and safe weren't pocket change. Maybe he would do both.

He glanced at the minivan as he climbed out of his cruiser and considered what kind of replacement might appeal to her. It should probably be a family-sized SUV or another minivan. Definitely big enough for four, but preferably roomy enough for a carseat or two. He loved Jenny and Becca, but it would be nice to have a couple more. Babies he was responsible for making.

He wanted to watch Kate's belly grow round and put his head against it to listen for a heartbeat. He wanted to be there when his baby entered the world, and he wanted to watch Kate aglow with love for the baby they'd made together. He'd been more jealous of Ethan than he'd previously acknowledged, even to himself. He wanted it all.

Max met him at the door, wagging furiously. Jon scratched him behind the ears, and then put his car keys and weapon away before bending to untie his shoes, fending off Max's eager tongue. When he straightened and crossed the hall with Max prancing at his side, the faint sound of Jenny practicing her violin came from the upstairs and an enticing aroma wafted in from the kitchen. He scooped up the mail that had been left on the table for him and smiled. Coming home had never seemed sweeter.

Max padded off toward the kitchen and Jon headed for his study, hesitating when he heard Kate's voice. She stood by the window, her back to him with her cell phone pressed to her ear. Rather than interrupt her call, he remained just inside the doorway and started going through the mail. He smiled at his aunt's neat handwriting. She was the only person he knew who still wrote handwritten letters and refused to even consider email as a civilized form of communication. He lifted the flap and began to read a recital of her fiftieth high school reunion.

Half way through a sad passage on how many of her classmates were no longer alive, the excitement in Kate's voice caught his attention. Eavesdropping wasn't his style, but he couldn't help noticing the eagerness in her voice.

"I never in my life expected—" she paused. "Of course. Next week? Sure. But it will have to be after Election Day."

Whatever it was, Kate was pleased. Very pleased.

"Thursday? Let me get back to you after I check available flights."

Another trip? Where was Driscoll sending her now? Depending on how long Kate would be away, he might have to get someone else to watch the girls. Taking too much time off with everything hanging in the balance at the station wouldn't be a good strategy for advancing his career.

He moved to his desk and set his aunt's letter and the rest of his mail on the corner.

Kate remained facing the window, but her call had ended. He waited for her to turn, but when she didn't, he took the last few steps and slipped his arms about her waist. She jumped and spun to face him.

"Jon! Where did you come from?"

"From work. Where else would I have come from?"

"But—" she glanced at her watch and then at his stocking feet. "Aren't you a little early?"

"I couldn't wait to get home to my best friend." He pulled her closer and kissed her. She twined her arms about his neck and the kiss deepened. He broke it off before things got too heated. "So? What's up?"

She shrugged. "N-nothing. Just same old same old."

"You're going somewhere?" he prodded.

"Oh . . . just business. Just . . . I have to go to New York next week. Only for a day and a night. Will you be okay with the girls, or should I talk to my mom?"

She was being strangely vague. The excitement in her voice when she made the date had been unmistakable, but now it held a note that sounded more like guilt. Or was he just reading too much into it?

"What day?" he asked, careful not to give away what he already knew.

"Thursday. I'll fly up Thursday and be home Friday."

"If something comes up, I can always call your mom later." Jon kept his voice even so his disappointment wouldn't show. She wasn't lying to him, exactly. Just omitting something. Something she didn't want to share with him. Her reluctance to confide in him hurt more than he'd thought possible.

"So, how did your day go?" She changed the subject.

"More of Allison's threats, but nothing really important. Unless you call Gracie's cat getting stuck in a tree again memorable. I found Old Man Moffett wandering around by the library, more vague than usual, but I took him home and all is well. What's for supper?"

"Something Jenny concocted. She wanted to surprise us."

"Excellent. Two cooks for the price of one." Jon kissed Kate's nose and she chuckled.

"If I didn't already know that you like to cook yourself, I'd consider that a sexist remark."

"Call it whatever you want, but then give me a proper kiss to welcome me home after a long day."

Even if there were secrets she still wasn't sharing, he'd claim this right. He'd waited all his life for her, and he'd be damned if an unexplained trip to New York was going to derail what they had now.

She grabbed his ears and tugged his face down to hers, kissing him so thoroughly that he forgot about everything else.

AS SOON AS Jon left for work and the girls were on the school bus, Kate let Max out to poke about the yard while she headed down the hill to her old house. Jake's crew were all there and the driveway full of pick-up trucks, but there was no sign of Jake.

A wave of guilt washed over her when she thought back to her evasiveness with Jon. He deserved candor, but for some reason, she hadn't told him why she was going to New York.

He'd said before that as long as she was a part of his life, he didn't care where he lived. Of course, that was when they were discussing his working in Wilmington if Allison took over the Tide's Way Police Department. And they probably wouldn't have have to move at all. Or maybe they would if the Wilmington PD expected their officers to live within the city limits. But that wasn't the same as moving to New York.

The idea of moving back to New York was what had started the argument with Ethan that ended with his death in the parking lot of his restaurant. In retrospect, she didn't blame Ethan for not wanting to toss all those years of hard work building Ethan's Ribs into a popular restaurant just so she could start at the bottom of the ladder again in New York. Of course, there had been other reasons Ethan had wanted to stay in Tide's Way. Maybe Jon would have the same reservations.

But just because the girls were used to living in a small town didn't mean they wouldn't fall in love with the vibrancy of the Big Apple. They'd have to acquire a few street smarts. And Jon was a cop. New York needed good cops even more than Tide's Way or Wilmington. In any case, it was only an interview. Not a sure thing. Maybe that was why she hadn't shared the interview invitation with Jon. Until she knew for sure.

The back door was open, so she didn't need her key. Tarps and heavy, mauve colored paper lined the floors and the stairs. The huge tree trunk had been removed from the upstairs hallway and the ceilings had been repaired. New Sheetrock covered the walls of the master bedroom, and all the furniture that had been salvaged was gathered in the center of the room under a paint-stained drop cloth.

Kate slipped sideways past the corner of her bureau to get to the closet. She pushed aside the things she hadn't taken to Jon's because they were out of season and reached for a garment bag she hadn't opened since she'd returned from New York thirteen years ago. She hoped the suit she was looking for still fit.

Unzipping the garment bag, she pulled the navy-blue suit out and held it up. Nothing like quality to keep its style. Just in case she needed more than the one, she grabbed the gray suit as well. It wasn't her favorite, but she didn't like to wear the same thing two days in a row if she was trying to impress someone. Living and working in Tide's Way and Wilmington, she'd never gotten that dressed up for work. She'd worn gray slacks and a silk blouse to her interview with Steve Driscoll, and even that had felt a little overdressed. The dress code for the Big Apple was something she'd have to get used to again. She hung both suits on the hook on the back of the door while she rummaged around looking for the right shoes.

November. She probably needed her coat, too. Where had she put it? Downstairs closet? She grabbed the garment bag that matched her carry-on suitcase off the top shelf, unzipped it and slipped the suits inside. Just one night so she didn't need the larger suitcase that was up at Jon's, just the weekender. She pulled it out, put the shoes inside and shut the door.

She hauled the garment bag and weekender back around the collection of furniture to the door and down the stairs. Her dress coat was in the hall closet along with the girls' cool-weather coats. She grabbed all three and folded them into the weekender to get them back up the hill. She should have driven the car around.

Max greeted her at the border of poplars that separated her property and Jon's and escorted her back to Jon's house.

In her room, she unpacked everything. Slipping out of her jeans, she wriggled into the navy-blue skirt. It fit. Thank God. She turned this way and that, pleased by the reflection in the mirror. Why hadn't she worn it all these years? It made her look slender and sophisticated. And very professional. Maybe she'd stop at Francine's Frocks and get a new blouse. Excitement about the upcoming interview grew. Time to call Jacqui and schedule a trim and a manicure on Wednesday so she would be looking her very best.

Chapter 28

KATE SHOOK HER pen as if that would replace the ink that had finally dried up. The man she was interviewing kept talking, apparently unaware she'd stopped taking notes. She dug in her messenger bag, searching for a replacement, and thankfully, found one.

"What was your main reason for choosing Miss Jones? Don't you feel that Gordon Quinn has done a good job?" she asked when the man stopped speaking.

The lanky gentleman answering her questions was a day manager at the local grocery store and had come to the polls after work like much of Tide's Way. He ran his bony fingers through his thinning hair and glanced past Kate as if the answer to her question were somewhere in the distance.

"He has," he finally answered. "Quinn's done a fine job, but he's been sitting in the mayor's office for a long time. Maybe it's time for some new blood. New ideas. You know?"

"Have you heard about Miss Jones' plan to create a facility for troubled young men here in Tide's Way?"

Brad Richards grinned suddenly. "Well, Ms. Shaw, it would have been hard to miss your story, now wouldn't it? Took up most of the front page. I don't want you quoting me or anything, but your story changed my mind. Just don't want the wife to know I'm not in her camp on this anymore. Changed a lot of minds, I'm betting. I'm looking forward to meeting that Trevlyn fella at the next town meeting."

A warm feeling of satisfaction pooled in Kate's chest. Of course, her story would have been hard to miss for anyone who regularly read the paper, but that it had the power to change minds was quite an ego boost. The fact that her former boss in New York had been impressed had glowed like a warm fire all week since she'd gotten the call, but today it had amazed her how many of her hometown citizens had been impressed as well.

"When we left the last town meeting, there was a lot of grumbling and not many in favor, I'd guess," Richards went on. "But now, I'd be surprised if—" He broke off suddenly as a tiny bird of a woman who didn't even reach his shoulder appeared at his side.

"What are you doing mouthing off to a reporter?" Mrs. Richards slapped her husband's forearm and shot an unfriendly glance at Kate. "Come along now," she said, turning on her heel and marching toward the parking lot.

Brad winked in Kate's direction and put a finger to his lips before following his wife.

"Well, you can't win them all," Kate muttered as she slipped her notebook into her bag.

"Were you trying?"

Kate jerked around to find Jon grinning at her.

"That's what my story was aimed at doing as you very well know." She placed a hand against his chest and tiptoed to kiss him. "Did you just vote?"

"Yeah. And now I get to stand here looking official until the place closes. Are you done for the day?"

"Not until I get my notes typed up and sent off to Steve. I want to stop in and see JJ if they've called it by the time I leave the office. Mom won't bring the girls home until bedtime, so it's just us. Do you want me to wait supper?"

Jon shook his head. "No telling how late I'll be, and I just wolfed down a sub. Just wish I could make better use of an empty house." He gave her a thorough going over as if he were undressing her in his mind and wagged his eyebrows.

"We'll improvise. See you later, stud!"

Without waiting for his reply, she turned and hurried toward her car.

He whistled after her.

She grinned but didn't look back. Being whistled at felt good. It made her feel young, carefree, and attractive. And very much in love. Things that, such a short time ago, she never thought she'd feel again.

KATE WOKE WITH a start alone in Jon's big bed. It was later than her usual. How had she slept through Jon's getting up? She scrambled out of bed and hurried to the bathroom. Voices in the kitchen told her Jenny and Becca were already up, but there was no deep rumble of Jon's voice.

She'd interviewed JJ right after the results had finally been announced. Today she had an appointment with her sister-in-law and Tony Jenkins to talk about what was next for the Jolee Mansion now that the town had approved the bond issue to restore it. And an appointment with Jacqui ahead of tomorrow's trip to New York.

"Good morning, Mommy," Becca gave Kate a hug when she walked into the kitchen. "Uncle Jon said I could have Natalie for a sleepover this weekend. Do you think we could get a couple new movies to watch?"

"I'm sure we can," Kate answered absently. Jon was nowhere in sight. "Where is he?"

"He got a call and had to leave in a hurry," Jenny informed Kate as she slung her heavy backpack over one shoulder and headed for the door.

Having her new morning routine disrupted was a little disconcerting, but Kate guessed she'd have to get used to it. No matter where Jon did his police work, there would be times he'd have to leave without any warning and she might not always know where or what he was doing. Or if it was dangerous.

Her heart skipped a beat at that thought. Law enforcement was a hazardous profession. Living in a small town had lulled her into forgetting that officers' lives were sometimes in the line of fire. In today's world, people with an axe to grind often aimed their discontent at first responders for no better reason than that they were the first to arrive on the scene.

Kate sat down as the reality of Jon's profession and how it would impact her if they lived in New York City slapped her in the face.

"It's okay, Mommy." Becca patted Kate's shoulder. "Uncle Jon promised he'd call you later."

"Of course." Kate plastered a smile on her face and helped Becca slip her arms into her backpack. She kissed Becca and turned her toward the door. "Better hurry or you'll miss your bus, and I'm not even dressed yet so I can't drive you and get you to school on time."

Becca blew her a kiss and hurried out, letting the screen door slap shut behind her.

In her eagerness over the possibility of landing a prestigious job and moving her family and Jon to New York, Kate hadn't really given much thought to the difference in big-city policing. New York was the kind of place where a man could be targeted just because he wore a uniform. Jon was used to dealing with people he'd known all his life. But cops were being targeted everywhere, weren't they?

Besides, it wasn't like she would be starting out at the bottom of the ladder like she would have back when she and Ethan had argued about it. Her old boss wanted Kate to take over the position held by a woman Kate had once worked for, who was leaving for health reasons. It was the opportunity of a lifetime with a salary big enough to support them while Jon got reestablished in any line of work he wanted. Maybe he'd want to go back to school and do something entirely different.

JOHN HADN'T MADE it home for supper due to a call-out over on the island to find a missing child. The girls were asleep and Kate rocked anxiously in big wicker swing on Jon's veranda, on the lookout for the cruiser's headlights.

She was tired, but she needed to talk to him. She needed to tell him about the interview before she left in the morning. He deserved her complete honesty. He was going to be her husband and he deserved to be included in decisions that would change his whole future.

She must have dozed, because the next thing she knew, Jon was stepping up onto the veranda.

"Kate?" He detoured from his beeline toward the front door and headed her way. "I thought you'd be in bed by now, getting your beauty sleep for tomorrow's adventure."

She reached for his hand and drew him down beside her on the swing.

"We need to talk."

He stiffened and she squeezed his hand tighter.

"I'm not calling off the wedding or anything. I just need . . . I should have . . . You have a right to know why I'm going to New York tomorrow."

He let go of her hand and wrapped his arm about her shoulders as he settled into the swing and pulled her against his side.

"Did you find the kid?" Kate asked, suddenly realizing she'd been so wrapped up in what she needed to share that she hadn't asked how his search had gone.

"We did. And he's going to be okay." Jon lifted one foot and placed it across his knee while he gave the swing a gentle shove. "He hadn't gotten very far, but he'd slid into a hollow in the dune and couldn't get out. He was scared, but unhurt. The family is reunited and all's well in Tide's Way again. Now about that trip to New York?"

He continued to gently push the swing to and fro while Kate searched for the words to tell him what she should have shared with him right off.

"I was asked to come for an interview. With my old paper," she finally said in a rush. "The woman I used to work for had to retire early because she was diagnosed with ALS, and I'm one of the people they are considering to replace her."

"That—sounds—pretty exciting."

"Well, it is. And it isn't," Kate hurried on in the face of his hesitation. "I mean, it's an exciting possibility. It was exciting just to be asked to come for an interview. But . . . It would mean we have to move to New York. You'd have to move to New York, and maybe you don't want to."

For a long time Jon didn't say anything as he continued to push the swing back and forth. His free hand kneaded the fabric of his trousers, then smoothed the rumpled cloth against his thigh before he finally looked at her. In the faint light coming from inside the house it was hard to read his expression.

"I don't know," he finally said. "Only time I've been away from Tide's Way was my stint in the Marines. And even that never had me posted in a city. Or even close. I'm not sure I'm cut out for that kind of life. But what about the girls? How will they feel about leaving everything they've ever known?"

"Kids are resilient," Kate argued reasonably. She'd used the same argument with Ethan and it hadn't swayed him, but she'd expected Jon to be different. She'd hoped he would say he'd go wherever she went. But maybe expecting him to give up his whole way of life was unrealistic.

It was kind of sudden and out of the blue. Just the other day the four of them had been talking about living here in Jon's house on the hill overlooking the waterway. And there was no ignoring how much he wanted to become chief of Tide's Way police in spite of the odds against it now that JJ had won the election.

Or maybe he just needed more time to come to terms with the idea. To consider the possibilities.

She opened her mouth to start listing some of them when he leaned toward her, closing the gap between them before she could speak. His mouth wasn't gentle on hers as he dropped his foot to the floor and dragged her into his lap.

"I want you to be happy," he whispered against her mouth when the passionate kiss ended. "It's a fantastic opportunity, and you should be excited. I don't know how I fit into it, but I'm sure you'll make the decision that's best for you." Then he claimed another kiss as urgent and demanding as the last.

JON STARED AT his computer screen without really seeing it. Kate had left for New York three hours ago. She'd woken him up, fully dressed and ready to leave. He was disappointed that she hadn't woken him before she climbed out of bed, His day hadn't started with the same warm ball of happiness that he'd begun to count on, but after her revelation last night maybe it never would.

He was thankful she had trusted him enough to tell him why she was going, but distressed about the likely outcome. The idea of moving to New York, coming with no warning like it had, caught him unprepared. His heart ached just thinking about it.

It was Kate's dream to work for a newspaper in New York. It had been that dream and her desire to move back to New York to make it happen that had precipitated the argument that ended in Ethan being in the wrong place at the wrong time. Yet in spite of her oft expressed guilt, the dream hadn't died.

Was he making the same mistake? Clinging to a job and a place that shouldn't mean so much?

Allison would more than likely take over the Tide's Way police department on the first of the new year, and he'd be looking for employment anyway. He touched the badge pinned to his chest and glanced around the familiar office.

Did he love Kate enough to give up a way of life he was comfortable with for her and never look back?

"It's not fair!" Allison stormed past the office door, jerking Jon out of his troubled thoughts. She'd been closeted with her aunt in one of the interview rooms for the last half hour. Jon had pictured her smirking in satisfaction, but she wasn't smirking now.

"May I have a moment?" JJ appeared in the doorway looking cool, efficient and classy in a maroon suit with a pencil skirt and a floral scarf decorating the neckline of a cream colored blouse.

Jon popped to his feet. "Here? Or—?"

"Here is fine." She stepped into the cramped quarters and wheeled the chair behind Allison's desk around to sit facing him. She folded her hands in her lap and met his questioning gaze.

"Please sit down before I get a crick in my neck."

Jon sat.

"I guess you heard Allison's discontent?"

He nodded. He wouldn't say anything negative about his coworker to her aunt.

"She's not cut out for the job she thinks should be hers, and I told her so."

Jon did his best not to let his surprise show.

"She hasn't had enough experience to start with," JJ said with a sad shake of her head. "She also doesn't have the temperament. As her behavior just now confirmed. She forgets I've known her all her life. I know her better than perhaps she thinks I should."

Having no idea where this conversation was going, Jon said nothing. Agreeing with JJ would be impolite at best. Disagreeing would be a lie.

"I would like to appoint you as our new chief when Don Atkins retires."

He couldn't hide his shock.

"You're surprised?" JJ smiled at him knowingly.

"Well . . . yes," Jon said as he finally found his voice.

You've got the experience. Both here and in Wilmington. Your time in the Marines adds to your qualifications in my estimation. And the people of Tide's Way like and admire you. I'd be honored to have you serve as my Chief of Police." She waited with a serene smile on her face, her hands still folded.

"I—" he swallowed. He wanted to say yes and pump JJ's hand to seal the deal. But, if today's interview went well, Kate would have other plans for his future. "I am the one who's honored, ma'am. But I'd need to discuss it with Kate first."

"I would expect nothing less." The calm smile stayed in place. "Have you two set a date yet?"

"December twenty-third. It will be a small affair, but we'd be honored if you were able to attend." He hoped Kate would be honored. She'd become JJ's ally on the Second Chance project. Correction, Leonard's Place. Presumably she would be pleased to have JJ attend their wedding. If there was a wedding.

"I'll be there with bells on as my grandmother used to say." JJ smiled and got gracefully to her feet. "I've got a couple months to come up with an alternative, but I really hope you'll take the job. You're the best man for the job, and I think we could work well together."

With that parting shot she walked out leaving Jon still stunned by the turn of events. He'd loved Kate for as long as he could remember, but leaving behind the one job he coveted more than any other would be a wrench.

He stood and crossed to the window. Shoving his hands into his pockets, he stared at the familiar view without really seeing it. His heart and head were in a turmoil from which there seemed no easy exit. He fully expected Kate to come home bubbling with her own good news. How was she going to react to his?

Chapter 29

KATE TOOK THE Air Train to Jamaica and transferred to the Long Island Railroad which would take her into Manhattan. The trains were busier than she recalled. Filled with people who paid more attention to their smart phones than the people they might be bumping into or inconveniencing. Had it always been like this and she'd just never noticed before?

Penn Station was a madhouse of commuters bustling in every direction. Already she was regretting the high heels she'd chosen. All the women hurrying past her with bulging designer totes wore running shoes. No doubt, they had work shoes parked under their desks waiting for them, but she didn't have an office – yet. And she'd wanted to put her best foot forward so to speak.

As she exited the station she stopped on the sidewalk, shocked by the size and hustle of the city around her. It seemed so much bigger, so much busier and so much more overwhelming than she remembered. She didn't recall feeling this small and out of place the first time she'd come here on her way to NYU for her freshman year of college. Of course, she'd been with Ethan then. And they'd been young and so full of themselves.

"Miss Cameron?"

Kate hesitated at the sound of her maiden name before reacting and turning toward the voice. A sandy haired man with a big smile on his face stuck his hand out.

"You don't remember me, do you?"

She didn't. Not even vaguely. He looked about her age. Slender, a runner's body, thinning hair, and an engaging smile. It felt like she should remember him.

"Andy Bolton. NYU School paper?" he hinted as she slipped her hand into his waiting one.

"You were the computer guy." Kate shook his hand thankful to have her memory jogged. "You still live here in the city?"

He nodded. "Yup. You look a little lost."

"I'm headed to 8th Avenue. For an interview."

"I'd walk with you, but I've got an appointment in the opposite direction. Good luck. It was good to see you again." He touched his brow with a finger in a vague sort of salute, and then hurried past her disappearing into the crowd of pedestrian commuters.

Kate glanced at her watch and realized she had an hour to spare. In spite of the pinching shoes, she could walk to her interview and maybe the bagel place would still be where she and Ethan had met for breakfast so often. She hitched her overnight bag higher on her shoulder and headed for the crosswalk. Maybe she'd find time to come back and do a little shopping at Macy's on her way home. Her flight was mid-morning though. So maybe not.

Just as the walk light lit up, a police cruiser came tearing around the corner, lights and sirens going. She backed up onto the sidewalk and watched as it screeched to a stop just a hundred yards down the street. Two officers leapt from the vehicle and hurried into a shop with their guns drawn.

That could be Jon's life if they moved here. Suddenly it was hard to imagine Jon working in this environment. She stared at the shop front wondering what was going on inside. The walk light lit again and a dozen people pushed past her and crossed the street. Belatedly, she jerked into action and followed them.

As she approached the shop the police officers had run into, one of them came out with his hand wrapped firmly around the upper arm of a cuffed man in a jogging suit. The officer escorted his prisoner to the cruiser, opened the door, and put his hand on the man's head to guide him into the rear seat. Then he shut the door and leaned against the cruiser, apparently waiting for his partner to finish questioning the people still inside the shop.

Jon hadn't worked with a partner for all the years he'd been on the Tide's Way force. Nor had he, to her knowledge, ever responded to what she assumed had to have been a robbery in progress. She knew he'd never drawn his gun on the job. The most dangerous thing he'd ever mentioned was intervening in a domestic dispute. Not that they weren't dangerous when emotions and guns were involved, but still. The job had been a little livelier when he was on the Wilmington force, but he always said he loved being a big fish in a very small pond. A small pond where all the fish knew each other.

She considered another alternative.

If they lived outside the city, she could commute and Jon could serve on a suburban force. It wasn't the same as Tide's Way, but then nothing would be. But maybe it would be a good compromise. If Jon was willing to compromise. When confronted with her news, his reaction had been hesitant and in the end, he'd only said he expected her to make the right decision for herself. He hadn't included himself in that assurance.

She hurried past, not wanting to dwell on the scene she'd just witnessed or think about the sacrifice Jon would have to make. The bagel place looked different, but it was right where she remembered it being. She went in and got in line. The sign and ownership might have changed, but the scent of fresh brewed coffee and fresh New York style bagels hadn't. When she'd paid for her purchase she moved to take a seat on a high stool at a counter stretched along the window where she and Ethan had spent so many Sunday mornings between St Patrick's and their school campus.

It seemed like a lifetime ago that they'd come to this little shop the first time. They had been so excited to be on their own and living in the city. Ethan had been enrolled in pre-law classes. His brother Garrett had joined the Navy and their dad wanted at least one of his sons to follow in his footsteps. Kate hadn't had a clue what she wanted except to be wherever Ethan was. Working on the college newspaper and then getting the internship at a real newspaper had seemed like an adventure because of the places it got her into when she wasn't with Ethan.

In the end none of their plans had turned out to be very permanent. His dad had passed away and had not been around to be disappointed when Ethan switched his major and began working nights at a restaurant. Then her difficult pregnancy and slow recovery had given Ethan all the reason he'd needed to turn his back on the city he no longer enjoyed and pursue something that he'd found far more rewarding.

Getting his brother to help finance the purchase of a run down rib joint and turning it into Tide's Way's best restaurant had been his dream job. He'd loved every minute of the years he'd devoted to making Ethan's Ribs the local hot spot in Tide's Way while she'd felt cheated of her chance to shine in her chosen field.

As she sat at the counter sipping her coffee and nibbling on her bagel, she realized that lifetime seemed very long ago. There had been so many firsts without him these past two years, so many birthdays and events with just her and the girls. Her recollection of how it had been before a faded and dwindling memory. So much heartache and so much healing.

And now there was Jon.

The hole Ethan's death had left in her life had been filled by the unexpected new relationship with Jon. She had loved Ethan with all her youthful innocent heart, but now she loved Jon with something just as compelling. Something that felt more solid and abiding. She was still getting used to the way he'd suddenly slip up behind her and slide his arms about her or kiss her on the back of her neck without warning. She was still getting used to his sometimes tender, sometimes fiery lovemaking, and sleeping within his embrace.

Relying on him was not so new. He'd always been there, always been her best friend. He'd always been the first one she told with every new triumph in her life. How much it must have hurt him when she dashed next door to show him her acceptance letter to NYU, knowing she was only eager to go there because Ethan was already enrolled. He'd hid his own disappointment and hugged her in congratulations. He might have gotten drunk afterwards, but he'd been there with a smile on his face for her wedding, too. And he'd been there for the worst of her days of her life with the same unflagging support. He'd even been the first one she'd told of the miscarriage between the births of Jenny and Becca. So unselfishly had he loved her all these years.

But he wouldn't love the hustle of New York City. Did he love her enough to give up everything and move here?

She hadn't even been to her interview and already she was having doubts. Everything about the city was just as she remembered it. And yet, nothing felt the way she remembered it.

Had she changed that much?

She swallowed the last of her coffee and dabbed her napkin over her lips, then slipped off her stool and headed for the door. It was time to meet Cécile.

KATE DROPPED HER overnight bag on the bed in her eighth floor room at the Four Points Hotel and kicked off her shoes. She crossed to the window and gazed down at the busy street below, trying to imagine living here again. Trying to picture herself as part of a vast and well-known news organization, with demanding deadlines and a chance to make a name for herself.

On the flight up here, she'd been so certain this was the chance of a lifetime, and she needed to just reach out and grab it. She'd shoved aside niggling doubts about Jon's willingness to move to the city or her daughters wishes in the excitement Cécile had filled her with during that totally unexpected phone call. She'd interned at this newspaper and gotten hired there right out of college, and loved every minute of it.

The job description and the expectations outlined in today's interview suddenly hit her. The freedom to take a half hour off and drive Jenny to her violin lesson or watch Becca play soccer wouldn't be a part of it. Maybe, if Jon did work in the city, there would be opportunities to meet for lunch, but it would be a rushed lunch, crammed between other more demanding responsibilities for both of them. *Is that what I want our life to be like?*

Instead of walking down the street being greeted by folk she knew, she'd be rushed along on a tide of humanity that never really connected. Abby's Book Nook might not have the best bagels in the world, but her favorite bagel place in New York didn't have a sagging old couch by a fireplace where she could have shucked her heels for a few blissful minutes.

Maybe it was true you could never go back, that things could never be the same. She would certainly never be twenty-two again, or as carefree and untouched by tragedy. And maybe Jon was right about being a big fish in a small pond. Here, she would just be one of hundreds of thousands, rushing through life without ever stopping long enough to enjoy what she had.

Suddenly she needed to talk to Jon. She slipped her phone from her pocket and woke it up. His face, smiling beneath the brim of his patrol cap, greeted her on the lock screen.

She clicked on his number and waited for the connecting ring tone.

He didn't pick up.

She ended that call when it went to voice mail and tried the house phone.

No answer.

Not even Becca or Jenny. It wasn't violin night or soccer night so where were they? And why wasn't Jon answering his cell? Worry began to edge into her heart. What if something had happened in her absence?

She forced herself to stop worrying and decided Jon had taken the girls out for supper somewhere and maybe his cell was dead. Or maybe he hadn't wanted to take a chance on being called into work and left it at home. That sounded more like the Jon she knew. She relaxed her shoulders and turned away from the window.

In a few minutes she'd have to put her shoes back on and deal with the blisters on her heels because she'd promised to meet Cécile for a cocktail at a lounge just around the corner to talk more about the job that was hers if she wanted it. Cécile would be bubbling over about the future of working together again, and sharing a cocktail often as they compared notes and discussed the stories they were tracking down.

Kate looked once more at Jon's smiling face, felt her face smile in return, and then slid her phone back into her pocket.

BECCA AND JENNY walked along the water's edge kicking up sprays of seawater while Jon kept his eye on them from the blanket where they'd enjoyed a picnic supper. He'd left his phone on his dresser specifically to avoid the off chance he'd get called to handle some police emergency, but now he wished he'd brought it so he could call Kate. He wanted to hear her voice. He wanted to tell her about his day and hear about hers. Anguish about the sacrifice one of them was going to have to make still roiled in his gut.

241

He didn't like the idea of moving to New York, and wasn't sure if he could bring himself to accept it if that was what Kate wanted. But after loving her all these years, and finally having her love in return, could he let her go again?

They hadn't discussed where exactly they might live if she got the job. She'd probably want to stay in the city, in the heart of all that hustle and incivility. He thought about the house of the fictional chief of police on the television show, *Blue Bloods*. It wasn't Tide's Way by a long shot, but it wasn't downtown Manhattan either. There were sidewalks, and lawns, and back yards to enjoy. And leafy streets. He had no idea where Frank Reagan supposedly lived, but it looked like a place he might be comfortable with. But even if Kate didn't insist on living in a super expensive, but cramped apartment with the constant sound of honking horns, blaring sirens and the cacophony of city life, he'd miss the scent of salt air and the distant rote of the sea.

And the hardest part would be telling JJ he wasn't going to be her chief of police after all. The soul-deep satisfaction of being offered the job he'd spent his whole life working toward was gone, replaced by the sinking feeling he would never enjoy policing the streets of New York.

Chapter 30

WHEN KATE WALKED out of Wilmington's small airport into the blazing sun it was not her mother's blue Buick waiting in the pick up lane, but Jon's familiar gray and white cruiser. Jon leaned against the fender with his arms folded across his chest and a warm smile on his face. He uncrossed his arms and opened them as she approached.

Coming home had never felt so incredibly right.

Kate dropped her overnight bag and flung herself into his embrace.

"I thought my mom was coming to pick me up," she said as soon as his lips left hers and she caught her breath.

"I called your mom and told her I'd come after you. I've gotta get back to work by one, but I couldn't wait until tonight to see you. Did you get my message? I didn't sleep much last night. I thought about it and about us, and I'm going to tell JJ I can't—"

She pressed her finger over his lips, then replaced it with her lips. "Me first," she whispered against his mouth, and kissed him again. "But shouldn't you move your cruiser?"

"I know these guys." He gestured toward the security officers keeping watch on activity in the pick up lane. But he let her go and turned to open the passenger door. He picked her bag off the ground and tossed it in the back before circling the vehicle and folding himself into the driver's seat.

"I got the offer I was hoping for," she blurted even before he'd pulled away from the curb and followed a red pickup truck onto Airport Boulevard.

He glanced across at her with a smile tipping up the corners of his generous mouth. "I knew you would."

Kate wasn't sure exactly when her decision had been made, but somewhere between listening to Jon's voice mail message telling her JJ had asked him to be her chief of police and seeing him waiting for her outside Wilmington International Airport, her heart knew it was the only one she could live with. Jon didn't belong in New York and neither did she. The nagging doubt that had followed her into the city was gone and in her soul she knew it was the right decision. The only decision. For all of them.

"I thought I missed New York, and this was my big chance. I thought I was missing out on—"

"You don't have to miss out on anything," Jon interrupted as he clicked his blinker and turned onto the main road headed toward Tide's Way. "I'll go where you go."

"But that's the thing. You shouldn't have to." Her voice went husky with emotion.

Jon glanced at her again, and then quickly pulled the cruiser onto the shoulder of the road and put it into park. He shifted to face her.

"Kate, you are the most important thing in the world to me. I love Tide's Way, and I'd love the chief's job, but I love you more." He reached a hand behind her head and pulled her toward him for a kiss. "Home for me is wherever you are," he murmured when their lips finally parted.

With the dash-mounted computer crowding in on one side and the console between them, she couldn't fling herself into his arms as she so desperately wanted. She leaned her forehead against his.

"Home is at the top of a hill in a wonderfully restored old house with creaky floors and a view of the ocean," she whispered. "That's what I'm trying to tell you, Jon. I thought

I missed New York, but I was wrong." She tipped her head away and met his steady green gaze. "Everywhere I went it just didn't seem the same as I remembered. I mean, it looked the same. Mostly. But it didn't feel the same. Everyone was in such a rush and everyone is so rude. Nobody knows anyone. You would hate it there."

"I wouldn't hate anywhere that you are."

Kate's eyes flooded with tears and her throat ached. His declaration was more than she deserved. She hadn't given his needs nearly as much consideration before getting on that plane with the single-minded focus of landing a prestigious New York journalism job. She swallowed hard and blinked furiously.

"Well, we won't have to put that to the test. I didn't give Cécile an answer yet, but I'm going to call her as soon as we get home. On second thought—" Kate broke off and fumbled in her purse for her phone. She located Cécile in her contacts and initiated the call.

With one arm stretched across the seat backs, his fingertips touching her shoulder and the other wrist resting on the steering wheel, Jon watched her, his face soft with love and wonder.

"Hi. Cécile? It's Kate. Look, I hate to disappoint you, but the answer is no."

Cécile didn't respond right away. She was probably in shock. When they'd parted last night Kate had been talking about how long it might be before she could start.

"Why?" Cécile finally said in a stunned-sounding voice.

"New York isn't home," Kate answered, gazing at Jon through watery eyes. "I'm flattered that you thought of me and thank you for giving me the chance to consider it. But my life is here." With Jon. She reached across the gap to touch Jon's face.

She winked as Cécile expressed her sincere disappointment. A huge smile began to spread across Jon's expressive face. Finally Cécile said goodbye and Kate ended the call.

Jon would have given up everything and gone anywhere to be with her and that promised her a lifetime of love and unfaltering support. The happiness on Jon's face echoed the contentment suddenly in full bloom in her heart.

Jon kissed her fingertips and grinned. Then he put the cruiser in gear and pulled back onto the road. When he glanced over at her his green eyes danced and the spray of laugh lines at the corners of his eyes crinkled.

"In that case, how do you feel about being married to Tide's Way's chief of police?"

Epilogue

KATE RAN HER thumb over the back of her sparkling engagement ring now joined by a gorgeous white gold wedding band and glanced about her. Philip and Elena's son Alex, just shy of a year, clutched at her knees as he made his determined way along the line of relatives to his father who scooped him up in an enthusiastic hug. For the first time since Philip had joined the Marines she and all of her brothers were together in her parents' beach house living room for Christmas.

She leaned back into the curve of Jon's arm and stretched up to whisper in his ear. "I love you."

"Love you more," he whispered back.

Her heart swelled with emotion. He probably did love her more, but that was only because he had the biggest heart of any man she knew.

"Don't go weepy on me." He chuckled. "We're newlyweds. We're supposed to be happy."

That made her laugh and the heavy moment of emotion lifted. She gave him a kiss and let it linger until someone cleared their throat. She laughed again and turned her attention to Meg and Ben's twins who were shrieking with delight over the princess dolls from their favorite aunt and new uncle.

Sam and his cousins were out on the deck figuring out how to get the little drone Will had given Sam into the air and Ava and Julie, the only teenagers in the family, had disappeared into the bedroom they were sharing. Sandy and Cam sat in their matching recliners holding hands and behaving more like young lovers than the newly retired grandmother and grandfather they actually were.

"Bet you never thought we'd all be together for Christmas again," Philip commented as he set his son back onto his feet.

"I always believed it would happen," Sandy smiled complacently. "When you all got the wanderlust out of your system."

"Don't speak for me," Jake laughed. "I only moved across town."

"I just went as far as Wilmington to college," Ben added.

Kate let her gaze move around the room, hesitating first on Jake and Zoe cuddled on the end of the long couch, then on Meg seated between Ben's legs on the ottoman helping her daughter to remove a princess dress, to Will with his arms draped about Bree's shoulders and his chin resting on top of her head as she cradled their sleeping 8 month old daughter and finally Philip as he bent to kiss Elena and curve a possessive hand over her growing belly.

This house she'd grown up in was bursting at the seams with love, laughter and children. Her mother's greatest wish had come true. And, as it turned out, Kate, glanced over her shoulder into Jon's warm green gaze, hers too, right here in Tide's Way.

She'd wanted her life to make a difference, but she'd never considered the importance her presence made in her parent's lives or her brothers or daughters. And now there was Jon, who told her every day that her love meant everything to him. Three days ago, she'd been invited to take over Steve's position at the paper so he could retire and care for his ailing wife. And in January she would attend her first meeting of the newly formed board of directors for Leonard's Place and begin to make a difference in the lives of men who desperately needed a second chance. She could hardly wait to begin.

Pecan Praline Shortbread Cookies

Shortbread
 ½ lb butter
 ½ cup confectioners sugar
 2 ½ cups flour

Mix together and kneed dough until smooth. On a lightly floured surface, roll dough to ¼-inch thickness. Shape as desired, rerolling scraps no more than twice.

Bake at 350 ° for 10 minutes

In a small saucepan, combine 1 (11 ounce) package of caramel bits and ¼ cup water over medium heat. Cook, whisking often, until bits are melted and mixture is smooth.

Let cool to room temperature.

Spread approximately ½ teaspoon caramel mixture in the center of each cookie. Press a praline pecan on each cookie. Garnish with sea salt, if desired. Place cookies on parchment paper to cool and harden caramel.

Acknowledgements

Writing is often a lonely task, but rare is the author who can claim to have done it all without the input of others and the support of family and friends. Folk without whom the story would not be possible.

While I have visited and love the North Carolina coast, I owe a big thank you to Gayle Glass, aka Lilly Gayle who provides me with such odds and ends as what a child might call their grandmother or what plants are in bloom with the story is taking place and dozens other things. Inspiration for my hero's career came from Debra Dixon and her dad, Jack Berry, whose book, *When You're the Only Cop in Town* painted a wonderfully thorough picture of what it's like to be law enforcement on a small town police force.

A huge thank you to the Sandy Scribblers, my brainstorming buddies: Nancy Quatrano, Pegeen Brant and Glo Ferguson who helped fill holes when I fell into them and inspired me to be a better story teller. Thanks as well to Betty Carpenter Johnston who sheltered me during Hurricane Matthew and spent some of those hours conjuring up names for my characters and in general read and cheered me on as the story unfolded.

And, of course, to my kids who are my most enthusiastic cheerleaders: Rebecca, Bobbi, Alex and Lori.

About the Author

Skye Taylor, mother, grandmother and returned Peace Corps Volunteer, loves adventure and lives in St Augustine Florida where she enjoys the history of America's oldest city and walking on its beautiful beaches. She posts a sometimes weekly blog and sends out a monthly newsletter, volunteers with the USO, and is currently working on a new mystery series. Her published work includes: *The Candidate, Falling for Zoe, Loving Meg, Trusting Will, Healing a Hero, Iain's Plaid* and *Keeping His Promise*. Short stories*: Loving Ben, Mike's Wager and Saving Just One* and non-fiction essays of her experiences in the Peace Corps (Available on her website: www.Skye-writer.com.) She is a member of Romance Writers of America, Women's Fiction Writer's Association, Florida Writer's Association and Sisters in Crime. She loves hearing from her readers at Skye@Skye-writer.com